D1459719

MATRICIDE AT ST MARTHA'S

MATRICIDE AT ST MARTHA'S

Ruth Dudley Edwards

St. Martin's Press
New York

MATRICIDE AT ST. MARTHA'S. Copyright © 1994 by Ruth Dudley Edwards. All rights reserved. Printed in the United States of America. No part of this book may be used or reproduced in any manner whatsoever without written permission except in the case of brief quotations embodied in critical articles or reviews. For information, address St. Martin's Press, 175 Fifth Avenue, New York, N.Y. 10010.

"A Thomas Dunne Book"

Library of Congress Cataloging-in-Publication Data

Edwards, Ruth Dudley.
Matricide at St. Martha's / Ruth Dudley Edwards.
p.   cm.
"A Thomas Dunne book."
ISBN 0-312-13122-4
1. Universities and colleges—England—Cambridge—Fiction.
2. Cambridge (England)—Fiction. I. Title. II. Title: Matricide
at Saint Martha's.
PR6055.D98M38   1995b
823'.914—dc20   95-2072   CIP

First published in Great Britain by HarperCollins Publishers

First U.S. Edition: May 1995
10 9 8 7 6 5 4 3 2 1

To Martha, of course, but to John as well

When the Himalayan peasant meets the he-bear in his pride,
He shouts to scare the monster, who will often turn aside.
But the she-bear thus accosted rends the peasant tooth and
    nail.
For the female of the species is more deadly than the male.
  . . .

Man, a bear in most relations – worm and savage otherwise, –
Man propounds negotiations, Man accepts the compromise. ·
Very rarely will he squarely push the logic of a fact
To its ultimate conclusion in unmitigated act.

Fear, or foolishness, impels him, ere he lay the wicked low,
To concede some form of trial even to his fiercest foe.
Mirth obscene diverts his anger – Doubt and Pity oft perplex
Him in dealing with an issue – to the scandal of The Sex!

But the Woman that God gave him, every fibre of her frame
Proves her launched for one sole issue, armed and engined for
    the same,
And to serve that single issue, lest the generations fail,
The female of the species must be deadlier than the male.

From: 'The Female of the Species',
by Rudyard Kipling, 1911

PROLOGUE

'Balls!' said the Bursar and continued skipping vigorously. As her skirt rode higher, vast quantities of satin eau-de-Nil directoire knicker were exposed to Amiss's enchanted gaze. 'Sod this!' she shouted a couple of minutes later. Flinging the skipping-rope into the corner of her office, she marched back to the desk, threw herself into her chair and lit one of the pipes that peeped out from under the litter of papers.

'You've lost me, Jack. What precisely was it I said that you consider to be balls?'

'That blather about the tranquillity of Cambridge after the hurly-burly of London.'

'I was just being polite,' said Amiss testily. 'One has to say something.'

The Bursar yawned, leaned back in her chair and planted her feet on her desk. She took another deep pull on her pipe. 'Drink?'

'It's a bit early for me.'

'God, you're so prissy.' She swung her legs off the desk, reached down to the drawer on her right and pulled out a bottle of gin. Two glasses followed. She poured a generous slug into one and let the bottle hover over the other.

'Oh, all right,' said Amiss. 'But weak, please, and may I have some tonic?'

She sloshed what to Amiss's anxious eye looked like a treble into the second glass, shook her head and reached down to the left-hand drawer to get the tonic. 'Ruins the taste of good gin, you know. Always take mine neat. Learned that trick in the Navy. You young people are all such wimps.' She shoved the glass over to him. Amiss took a small sip and choked. He grabbed the tonic bottle and filled the glass up to the top. The Bursar took a mighty swig and smacked her lips appreciatively. 'I like gin,' she said.

'That is patently obvious. Now what's this all about, Jack?'

'Less of the "Jack". You're going to be very formal with me here. I maintain my distance from colleagues. It all helps to put the fear of God into them. I don't want anyone to know that we're friends. Spoil the whole effect.'

'Bursar!' A note of desperation was creeping into Amiss's voice. 'Why am I here?'

'Because I need an ally to sort out this, this . . .'

'Mess?'

She shook her head irritably, 'just searching for the *mot juste,*' she said. 'Try another.'

'Imbroglio?'

She shook her head. 'You don't know a word for witches' brew?'

'Sorry, I think it's normally known as a witches' brew.'

'Oh, anyway,' she said impatiently, 'the nub is that St Martha's is in such a state that even I cannot tackle its problems alone.'

'And in essence what are they?'

'Money and politics.'

'No sex?'

The Bursar knocked out her pipe with some savagery on the heavy brass ashtray. 'Here, sex is politics and politics is sex.'

Amiss felt his head swimming. The Bursar's darkly impenetrable briefing, the gin and an empty stomach were cumulatively taking their toll.

'Where do I come in?'

'I'll get you in. Do what I tell you and you'll be a Research Fellow by next week.'

There was a knock on the door. The Bursar's roar of 'Enter!' was loud enough to make Amiss jump. A tiny, elderly, whiskery woman tottered in. She was wearing district nurse's shoes, thick grey woollen stockings and something grey and woolly underneath her threadbare gown. Much of her hair was confined within a bun on the top of her head, but although it was encased in a brown net which contrasted rather oddly with her white hair, enough had escaped to make her look deranged.

'That minx, Bursar! That dreadful, dreadful minx!'

'Which one?' asked the Bursar wearily. 'Sandra or Bridget?'

'Sandra, of course. I said the minx. Bridget's the hussy.'

'What's she done?'

'She sent me this commentary on my reading list–' she brandished several sheets of paper– 'and it's full of all that awful gibberish, you know.'

'Don't tell me,' said the Bursar. 'All that DWEM stuff again.'

'I don't understand any of it. It's all full of words like "Anglo-centric" and "neo-colonial perspective" and "patriarchal dominance".'

'So what's new?' asked the Bursar. 'Why don't you just ignore it?'

'She's circulated it round all my students and you know what will happen.'

'Have you talked to the Mistress?'

'Not on a Tuesday morning.' She sounded shocked.

'Sorry,' said the Bursar. 'One forgets. Leave it with me, Senior Tutor, we'll have a word about it later on today and don't let the . . .' she paused for a second, 'minxes, get to you.'

The door closed on the afflicted don. The Bursar hurled the papers viciously into the corner. '"Minxes", indeed. "Vipers" would be more like it. They've got that poor midget in a fearful state.'

'Do I gather you are suffering an outbreak of political correctness?'

'You can say that again. They've gone to war and the enemy is the Dead White European Male. The battle cry is, "Get the DWEMs off the reading list and bring on the one-legged black lesbians."'

'But that's a pretty normal scene on many a campus these days, isn't it?'

'This time the whole future of the college is at stake. Come on, drink up and I'll take you out for a decent lunch. I'm fed up with this health kick.'

'What health kick?'

'Well, I'm trying to lose weight,' said the Bursar stiffly. 'Why do you think I was skipping?'

'What about the gin?'

'Gin isn't fattening. How could it be? It's a clear liquid. Anyway, I've got to keep my strength up.'

'Why are you trying to lose weight?'

'Well, look at me. How would you describe me?'

'Plump?' hazarded Amiss politely.

'God, what a mimsey word. Portly is more like it. I'm portly. Mind you, in this bloody place I'm not allowed to be portly. "Differently-sized", that's how that half-wit Sandra described a fat student the other day. Anyway, I've been doing a bit of huffing and puffing climbing the stairs so it's time I did something about it. Come along. I know where we can get some excellent bloody roast beef and a decent bottle of claret.'

1

The trouble with Jack Troutbeck, wrote Amiss to Rachel, is that though she is a particularly splendid old bird, and one with whom I worked and occasionally caroused very happily in the civil service, once she has decided you're intelligent it's almost impossible to get any information out of her: she assumes you pick up everything by osmosis. However, I applied myself to extracting the salient details and have now got a grip and awfully entertaining it all sounds.

St Martha's has been staggering along on a shoestring in an undistinguished sort of way for 80 years or so. It's the least well-known of the Cambridge colleges for reasons which I haven't yet sussed out. Jack said something darkly about the founder wanting them all to be seamstresses rather than scholars. They seem, these days at least, to have people who can't get in anywhere else and don't really want to come to them in the first place, and that applies to dons as well as students.

Now the even tenor of St Martha's life has been disrupted by a shattering event. An old girl has left a bequest of ten million quid to be used at the discretion of the Mistress for a specific project. This is the root of the problem: apparently the benefactor, Miss Alice Toon, was not one of those who fears lest her left hand find out what her right hand has been up to. She wished her light to shine free of bushel, hence the stipulation of something that can have her name attached. Forget minor improvements and running costs. What St Martha's really needs is money to cure the dry rot in the loo seats and the rising damp in the under-gardener, with a bit of money thrown in for scholarship. But that isn't the sort of thing Alice Toon had in mind. She saw it more in terms of the Alice Toon Memorial Ante-Room or the Alice Toon Chair of Cosmic Understanding or whatever.

The decision has to be taken by the end of this term, and the Fellows are at war over what it should be. With her customary delicacy, Jack describes the two main tribes as the Virgins and the Dykes, with a minority party called the Old Women.

The Virgins are what you might expect. Head Virgin is the Mistress, Dame Maud Theodosia Buckbarrow, who is a medieval historian – a 'decent old biddy', according to Jack, who was contemporaneous with her at St Martha's forty years ago, but not a bag of laughs. She lives, breathes and exhales footnotes and lives a life of abstraction, purity and fixed routine.

Equally virtuous is Emily Twigg, the pint-sized Senior Tutor, who is an authority on Beowulf, looks like an intellectual grey squirrel and, according to Jack, is a complete innocent about everything except, of course, English literature. There are a few other similarly chaste and dedicated ancient bluestockings in the college, all minded to keep the fires of rigorous scholarship alight. To this end they are devising the Alice Toon Postgraduate Scholarships in Theology, Palaeography, Medieval Law and so on. Dame Maud Theodosia is compiling a definitive list at present of the most unpopular subjects anyone can think of.

The second lot, the Dykes, are fewer in number but they're better street-fighters. For instance, their leader, Bridget Holdness, was clever enough to get a Visiting Fellowship for her frightful sidekick Sandra Murphy, who turned out later to stand for everything that Dame Maud hates. Jack thinks Holdness is an apparatchik who is using the politically correct movement entirely cynically and marshals her troops well. Her lot want to spend the money on a centre for Gender and Ethnic Studies.

The Old Women are in fact men. I don't know how they came on the scene but there are three of them, who also have some nascent support among the uncommitted Fellows. The one Jack mentioned, Francis Pusey, inspired her to a rush of expletive-spattered denunciation which escapes me now but the gist of which was that he was a namby-pamby mummy's boy who spends most of his time doing embroidery. What Pusey and his pals want is to call the whole college after Alice Toon and spend the money on making it extremely comfortable for the Fellows – rewired, replumbed, equipped with a decent wine cellar and a good cook. Jack is morally on the Virgins' side, in her heart she's on the Old Women's side – but all that matters is to do down the Dykes.

I'm being dragged into this simply because Jack is ever a woman to seize an opportunity and I am that opportunity. Jack had screwed out of her ex-colleagues in the civil service the money for a temporary Research Fellowship to study the relationship of government and academia: the holder is to examine the situation on the ground, as it were, and come up with a thinkpiece on how Whitehall and academe could snuggle up together more productively. The person chosen has dropped out at the last minute and having heard from a mutual friend that I was resting, she thought it would be a good wheeze to get me along to hold her hand through the weeks ahead. She's persuaded her civil service contact to insist that work start on the agreed date, i.e. at the end of the next week, so she's been able to cut corners in getting a shortlist together for the selection committee to meet next Tuesday. She's rigged it to the best of her ability and now I've got to pass muster with a rather disparate group which includes one of the Dyke faction and the midget (sorry, vertically-challenged) Senior Tutor. My instructions are to be cunning, play it by ear, and dress the part. 'What part?' I asked. 'Work it out', she said and abandoned me to my fate.

Of course, I'm going to give it a whirl. It will be a good billet, if I get it, from which to job-hunt and besides, I like old Jack. I still remember with deep pleasure the occasion when she became even more frank than usual at a Permanent Secretary's sherry party and told a Treasury mandarin where to put his Public Sector Borrowing Requirement: the only effect alcohol ever seems to have on Jack is to make her even less inhibited.

Now I'm off to choose my wardrobe for Tuesday, working on the principle that the Virgins won't notice what I wear, so I'd better dress for the Dykes. I can see I'd better take advice.

2

Amiss was quite pleased with the general effect. The black woollen collarless shirt and trousers were the clothes of an earnest person: over them he wore a donkey jacket, purchased in the local charity shop. Yet some touches were needed to compensate for his overall unrelieved white Anglo-Saxon maleness. It was obviously imperative to cloak his other twin disadvantages of heterosexuality and good health.

He had spent a long time agonizing over the choice of book to carry with him: even the Dykes presumably wouldn't be gullible enough to be taken in by a volume of poems by 'Black Sisters in the Struggle'. In the end he took Ellmann's *Oscar Wilde*, unsubtle but credible, and, besides, a book that he would actually enjoy reading on the train to Cambridge.

Amiss had practised his limp assiduously and as he inspected his hobbling figure in various shop windows he congratulated himself on the general effect. However, by the time he had got halfway up the long drive of St Martha's he was beginning to wish he had taken a less tiring route to winning the sympathy of the selection board. The slowness of his gait gave him ample time to make a judgement on the architectural merits of St Martha's, which were nil unless one happened to have a penchant for neo-Gothic piles with overhanging turrets and lots of narrow windows peering out of the scarlet brick. He could appreciate the Bursar's *crie de coeur* about the need for an extra gardener. In a city crammed to the gills with rolling swathes of manicured perfection, St Martha's lawns, by contrast, were a sorry spectacle of ragged vegetation. Great dark hedges and bushes of evergreens were clumped glumly here and there and all were in need of a good trim: the dangling ivy cluttered around bits of the building lacked both restraint and direction.

St Martha's architect had clearly been enjoined to provide adequate protection for the precious inmates: the front door was made of an oak so heavy and thick as to be capable of resisting a phalanx of mad axe-men. As on Amiss's last visit, it was open: once again, his nose wrinkled in distaste at the pervading institutional smell provided by a kitchen free of air-conditioning and a great deal of polished linoleum. He rang the bell marked 'Office' and the college secretary came rushing into view.

'It's Mr Amiss again, isn't it?' she asked brightly. 'Now what have we done to ourself? Why have we got a stick?'

'An old complaint, Miss Stamp. Polio as a child and all that. Get a recurrence sometimes – a bit like malaria. Don't let's talk about that.' He silently applauded the stoicism that shone valiantly through his cheery tone. Shamelessly, he continued. 'Let's talk instead about that nice jumper you're wearing. Absolutely beautiful.'

Miss Stamp simpered and gazed down at her tiny chest, which was encased in a remarkably elaborate construction of blue and pink embroidered butterflies on a white mohair background. In itself it wasn't bad, thought Amiss; it might have looked quite fetching on an eight-year-old girl.

'Francis, I mean Dr Pusey, made it for me. Well, that is, I knitted it and he embroidered it. We help each other out in our sewing circle. Can you sew or knit, Mr Amiss?'

''Fraid not. I'll have to get you to teach me – if I get this job.'

'Oh, then we'll have to see that you do.' Giggling girlishly, she led him down the hall.

'The others are in here already,' she said. 'Now I'll go and get the Bursar and I'll see the three of you at lunch.'

She tripped away. Amiss smiled at his rivals.

The Bursar had assured him that she had misused her position as applications supremo to claim that the only contenders available for consideration at this short notice were these two carefully selected lemons who were unlikely to

16

appeal to any of the three factions. Certainly he felt that sartorially they were on a hiding to nothing. The woman's smart City suit was ideologically incorrect for the Dykes (aping the patriarchal), too smart for the Virgins and lacking the little feminine touches that would have appealed to the Old Women. The chap was kitted out like a prep-school master from his leather-patched tweed jacket to his brogues, which made him bad news for Dykes and Old Women, though OK with Virgins.

Conversing with them gave him even more confidence. The chap, it emerged, had never been to university and wondered what was the point of studying all these dead languages: the woman was clipped and businesslike and talked about meeting the needs of the marketplace. By the time the Bursar plunged into the room and interrupted, Amiss was moved to smile at her with complicity and approbation. He received a stony look in response.

'Come on you three, must get on, must get on. Off to lunch now with your interrogators so we can all suss out if you know which fork to use for the asparagus.' The booming laughter with which she always greeted her own sallies rang out at a volume which rattled Amiss's companions.

'Hold on,' called Amiss, as she accelerated out the door. 'I'm afraid I won't be able to keep up with you.'

The Bursar turned round and surveyed him and his stick. 'What's the matter with you?'

'Nothing, nothing, it's just an old trouble.'

'Well you weren't a bloody cripple when I interviewed you last week. If you had been I'd have thought twice about putting you on the shortlist, I can tell you. Well come on, drag yourself along as fast as you can.'

Amiss had the satisfaction of observing the prep-school master and the City type falling into a condition of paralysed embarrassment.

Lunch was held in a cavernous dining room which could at a pinch have fitted a hundred and fifty, but today contained only the guests, the selection committee, Miss Stamp and half a dozen undergraduates. Amiss was put sitting between the Bursar and the Senior Tutor and opposite an

17

earnest anorexic-looking blonde with an American accent who was introduced as Sandra Murphy.

'There's steak and kidney pudding. Fill you up a bit now you're crippled,' said the Bursar solicitously. 'It's not on his application form, but he's a cripple,' she explained to Sandra.

'It's nothing, it's nothing,' said Amiss. 'Honestly, since I grew up it only occasionally recurs.'

'Excuse me, Bursar,' said Sandra. 'Like, it's very hurtful to use that term.' Amiss tried to look hurt.

'Oh God, what's it supposed to be, handicapped?'

'Differently abled, Bursar. Our condition is no better than Mr Amiss's condition. It's just different. OK?'

'That's a lot of bollocks if you ask me,' said the Bursar. 'If he's crippled he's crippled, so he isn't as abled as us. Stands to reason.' She shook her head at her colleague's stupidity.

Amiss composed his features in what he hoped was a grateful, non-sexist, non-sexual smile and shot it across the table at Sandra, on whose solemn features it had no discernible effect.

'Right,' said the Bursar. 'What d'you want? We have to go and get the food from the hatch and I suppose I'll have to go and get it for you, since you're whatever you are. Steak and kidney pudding or that health muck they've introduced recently.'

'Which is what?'

'Root vegetable and dried fruit salad,' said Sandra. 'It's really great.'

'I think I'll have that,' said Amiss faintly. The Bursar looked at him incredulously and stomped off muttering 'pansy' loudly enough for everybody at the table to hear. Amiss affected not to and began to ask Sandra politely about her area of study. 'I'm working on phallocentrism and homophobia in *Adam Bede*,' said Sandra. It was one of those answers that made Amiss wish he'd asked about the weather, but he struggled gamely on. 'And what are your conclusions?'

'Yeah, of course it's phallocentric. I mean, that's obvious. Any woman who takes a man's name to write a book has to be yielding to a phallocentric culture so therefore the book must be too. OK? And as for the homophobia . . .'

18

'Oh Christ, not that again,' said the Bursar, slamming Amiss's plate down in front of him. 'George Eliot as queer-basher, is that what we're on about? I suppose you go along with that crap too?'

She dug deep into her pudding, found a kidney, grunted with pleasure and chomped it noisily. Gazing around with a seraphic smile, she focused on Sandra. 'I like kidneys,' she observed. 'It's no wonder you look so washed out, never eating anything decent.' She turned to Amiss. 'Girl's a vegan. Can you believe it?'

'Excuse me, Bursar, I've explained before that it's demeaning to speak of any woman past puberty as a "girl".'

'You never give up, do you?' The Bursar speared another kidney. 'I'll hand it to you, Sandra. You're some persistent dame,' she said gaily. 'Now, enough of this rubbish, I need a word with you about the afternoon's arrangements.' As she turned her back on Amiss, he took two forkfuls of diced turnip and raisins and tried to stay brave. He drank from the glass of water which was the only substance on offer and turned to the Senior Tutor, who was apparently on auto-pilot as she nibbled on her salad. She was an easy target; within two minutes he had her burbling happily about the critical edition of Beowulf that she had been working on for thirty years. Amiss won her over completely with a murmured expression of regret that so little Anglo-Saxon was learned any more; by the end of lunch she had confided in him how she hoped that that would be remedied with the help of the Alice Toon bequest.

It was a bonus that Sandra had been unable to hear this exchange. The Bursar had drawn the City slicker into their conversation and by an exercise of *force majeure* had got her to agree that all this feminist business had gone much too far. Amiss couldn't hear what was happening between the prep-school master and Pusey, but they both looked encouragingly miserable – certainly not like two chaps who were going to rush off and swap knitting patterns.

The interview, if it could be called that, went well. Sandra asked him solicitously about special needs in relation to his mobility impairment, which he managed to interpret swiftly enough. The Bursar then helped out by adopting a tone of deep sarcasm and asking if he'd like some ramps installed, or, perchance, a lift. Amiss had managed to sidestep all this by explaining that his present condition was as bad as he ever got and that most of the time no one would know there was anything wrong with him. The Senior Tutor, making an effort to address herself to the central issue, asked Amiss what his views were about the relationship between government and academe, in response to which he had burbled fluently about cooperation, mutual learning, scholarly heritage, but above all the necessity for keeping an open mind. Sandra had then pointed out that open minds could be overrated and that surely no work could be undertaken without starting with a set of beliefs.

'I mean, you know,' she said earnestly, 'you aren't going to say that government shouldn't ban all kinds of discrimination on campuses.'

'As long as there is no undermining of academic standards,' piped up the Senior Tutor.

Amiss had responded to that one with a flow of gobbledygook about learning from others' experience, challenging preconceptions and reconciling human and scholarly values. It was, the Bursar later told him grudgingly, one of the finest examples of meaningless but convincing bullshit she had heard in many a long year. Certainly it appeared to have silenced and contented both the Senior Tutor and Sandra. Francis Pusey had then asked Amiss how he felt about continuing cuts in government finance for education, on which Amiss, feeling safe on this one, had waxed concerned and eloquent and had talked about disturbing philistine trends.

Was there not too, Pusey had asked, a tendency for government to see education purely in terms of the acquisition of qualifications? Surely the quality of life at university was as important to the student as the quality of teaching. Should not the purpose of a university be also to introduce the student to beauty, to sensual experience, to art, to the spirit?

Sandra had interrupted to warn of the dangers of such

experiences being elitist; art should not be seen as objectively good or bad. Amiss began to flounder slightly on this one but was rescued by the Bursar, who explained she was bored to tears with all this claptrap and proposed to throw Mr Amiss out unless somebody had something else practical to ask him. Nobody had.

'Just one thing before you go,' she said. 'Are you married?'

'No.'

'Girlfriend?'

'No,' said Amiss, hoping he was getting this right.

'Thought not,' she said. 'Hobble off then. Don't call us, we'll call you.' She snorted loudly at her own wit as he nodded his goodbyes and limped to the door. As he shut it behind him he heard her saying, 'I don't think we want any more poofs in this place, do we?' and he knew the job was his.

3

'I played a blinder on that one,' said the Bursar complacently as they conducted their postmortem on the telephone later that evening.

'What about me? I thought I did rather well.'

'Not a bad touch with Oscar Wilde and the stick, but I thought my approach was rather more subtle.'

'Subtlety, Jack, is not the first word which comes to mind when thinking about you.'

'Just because I'm loud and a bit of a ham doesn't mean I'm not subtle. And how many times do I have to tell you to cut out this "Jack" business. It's imperative that you think "Bursar".'

'What's Jack short for anyway, or instead of?'

'Never you mind. We girls have to have some secrets.'

'Oh, blast you, be mysterious, then. Can I entice you into sharing with me what happened to the other two?'

'Oh, a touch of the blood sports really. Sandra impaled the poor bitch with the padded shoulders on the spike with which I had provided her. She was asked to explain her position on feminism with particular relation to dealing with sexist language, sexual harassment, sexism in the workplace and sexism on the syllabus. Poor bitch never had a chance. She tried to shift her ground at one stage and became a bit radical, so she managed to upset Emily by saying that relevance in education was very important and must take account of changing trends.

'Francis didn't take much interest in her. He was holding himself in readiness to tear the other poor schmuck apart, which he did in a rather splendidly feline fashion. I have to say that Francis, though undoubtedly a twerp, is quite a shrewd twerp, and he quickly revealed our poor tweedy friend to be both dumb and ignorant. Mind you, Sandra's both dumb and ignorant and would probably think it elitist to require brains and knowledge in a Fellow, but she had already decided against him. She's a maternal little soul who had been won over by your sufferings and my insensitivity.'

'How do they put up with you?'

'Why shouldn't they? The civil service did. Anyway quite apart from my three-year contract being watertight, I'm so good at the job the majority of the Fellows know they'd be mad to do without me. Besides, I think I bring a bit of cheer into their dreary lives; they can swap stories about my latest grossness.

'Now, to our muttons. What sort of accommodation do you want?'

'What can I have?'

'Medium-sized and uncomfortable, or large and very uncomfortable.'

'No small and comfortable?'

'Don't be ridiculous; this is St Martha's.'

'Medium,' he sighed. 'I suppose that means no bathroom.'

'You're lucky there's one on your corridor.'

'Who are my neighbours?'

'Francis Pusey and the Reverend Cyril Crowley, you lucky chap. Men get tucked away in corners by themselves for reasons of propriety.' She gave a loud cackle. 'When are you coming?'

'Soon as you like.'

'Tomorrow?'

'No. First I've got to go and find a cattery for my cat.'

'Why not bring it?'

'What, Plutarch?'

'I like cats. It would be quite nice to have one around the place. Add a bit of grace and elegance.'

'Listen, Bursar, that cat has about as much grace and elegance as you have.'

'Why then, you must certainly bring it. See you tomorrow, in time for guest night.'

'What happens on guest night?'

'You'll find out,' and with another loud cackle she rang off.

On the train to Cambridge, Amiss cursed himself for having given in so feebly to the Bursar about Plutarch, who had not ceased yelling throughout the entire journey.

'Should have given her a tranquillizer, dear,' said one elderly passenger. 'Poor little mite, she's terrified.'

'Madam,' said Amiss stiffly, 'it would take three circus strongmen to administer a tranquillizer to this . . . this . . . extremely large and bad-tempered animal.' He turned his face to the window and tried to pretend he had nothing to do with the rocking and relentlessly vociferous cat-basket.

By the time he reached St Martha's, he was exhausted from emotional tension and even Plutarch was beginning to show signs of weariness, but she started up again enthusiastically when Miss Stamp arrived at the door and began cootchy-cootchy-cooing into the wickerwork. This time she was sporting a lavender mohair jumper with a motif of musical notes. 'Dr Pusey's handiwork?'

Miss Stamp beamed and smiled. 'Yes, and I'm knitting him a waistcoat. One like the Bursar's got. You know, with a lot of pockets for his implements.'

Plutarch's needs were too pressing for Amiss to stop and seek further information on this baffling statement. 'Would you be very kind, Miss Stamp, and help me up to my room?'

'Well, yes, certainly, Mr Amiss. But you're a little early. I don't know if Mr Franks has gone yet.'

'Who?'

'Poor Mr Franks.'

'Why is he poor?' asked Amiss in some trepidation.

'Well, it's been ever so nasty over the last few weeks, all those allegations. Those girls, I don't know, really. I'm sure he didn't do any of those things.'

'What things?'

'Oh, er, it's not for me to gossip and I'm sure there's nothing in it. He never laid a finger on me.'

Not bloody surprised, thought Amiss ungallantly. 'What was his job?'

'He was the Household Management Fellow.'

'The what?'

'You know, like in Mrs Beeton.'

'Of course, quite, I see,' said Amiss, who was by now completely foxed. 'Well, my problem revolves around Plutarch, my cat. I don't want to let her out yet because she might never find her way back again. I thought I should introduce her first to our joint accommodation – let her get the hang of things gradually.'

'It's awfully nice to see a young man travelling around with his cat like this. Have you had her since a child?'

'No. She was, let us say, an unsolicited gift,' said Amiss grimly.

'Oh, you lucky thing. Now of course, with your poor leg you can't manage everything. I'll take your suitcase and you take Plutarch. I'm sure she'd be much happier with Daddy carrying her.'

His resentment at being categorized as the cat's father removed the guilt Amiss was feeling about letting an elderly lady carry his heavy case. Miss Stamp trotted up the stairs ahead of him and by the time they had climbed three flights, she, carrying the heavier burden, seemed in much better nick than he was.

'You're very fit,' he said enviously.

'I set great store by our Swedish drill. I hope you'll join in, Mr Amiss – 7.10 every morning, outside if it's not actually raining, otherwise in the hall. Nearly all the Fellows are there, Mistress to the fore.'

'Is it compulsory?' he asked faintly.

'Not quite, but the Mistress does like us all to be there. Of course, the students won't do it. You know what they're like nowadays. Anyway, here we are.'

She knocked on the door and a shout invited them to enter. 'Mr Franks, this is Mr Amiss. He's come to investigate how we can have a better relationship with the government. Now I've got to dash. Perhaps I can leave you two young men together.' Girlishly she skipped away.

'Sorry to intrude,' shouted Amiss over Plutarch's screeches.

'I think you'd better let that thing out,' said Franks, an agreeable-looking man in his late twenties. Amiss looked nervously around. 'Do you have any valuables within reach? She tends to be a bit frisky when released.'

'No,' I've finished packing and, as you can see, this place is decorated very simply.'

'It certainly is. Nay, monastically or more properly – conventually.' In a room that could have fitted fifty people standing, the only objects were a narrow bed with a plain beige bedcover, a spartan wooden desk and wooden chair, a small wardrobe, tiny bookcase, hideous armchair and a washbasin. The walls were white, the curtains were beige to match the bedcover and the floor covering was brown lino with a small grey bedside rug to brighten it up.

'Cheerless is not the word,' said Amiss.

'You've nothing to complain about. This is positively a luxury apartment. Washbasin? It's only people who are well in with the Bursar who get a washbasin, I can tell you. There's even an electric fire, which I've hidden in the wardrobe lest anyone sneak to the sisterhood that a man has been so privileged.'

Amiss had undone the straps of Plutarch's basket by now. 'Are you ready? I should stand out of the way if I were you.'

Franks flattened himself against the nearest wall, Amiss opened the lid and Plutarch went into her seek-and-destroy mode, which on this occasion found few targets. There were no decorations to knock over and her attempt to swing from the curtains failed dismally; they were too light to support her weight for long enough for her even to get her claws into them.

After a couple of minutes of leaping on top of flat surfaces and skidding along them, she got fed up, hurled herself on to the bed and moodily began to wash herself under her tail. Amiss averted his eyes and focused on his human companion. 'Why are you leaving?'

'Self-preservation. I keep getting nightmares that they'll castrate me next. I mean literally do a Bobbitt. They've been doing it metaphorically for long enough.' He looked pityingly at Amiss. 'I should take that cat with you everywhere you go. You'll be needing it for protection.'

'Could you supply me with a little more detail?'

'I'll supply you with a drink first. You probably need it.'

Franks fished a bottle of whisky out of his case, reached into a desk drawer and extracted two glasses. 'Neat?'

'No, I'd like lots of water in mine please. Got to be careful. It's guest night tonight.'

'Ah yes, I see. You're fearful of excessive alcoholic intake are you? I shouldn't worry too much.' He handed Amiss a glass of aggressively dark orange liquid. 'Cheers. And may God have mercy on your soul.'

'I can see you've been having a rough time.'

'Rough?' Franks's cry was so loud and agonized that Plutarch actually jumped. 'Sex was my downfall. Gross moral turpitude, that's what I'm being accused of, along with lookism, sexual harassment, date rape and we won't even go into the general ones of cultural and gender insensitivity. Oh yes, and the latest – misdirected laughter.'

'What's that, for Christ's sake?'

'I should define it as making a joke the ladies don't see, or possibly even making a joke they do see.'

'And the sexual stuff?'

'Oh God, well, the sexual harassment is straightforward. The list of charges includes putting an arm round an American neurotic called Sandra Murphy without requesting her permission first – Christ, I must have been drunk – being overheard saying that one of the undergraduates was a prickteaser and interrupting a woman twice at a college meeting.'

'That's sexual harassment?'

'That's sexual harassment.'

'And the date rape?'

'Well, I will not hide from you the fact that I have, er, had it off with the odd inhabitant of St Martha's. But strictly consentual sex, old boy. However, the sisterhood were keeping a tight eye on me and they nabbed me after a little contretemps with young Pippa.'

Amiss looked enquiring.

'I grant you young Pippa was a mistake.' He took a contemplative gulp. 'I've a piece of advice for you m'lad. Never shag a neurotic. But she was a very attractive neurotic and we got on awfully well when we met at a party one Friday night. We came back here and one thing led to another and awfully jolly it was too. Next day she decides I'm the love of her life, wants to have intense discussions about our relationship and explore each other's psyches; it's not the sort of exploration I go in for, I can tell you, old lad, so I say, "Look darlin', that was just a bit of fun. Anytime you want a bit of fun come to me, but I'm not in the market for the lovey-dovey stuff."

'So she gets pissed off and goes and cries on Sandra's shoulder. They have a great whinge session together, Sandra remonstrates with me, I can't see what she's driving at so I suppose I get a bit flippant. She goes off to Bridget, Head Bitch, she has Pippa in and cross-examines her.

'By now they've persuaded her that she never wanted to go to bed with me in the first place and an official charge is laid against me for date rape. When I point out that in order to go to bed with me she had to go about half a mile out of her way to accompany me to my room, it's explained to me that she was operating under the influence of alcohol and emotional duress. Then they throw everything else they can think of at me.'

'What comes next?'

'Oh God, there was going to be another one of those endless bloody rows and reference to this committee and that committee and Mistress's Appeal Court and I just threw in the towel. The Bursar bawled me out for being a lily-livered coward. She said it was typical of the bloody Old Women.'

'Who are?'

'Me, a nancy-boy called Francis Pusey and a creepy cleric called Crowley.'

'Why do you get lumped in with them?'

'Because the Bursar thinks we lack balls – she says we offend the Trades Description Act.'

'Doesn't sound from your adventures as if you do.'

'She meant metaphorically and she's right. I don't stand

up to the Dykes. I'm not as tough as the Bursar. I'm like Pusey and Crowley in just wanting a quiet life and some creature comforts.'

He looked pityingly at Amiss. 'I'm off. Take my advice and don't lay a finger on any of them. Keep your eyes on the ground and go to bed with your cat.'

He walked over and handed Amiss the whisky bottle. 'And hang on to this, you'll be needing it.'

4

Amiss had just fifteen minutes to unpack, sort out Plutarch's hygienic and culinary requirements and change for dinner. He cursed the Bursar for her usual failure to brief him on such matters and decided that this time – since presumably it was the Mistress he was trying to impress – more orthodox clobber was to be encouraged.

He arrived in his dark grey suit at the senior common room on the dot of seven and stood there alone for a few minutes trying to become interested in portraits of defunct Mistresses, all of whom combined in their expressions the grimness and austerity required in a university whose men had for sixty years permitted them to take examinations but not to receive degrees. The room itself was not too bad: decent panelling, inoffensive long, dark – if threadbare – velour curtains, a few armchairs that looked as if they might be almost pleasant to sit on and a nice view of the garden – though it would have helped if the garden had been nice to look at. The two flies in the ointment were the absence of heat and the contents of the drinks tray.

Being the product of a male Oxford college, Amiss had assumed pre-dinner drinks on a guest night would be two varieties of sherry. Instead, what the drinks tray seemed to offer was tap water or orange squash, a substance Amiss thought had disappeared – certainly from the adult scene – sometime in the late 1950s. He was gazing morosely at the water jug when the Bursar entered and let out a glass-shattering hoot of laughter. 'Bet that came as a nasty shock. Don't you fret, Jack Troutbeck will see you right.' She reached inside the jacket of her houndstooth suit, fumbled round her extensive chest and finally drew out two miniature bottles of gin, which she swiftly decanted into tumblers. 'Water, orange squash or neat?'

'You do offer the most delicious alternatives. Orange squash please.'

'Well you'll have to provide your own mixers. I'm not your bloody nanny, you know; my waistcoat isn't that capacious.'

'What else have you in there?' Amiss was about to commence a sartorial investigation when he heard steps coming down the corridor.

'That'll be the Mistress,' said the Bursar.

'How do you know?'

'Because it's exactly ten past seven, of course.'

The door opened and a tall sturdy figure, clad in what closely resembled a dark grey sack, entered, bowed and said, 'Good evening, Bursar.'

'Good evening, Mistress. May I introduce our new recruit, Mr Amiss – the chap who's going to sort us out with Whitehall.'

'Ah yes, Whitehall. You and the Bursar will no doubt have a lot in common,' said the Mistress vaguely, reaching for the water jug. 'I'm afraid I don't know much about such matters.'

'Oh, I don't know, Mistress,' said the Bursar. 'You're pretty clued up on bureaucracies.'

'I think they've rather changed. They didn't, for instance, have computers in the twelfth century; I'm sure they must make a difference.' Her sociological reflections were interrupted by the arrival of a clutch of women, including Sandra Murphy and the Senior Tutor, whose hair was now three-quarters out of her hairnet. As she had a habit of swaying to and fro when she talked, long wispy bits of hair waved distractingly about her head. Sandra smiled at Amiss and he moved to her side. 'I don't need my stick this evening. It's one of my good days.'

'That's great. And it's really neat that you've got the job. Now, come and meet Bridget. OK?' She shyly tugged him by the sleeve. Amiss obediently followed her across the room to where a handsome woman with long frizzy black hair was laying down the law to Francis Pusey. She acknowledged

Sandra's introduction, shook hands with Amiss, greeted him curtly and continued to address Pusey about the agenda for the following morning's meeting. 'A principle is a principle. This discrimination will have to stop: we'll have to have our intentions made part of institutional requirements.'

'For heaven's sake, Bridget,' squeaked Pusey, 'it's only a part-time tutorship in classics. Surely we don't have to go through all the paraphernalia of job descriptions.'

Sandra tugged Amiss's sleeve again and drew him away. 'Sorry. Bridget's pretty steamed up. She's feeling a lot of anger about the way you got the job. It not being properly advertised and all.'

'Wasn't it?' Amiss distinctly remembered being instructed by the Bursar to pretend he'd answered an ad in the *Guardian*.

'Yeah, well, you see, Bridget feels – and of course she's right – that as equal opportunities employers we should be advertising in the women's press and journals representing marginalized people. Like, there's lots of folks can't afford to read the *Guardian*. OK?'

Amiss thought of three answers and rejected all of them. He fell back on the weak smile which served him so well. 'Who's here tonight in addition to the Fellows?' he asked.

'Well, there's the guest speaker. Though she's a Fellow too – the new Schoolmistress Fellow. It's her first day.'

'Speaker? Do you mean there's an after-dinner speech?'

'Yeah, well, it's more of a lecture really. We do this on the first Thursday of every month – come back in here afterwards with the students and hear a visitor talk.'

'On what?' Amiss felt swamped in despair; the thought of having to sit through a lecture was always enough to bring him close to tears.

'Maybe old architecture or one of those subjects that the Mistress's friends are interested in. I'm afraid they're completely irrelevant to our agenda. Bridget's going to have that stopped. We've got someone coming in next time to talk about dictionaries.'

'Ah. She's a lexicographer?'

'Sorry?'

'Someone who defines words.'

'Sort of, I guess. She runs a course at St Barbara's Access College called "Freeing ourselves from Patriarchal Wordwebs."'

'Like what?'

Sandra looked at him in a puzzled fashion. 'Well, you know, like any of them. *Websters, Oxford,* all those paternalistic ones.'

'Sorry, Sandra. What's the alternative?'

'Why there are lots. Haven't you got **Mary Daly's** *Wickedary,* or even *The Dictionary of Bias-Free Usage?*'

'I can see I've got a lot to learn.' Amiss wished Jack was to hand with some more gin, but she was out of reach on the other side of the room, booming at a pot-bellied cleric.

'We'll help. It's all very exciting here at the moment. Bridget is so inspirational. She makes you so aware. She's so brilliant and so principled.' Sandra looked at her watch. 'Oh, it's nearly time. We'll be going in in half a minute.'

'You're very precise.'

'Well, it's the Mistress. You can set your watch by her.'

For an academic, thought Amiss, and an advanced feminist one at that, Sandra had a surprisingly pedestrian turn of phrase. He speculated on how someone of her limited ability could tackle a genius like George Eliot and remembered that large numbers of people were paid for a living to write about those who were their intellectual and possibly moral superiors. And, of course, if possible, tear them to shreds.

'*Ave!*' said a cheery voice as the crowd began to move out of the common room. The greeting turned out to belong to the pink-cheeked Schoolmistress Fellow, Primrose Partridge.

'I'm so excited,' she said, as they set off together, Sandra having scuttled off to attach herself to Bridget's coat-tails. 'It's my first day here. I've got a whole three months. I've really been looking forward to the intellectual challenge.'

'Do you know St Martha's?'

'Oh yes. I'm an Old Girl. When I was a student here I used to look up at those dons at high table and wonder if I'd ever be among them. I thought how wonderful it would be to have all that challenging conversation. Shake up the old brain cells and all that.'

'You haven't been back since?'

'No. Always meant to. But you know the way it is. *Tempus fugit* and all that.'

'Where do you teach?'

'A Yorkshire girls' comprehensive. Classics. When it was a grammar school we used to have fifty or sixty girls taking classics in the sixth form. Now I've got four. Just as well I'm getting close to retirement. In fact, I should have left already, but they couldn't find anyone to replace me. It's all a bit sad.'

'*Nil desperandum*,' said Amiss encouragingly. 'Classics will rise again.' As they turned to enter the dining room, the Bursar burst through the people behind them and dug a vigorous elbow into Amiss's back, causing him to miss his step and cannon into his neighbour.

'I beg your pardon,' he said to Primrose Partridge. 'Very clumsy of me.'

'*Ego te absolvo*,' she said lightly.

The Bursar was impatient with these niceties. She caught him by the sleeve and dragged him to one side. 'You're getting a bit intimate, Bursar, aren't you?'

'Not with you, duckie,' she said, smiling coarsely. 'I don't fancy woofdahs. And you're safe with most of the other Fellows as well.' She raised her voice. 'Dykes don't go for your sort, do you girls?' she asked, leering at Bridget and Sandra, who had moved into earshot. Sandra flushed, Bridget compressed her lips and they accelerated into the dining room. The Bursar chortled. 'Here.' She jabbed several small bottles into his hand. 'You'll be needing these.'

'Why does everyone keep saying that?' An awful thought struck him. 'You don't mean this meal is dry?'

'Of course it's bloody dry. This is a Temperance College. Cf Statute Number thirty-seven.'

'You took care to keep that hidden from me before you inveigled me into this, you old . . .'

'Diplomat?'

'Swindler would be more accurate. And what's more, you told me nothing of after-dinner lectures.'

'Stop making a fuss. It'll be good for you.' She headed towards the dining room. 'It's Primrose on the subject of Henry VIII and his Yorkshire connections. Should be a gas. Sit at the back and I'll fortify you if you're in serious need.'

The maternal instinct took women in interestingly different ways, reflected Amiss, seating himself where directed at the left hand of the Mistress and to the right of the clergyman, who turned to him, bowed and addressed him in tones so unctuous that they might have come straight from a 1950s Ealing comedy.

'Good evening. How refreshing to see another brother among our little flock.' Amiss returned the bow.

'You, I suspect, must be Robert Amiss. I am the Reverend Cyril Crowley, Chaplain Fellow – a man of the cloth with some small pretensions to being also a man of scholarship. Are you by any chance interested in local ecclesiastical history, about which,' he said, speeding up in the manner of the bore who is terrified that he'll get a wrong answer to the question, 'I may claim to have some small expertise, particularly when one comes to the records of the parish of Athelstan to which I have the honour of being also attached. You understand I perform ecclesiastical services for these ladies only on a part-time basis.'

'I'm surprised they don't have a woman,' said Amiss, hoping to head him off from his scholarly pursuits.

'Couldn't do the Communion, old boy. Couldn't do the Communion.'

'They can now.'

'Oh, you're one of these feminist chaps, are you? In favour of priestesses and all that?'

'Yes.'

'I have to disagree with you there, old man. The fact of the matter is – and my experience is not slight – not that I would dare say it to any of these ladies, some of whom are rather ferocious, I fear, that this sort of thing really is not women's work. As my dear late wife and I frequently said to each other, "If Jesus had meant women to be priests, why – he would have said so."'

'The scribes were all male, so we'll never know if he did or not.'

'I can see you're a bit of a Quisling in our midst, Robert.' He laughed heartily. 'Don't mind me. I'm only pulling your leg. I'm sure we won't fall out over a little matter like the ladies and the Church.' Crowley turned to Sandra. 'Quite a young feminist firebrand you've found yourselves in this young man, if I may say so.'

Sandra cast upon Amiss a smile of approval. Before either of them could speak, the Reverend Cyril returned to the charge. 'As I was saying, about parochial history, there is still a lot of work to be done on the records of the parish of Athelstan. And in my spare time – of which I have little, you understand, for a man of the cloth is always on call and even scholarship must give way to the demands of his congregation – I try to make my modest contribution. It is not an easy path that I have chosen, but I have my moments of relaxation and when I have I like to continue with work on my monograph.

'No doubt you too have your scholarly interests?'

'Oh, yes, indeed,' said Amiss. 'I'm completing my Ph.D thesis on the incidence of flatulence among choirboys in the parish of Chipping Campden in the late seventeenth century.' As he said it he was appalled by his own rudeness; either the Bursar's habits were catching, he thought, or the whisky and gin were getting to him. Fortunately the Reverend Crowley was unfazed.

'Oh ho ho,' he said. 'I see we've got a jester here. Jolly good. Jolly good. I often think a little healthy humour is perhaps needed. The ladies can be a tad serious, you know; they're just a little prone to be serious. I often say to them, "You should rest more, relax more. Get around the piano and have a good old sing-song. You can't be always labouring over these scholarly tasks, you know."'

A thin green soup was slammed in front of him by a slattern with a walleye, a hump and an exaggerated limp. The soup tasted of weed. Amiss observed the Bursar reaching inside her jacket and emerging with a small bottle, the contents of which she proceeded blatantly to empty into her soup plate. Covertly, Amiss scrabbled in his pocket, took out the little bottles therein, found the sherry and followed suit; if he was going to listen to a lecture on Henry VIII in Yorkshire, he reasoned, he might as well be entirely pickled. For most of the rest of the meal he listened to the Mistress, who addressed him coherently on the subject of the advantages and disadvantages of single sex colleges.

'Why did you decide to become mixed?' he asked, when there was a lull.

'We haven't. Well, that is, only in a couple of special cases. We had to have a male chaplain and we couldn't seem to find anyone else to take up the two statutory positions that Dr Pusey and Mr Franks have. Or, to be precise, Dr Pusey has and Mr Franks had.'

'Which are?'

'Why, Dr Pusey is the Fellow in Womanly Arts.'

'Oh, of course,' said Amiss. 'And Mr Franks was your Fellow in Household Management.'

'Yes, I realize that to outsiders it is a little odd,' said the Mistress, 'but the founder was very anxious that the traditional skills should not be lost simply because the girls were being given higher education, and frankly, there are very few people these days who are sufficiently qualified in either of those subjects and who are also highly qualified academically. We were really rather fortunate to find those two.'

'They have to have good degrees?'

'I am not prepared to tolerate a diminution in standards,' said the Mistress firmly. 'This college rests or falls on excellence. We do not all necessarily see eye to eye on this, but I am determined that we shall reach new heights when the Alice Toon bequest is put into effect.'

Soup gave way to shepherd's pie, with nut cutlets for the vegetarians. It was followed by a surprisingly good mature cheddar. In the case of the Bursar, the sherry had given way to wine but Amiss had had a failure of nerve and – unable to bring himself to produce the quarter bottle of Bordeaux under the Mistress's nose – had gone on miserably sipping the tap water.

The Mistress had ceased to keep his attention; there seemed no chance of stopping her from talking about the need to restore palaeography to its original position as the jewel in the college's crown. He observed that Miss Partridge was looking a lot less cheerful than she had been at the beginning of the meal. The neighbour on her right, a sour-looking woman in her fifties, was reading a book, and Miss Partridge was enduring alternately the Reverend Cyril's orotundities – bellowed across the table – and, from her left, a disquisition from Pusey on the subject of his passion for order, method and lists. He had, it appeared catalogued his books, *objets d'art*, his clothes and – naturally – all his research notes on the history of eighteenth-century Westphalian embroidery.

'And then, of course,' Amiss overheard him saying, 'there are my own little works of art. You must come and join us one of these evenings, we have such fun, and I'll make something for you.'

'I'm not very domestic, I'm afraid,' Miss Partridge said nervously, only to be interrupted by another hoot from the Reverend. Amiss feared the quality of conversation on high table was not perhaps all she had hoped for.

5

At 8.15 the Mistress rose and headed for the door. The
assembled company began to shuffle after her. Amiss lagged
behind to catch the Bursar, who was scoffing another piece
of cheese and taking a slug of port from a small bottle.

'Hope you enjoyed the cheese,' she said. 'I'm responsible
for that. I provide it myself as otherwise I'd starve to death.'

'Fat chance of that. What I want to know is a) why do
you have a waitress who looks like a female version of
Quasimodo?'

'Cor, don't let the Dykes hear you use a word like "waitress": she's an "attendant". Poor old Greasy Joan. It's all
that Fens inbreeding.'

'Greasy Joan as in "Greasy Joan doth keel the pot"?'

'Good lad. I'm glad someone's literate. Mind you, I don't
recommend your addressing her as that. She might be hurt.
Stick to Joan. And the answer to your question is that she
comes exceedingly cheap, being dim as well as undecorative.'

'B) do I have to attend this ghastly event?'

'Certainly.'

'And c) how do you get away with drinking alcohol in
front of all of them?'

'Because old Maud Buckbarrow chooses not to notice and
the others wouldn't dare say anything. The oleaginous Crowley hinted something once and I told him it was a matter
between me and my doctor. That shut him up. Blasted old
hypocrite. If he had his way, every penny of Alice Toon's
would go on luxuries for C. Crowley.

'Now come on, put a brave face on it. You're supposed to
be a bloody ally, not a wimp. Your job is to weigh up the

39

opposition and help me to develop a foolproof strategy.' She jumped up so energetically that the chair fell over. 'Come on.'

'I should have thought that a woman of your gifts could swat these enemies with one mighty blow,' said Amiss, as they hastened out of the dining room.

'I probably will,' she said carelessly. 'But in any case, a girl needs an admirer to look on and applaud her valorous deeds.'

Gloomily reflecting that this adventure was turning out to be more boring than he had been promised, Amiss decided on another quick anaesthetic. A swift search of his pockets revealed that the Bursar's bounty had amounted to – in addition to the small bottle of wine he had been too pusillanimous to open at table – a miniature brandy.

Amiss liked to think of himself as a civilized social drinker; brandy was for consuming slowly after dinner. However, with Henry VIII and Yorkshire in mind he swallowed the contents of the bottle in two gulps, entering the senior common room choking and coughing. Sandra rushed up to him full of concern and indicated by her body language a sympathy with whatever congenital disadvantage had brought this on.

When he was able to speak again he muttered bravely. 'Asthma. Old childhood complaint.'

'Do you want to sit here?' she asked solicitously, pointing towards an empty chair in the front row. Simultaneously, Amiss observed the Bursar gesticulating wildly from the back row.

'Sorry, Sandra, I wish I could, but the Bursar seems to want me for something. I'd better do what I'm told.'

'Sure.'

Clearly one could not get too wimpy to lose Sandra's sympathy. Amiss saw his role clearly: he must seriously work at being a New Man and extremely unhealthy to boot.

'What are you doing?' he hissed *sotto voce* to the Bursar as he sat down beside her. 'We're not supposed to be friends.'

'What?' she asked loudly. 'Say that again. I didn't hear you.' He glared at her.

'You're so neurotic. Now look here, I want you to come over to my office afterwards. We've got some administrative details to sort out and I'm all tied up on college committees tomorrow. We really should cut this lecture . . .' Hope flickered. 'But we won't.'

A moment later the Mistress, who had been chit-chatting in an intense sort of way with Miss Partridge, ushered her to a chair at the head of the table, sat down on the other one herself and said, 'Colleagues and students.' Amiss was impressed by her considerable presence. She spoke with the confidence of one who knows silence will instantly descend on the word of command. Even Bridget, who had been expressing herself forcefully to a dishy-looking black woman in the front row, shut up instantly.

'Now, I want to introduce to you my old friend, Miss Primrose Partridge, who is joining us for the term as Schoolmistress Fellow. She is a most distinguished old girl of this college, who in 1952 pulled off the treble of the Agatha Runcible Essay Prize, the Daisy Shrubsole Prize for Greek Iambics, and, if I may introduce a personal note, with our Senior Tutor, our Bursar, our friend Amy Braithwaite – alas, long lost from us to Canada – and myself, the Winifred Wristbardge Ladies' Rowing Challenge Cup.'

'You, no doubt, were the cox,' whispered Amiss.

'Don't be impertinent. I, of course, was stroke.'

'I'm sorry, Bursar.' The Mistress's tone was icy. 'I didn't catch that.'

'Sorry, Mistress.' The Bursar looked almost abashed. 'I fear I was enlarging to our young friend here on our girlish exploits.'

There was a small ripple of well-bred laughter from the older Fellows. 'A little nostalgia is no doubt in order on such an occasion,' said the Mistress indulgently. 'However, we must get on with more serious pursuits.

'Miss Partridge has been fighting the good fight for traditional excellence in transmitting to the cream of Yorkshire gels a veneration for some of the greatest treasures of civilization. I refer of course to the classics, to the tongues of Plato,

41

of Aristotle, of Homer, of Pliny, of Thucydides . . .' Seeming to recognize that she was going off into a veritable laundry list of distinguished Dead White European Males, she paused.

'But that is not all that Miss Partridge has accomplished. She has never been a narrow specialist. As a gel it was always her delight in her leisure time to read of the glories of our past, to visit our royal palaces, our great cathedrals, our fortifications, our noble architectural heritage.

'Since she went to live there, she has made Yorkshire her own. She will have much to tell us while she is amongst us, but tonight she will concentrate on her most recent series of fascinating discoveries about the links of Yorkshire with King Henry VIII – as expressed in its architectural fabric.'

The Mistress turned and smiled at Miss Partridge, who had been slightly nervously shuffling what Amiss saw to his alarm were extensive notes. She stood up. 'Thank you, Mistress, for that warm welcome. I can't tell you what it means to be back in the old spot once more. *Quis custodias ipsos custodes*? so often comes to mind when one reflects on those in charge of education today, but not when one thinks of this great college, where our Mistress is a custodian who needs no supervision.' There was a polite titter from three or four of the audience.

'So now, ladies and gentlemen, if I may . . .' There was a loud scraping of a chair and Bridget Holdness jumped up.

'Excuse me,' she said.

Miss Partridge looked flummoxed. 'Yes?'

'I'm afraid I have to register a protest.' Miss Partridge looked at the Mistress.

'What is it, Dr Holdness?'

'Well, for a start I resent being addressed in that offensive manner.'

Amiss was interested to observe that Miss Partridge's jaw actually dropped. She gazed helplessly to her left.

'Dr Holdness,' said the Mistress levelly. 'Miss Partridge is a guest and I think we should accord her the courtesy of an uninterrupted hearing.'

'Oh no no,' said Miss Partridge. 'I . . . I wouldn't want to

upset anybody. Please, somebody tell me what I've done.'
She sat down.

'"Ladies and gentlemen" is a form of address which is totally out of order.'

'I'm sorry. I don't understand.'

'"Lady" is a condescending term, designed to keep women in the position of servants.'

Seeing Miss Partridge's baffled expression, Sandra piped up helpfully. 'You see, Ms Partridge, the word "lady" implies that women are ornamental – not involved with the workplace. It's a way of keeping us out of things, you see, like we're not equal. It oppresses us.'

'So what are "gentlemen"?' Miss Partridge's brow was furrowed with an effort to understand. 'Surely the same applies there?'

'No, no,' said Sandra. '"Gentlemen", well, it's you know, well ... classist ... or like that men are gentle, and that's wrong because just look at their violence against women.' Bridget helpfully took over. 'These are anachronistic terms which reinforce stereotypes,' she said crisply.

'Well, what do you suggest I say instead?'

'Men and women, people, or colleagues. Unless of course there are some non-colleagues in the audience who might feel marginalized.'

The Mistress no longer seemed to be paying attention. Amiss assumed that she had gone off into some erudite day-dream.

'Very well then,' said Miss Partridge. 'Now may I continue?'

'I'm sorry,' said Bridget Holdness, 'but there is a more substantial issue here. What the Mistress said about the classics is deeply offensive to our new Fellow, Ms Denslow' – she gestured to the black girl beside her, who was staring at the floor – 'who should not hear Western civilization described as if it were in some way superior to others.'

This was too much for the Bursar. Flushed with gin, wine and port, she leaped to her feet and bellowed. 'Mary Lou's a bloody American. What do you think that means if it doesn't mean Western civilization?'

'Mary Lou,' said Bridget, 'is an Afro-American, which means that she hails from a civilization probably older and greater than anything understood in this ethno-centric institution.' Mary Lou continued to inspect the rug. 'And moreover, as women, we are all insulted by the very memory of Henry VIII. I find it extraordinary that a gathering of sisters can be subjected to the insult of being asked to listen to an address on a white serial murderer of women.

'It is time,' she said, raising her voice for the benefit of the undergraduates who were clustering round at the back, 'that this institution examined its own ethno-centricity, neo-colonialism and slavish aping of patriarchal attitudes.'

She turned her back on her victims and addressed the audience. 'Sisters, this college was founded by a paternalistic capitalist whose mission was to contain the female subversion that threatened the male establishment. Have we learnt nothing from the last hundred years? Are we to go on accepting our own inferiority, using the language of the oppressor, enduring the racial insults to our black sisters, addressing ourselves to the cultures of female-hating societies like Greece and Rome when there are the great matriarchal societies and the history of invisible women to explore and celebrate? Are we to bury ourselves in the past? Or will we go forth into a future where empathy replaces scrutiny, independence replaces subservience and above all – universality takes the place of elitism.'

A ragged cheer went up from some of the students. Bridget Holdness smiled, turned round again and said, 'I'm sorry Ms Partridge, but I cannot remain to experience further affront.'

She had positioned herself neatly at the end of a row so her walk-out was unimpeded. Sandra and Mary Lou trailed in her wake, followed by a couple of dozen students. Miss Partridge put her head in her hands and began to cry.

'It's all right, Primrose,' said the Mistress, awkwardly patting her on the back. 'If you'd rather, we'll have the paper another night.'

Miss Partridge lifted her head and gazed round the audience. 'But I thought I was coming home. Getting away from all those philistines.'

'I fear,' said the Mistress, 'that in higher education these days, philistinism is rapidly becoming a dogma.' '*Tempera mutantur*,' sobbed Miss Partridge, 'I should have known not to come back.'

The Mistress looked around the remnants of the audience. 'Ladies and gentlemen, I think we'll postpone this lecture to another evening.'

'I'm going to kill that bitch one of these days,' said the Bursar to Amiss. 'Now come along to my room and we'll talk over how to do it.'

6

'I suppose you could try using that elephant gun,' said Amiss, gaping in awe at the great blunderbuss on the wall of the Bursar's sitting room.

'Can't get the ammunition nowadays. I'm told Rigby's gave up manufacturing them a few years ago no doubt owing to the shortage of elephants. Drink?'

'Unwise.'

'Listen, since Franks got chucked out, I'm surrounded by carrot-juice drinkers, teetotallers and oh-well-I'll-have-a-small-sherry-seeing-as-it's-my-birthday types. Don't go all pi on me.' She waved the whisky bottle at him.

'Oh, very well then, but a very small weak one. I have to find my room, deal with my cat and try to behave like a New Man to any virago I meet along the way.'

'What's a New Man?'

'My God, they're right about you being out of touch with the times.' Amiss settled back comfortably in the vast armchair. 'New Men read the *Guardian*, change the nappies, bond with their babies, share their emotions with their partners, recognize the inhibiting aspects of their maleness and explore their own femininity, if you follow me.'

'Can't say I do. Are they any good in bed?'

'Well, they're certainly very caring. Unfortunately, recent surveys seem to suggest that women are doing the dirty on them by abandoning them in droves for brutish, hairy, selfish, libidinous throwbacks. Sexual politics is a nightmare, Bursar. Just as well for you that it passes you by.'

'Would that it could,' said the Bursar sighing. 'Everything was very happy in this absurd old backwater until the Head

Bitch arrived. It was uncomfortable but it was contented; it knew what it was about. What's wrong with a collection of old biddies spending their lives trying to get their footnotes right and pass on to a new generation some belief in scholarship and truth.'

'Narrow elitism?' queried Amiss.

'Oh yes, the charge of narrowness has substance. And I'm not really entirely impervious to the need occasionally to open up to new ideas. But bugger the business about elitism. If you don't have that in scholarship, you don't have scholarship.

'No, what the Bridget bitch is doing is levelling. If you level the way she's going about it, you destroy the good and put nothing in its place except half-baked platitudes parroted by morons like Sandra who haven't got the brains of a hen but apply the few they have to picking the nits out of the work of one of the greatest female geniuses of all time because they have concluded that she was a misguided apologist for a patriarchal society.' She sat bolt upright and quivering. 'Now let me test you to see if you've any notion how bad it is. Why is George Eliot *persona non grata*?'

'Well, male ideology and all that stuff, I suppose.'

'Christ, you have no realization of how simple-minded these cretins are. George Eliot was a woman, right?'

'Right.'

'She took on a man's name.'

'Yes?'

'And you and I know why she did that.' She looked at him expectantly.

'Because otherwise she wouldn't have been taken seriously, the 1860s being what it was.'

'Ah, yes. That's what you think and that's what I think, and we think that in adopting *noms de plume*, she and the Brontës were adapting to reality and in a way pulling a fast one on the chaps. Well, it doesn't seem that way to Sandra, because Sandra has a simple mind, and Sandra knows that when Marian Evans decided to call herself George Eliot she was denying her own sexuality.'

'You mean selling out to the enemy?'

'More than that. If I understand it correctly, Marian Evans was a dyke without the courage to acknowledge her dykeness. Therefore, subliminally, she expressed it by adopting a man's name, living with men whom she was only pretending were sexual partners and using her books to cover herself with a heterosexual patina that would hide her true feelings even from herself.'

'Does the word anachronism mean anything to people like Sandra?'

'Nothing,' said the Bursar gloomily. 'Nor does reason. For Christ's sake, Sandra persists in talking about ''herstory'', although I spelled out for her in words of one syllable the derviation of the word ''history'' and explained why it had nothing to do with men.'

'She didn't understand?'

'In that little whiney voice of hers she told me that perception was all.'

They fell silent. The Bursar leaned forward and poured some more whisky into Amiss's glass. 'What really pisses me off, the older I get,' she said, 'is that the world is full of talent and people with brains who get no chance, so serve out their lives using a tenth of their potential, while increasingly the universities seem to be full of quarter-wits educated beyond their intelligence. If I had my way I would swap half our undergraduates and Fellows instantly for an equivalent number of street sweepers, male and female, from Calcutta. Six months remedial teaching and we'd be on a winner.'

'Well, that's definitely an unethno-centric statement. Have you put it to Bridget?'

'The only thing I'm likely to put to Bridget,' said the Bursar breathing heavily, 'is the muzzle of my elephant gun. Up her arse.'

'And what about the mysterious Mary Lou? Is she as dim a hanger-on as Sandra?'

'Finding that out is one of your jobs. They won't have anything to do with me for the reasons I'm sure you've spotted. I haven't a clue about Mary Lou; she's a bit of a dark horse.' She smote her forehead. '''Dark horse''. Excellent: there's an expression Bridget would have me blackballed for.'

'You're doing pretty well with the politically incorrect terminology, old girl. Does it come naturally or are you doing it on purpose?'

'You don't need to do it on purpose. You can offend in this place by blowing your nose.' She suited the action to the words: the resulting explosion would have done credit to the elephant gun.

'As I was saying, Mary Lou was unanimously recommended by the Research Fellowship sub-committee which consisted of two Dykes and a Virgin, presumably because the Dykes forgave her having good academic qualifications because she was black and was conducting research on early twentieth-century myths about Sappho.'

'So far so stereotyped. Now why do you think she didn't throw herself into the fray this evening?'

'Maybe she's still finding her feet. I leave it to you to conduct your researches in whatever way you think fit. Now, would you care to see the agenda for tomorrow morning's Council meeting. I would particularly like to draw your attention to item 3 a), Sandra's draft equal opportunity policy statement. Listen.'

She declaimed rather than read out:

'"St Martha's awareness that groups or individuals may have been disadvantaged educationally or otherwise in the past, has led to a decision that the balance should be redressed. Positive steps have therefore been taken to ensure that on every shortlist for every appointment in the college a majority of candidates will be from members of groups who have hitherto shared the experience of discrimination. Disadvantaged groups can be identified according to race, colour, creed, ethnic or national origin, disabilities, sex, sexual orientation or marital status."'

'I don't believe it.'

She passed it over.

Amiss scanned it. 'My God, I hope for your sake they recognize fat as a disability.' The Bursar playfully threw a cushion at him. It knocked over his glass, the contents of which soaked both the equal opportunities paper and his tie.

'Dries out,' she said cheerfully, pouring him another. 'Read on.'

' "Often people are perceived to have had insufficient education because of preconceived opinions or judgements about what education is. St Martha's will endeavour to ensure that through the abolition of pre-set requirements, jobs will be open to the widest possible variety of candidate. Historic disadvantage will, however, be a relevant factor in the decision-making process . . ." Do I have to read the rest?'

'No, that's the nub.'

'Do I understand this as meaning that the Dykes want qualifications to be unnecessary to get an academic job in this establishment?'

'I think that's about the size of it. And worse. It's clear that they propose to apologize, through the appointments system, for historic wrongs against particular communities.'

'So it's bring on the one-legged black lesbians and only the one-legged black lesbians.'

'We're headed there. Mary Lou's the black dyke, you're supposed to be the crippled gay . . .'

'And you?'

'Oh, at the moment,' said the Bursar, 'I'm making the most of being fat and old and I'm keeping my sexuality even more of a secret than did George Eliot. Now drink up, it's time you went to bed.'

'I don't know how to find my room.'

'I will escort you and protect your virtue from any lurking sexual predators. I will also meet your cat. Now, I want you up at seven o'clock in the morning, in the garden or the front hall, to participate in the Swedish drill.'

'Why?' Even to his own ears, Amiss's scream was heartfelt.

'Because you've had too much of the Dykes since you've arrived and I think it's time you had a blast of the Virgins. You're not here, you know, merely to enjoy yourself. There is,' said the Bursar, smiling evilly, 'no such thing as a free temporary Research Fellowship.'

7

Plutarch awakened Amiss by kneading his chest in a particularly brutal fashion. Casting her aside with a loud oath, he established that the alarm was due to go off in two minutes and crawled miserably out of bed to dress for the physical jerks. He was relieved to see that it was raining and that he would be spared the dank dew of an early morning in the Fens.

He arrived clad in jeans and T-shirt and panting in the front hall at 7.09, having been delayed by Plutarch's demand for food and a contretemps with a can opener. There were a half-dozen or so women already there, dressed in interestingly individual garments. A dreamy-looking beanpole with cropped grey hair – later identified as the theologian, Miss Thackaberry – wore a long striped shirt inside out; the Bursar was simply turned out in knickers and vest; the Senior Tutor sported grey woollen stockings topped with an elongated grey woolly sweater; Miss Stamp, as ever, radiated brightness – this time in a tracksuit in Christmas-fairy pink with appliqued cats. 'I hoped you'd turn up, Mr Amiss. I wore this in honour of your dear pussycat.'

Amiss felt a momentary flash of resentment on Plutarch's behalf; a cat of such determined fighting spirit and ferocity of temperament should not be thus slandered. As he strove to make some appropriate rejoinder, the Mistress came downstairs, looking trim in a maroon gymslip.

She stood with her back to her followers and went instantly into action, swinging her arms forwards and backwards in a warming-up exercise which the others followed faithfully. Within a minute and with no warning she swung into the in-out jump. Amiss had not participated in an exercise class since school but he had once observed one in action on civil service premises. On that occasion, half a dozen or so women dressed in leotards had been leaping about aerobically to a frightful din of hard rock interspersed with screamed instructions from a tarty-looking, over-made-up blonde. He was not enjoying himself, but he was grateful that at least the Virgins did it quietly.

His ruminations were shattered by a swift and extremely painful blow to the back of his neck, which turned out to be the Bursar's delicate way of indicating that the assembled company had now moved on to toe-touching. Out of the corner of his eye he observed with pleasure that this exercise was giving her a little trouble. Even with the greatest exertion she could reach only as far as mid-calf. He was doing only slightly better, but the others – to a Virgin – appeared to be effortlessly hitting the spot.

The Mistress took them through four or five more movements and at 7.30 said, 'Thank you, ladies, and Mr Amiss,' and took the stairs at commendable speed. All followed save the Bursar and Amiss, both of whom were short of breath.

'I shall probably be unable to walk tomorrow,' groaned Amiss.

'That's all right,' she responded cheerfully. 'You're supposed to be a cripple.'

'No thanks to you I'm not dead; you nearly broke my neck.'

'All you youngsters nowadays seem to want to be treated like Dresden,' she said contemptuously.

'Well, you are certainly putting up a pretty good imitation of Bomber Command.' He stopped for a moment to catch his breath. 'Now what was I supposed to have got out of this new unpleasant experience? Oh, yes, I remember, snuggling up closer to the Virgins.'

The Bursar began to climb the stairs. 'What did you notice?'

'That they seem to be a united and happy team.'

'That's correct. Except for that old cow Deborah Windlesham . . .'

'Who?'

'The one who looks as if she's just sucked on a lemon.'

'Ah, and reads at meals.'

'That's her. But Maud keeps her in her place, so mostly she's perforce a team player. What you saw there was the quintessential spirit of the college – enjoying duty and accepting leadership gratefully. That's what I expect of you.' Smiting him on the back from a sheer excess of good spirits she turned down her own corridor. 'Breakfast at 8.00 sharp. Later, if it's dry, we'll see about the cat.'

When he entered the dining hall, Amiss decided to sit with the students rather the Fellows. Recognizing a prettyish face from the previous night's fiasco, he sat beside it. He introduced himself as unthreateningly as possible. She said 'Hello' in a more or less civil way but did not give her name.

He helped her solicitously to cornflakes and milk and she appeared to thaw.

'What's your favourite course?'

'Bridget Holdness's Special: "Matriarchy meets Patriarchy; the fight for visibility".'

'Interesting?'

'It's not just interesting, it's empowering. Once the scales have fallen from your eyes, everything becomes clear and you feel you can fulfil your potential and share in releasing the spirit of the sisterhood.' Her eyes radiated devotion in a manner reminiscent of Sandra; it made her look rather attractive. 'Otherwise . . .' She shook her head. 'I don't like the rest of what I'm doing. It has nothing to do with me or my experience.'

'What's your subject?'

'History.'

'What? You mean you don't like any of the other courses?'

'Most of them are given by men, for heaven's sake.'

'Well, you must have known before you came here that the university teaching staff is predominantly male.'

'I didn't realize what that meant, then. That was before I understood. I was brainwashed at school. Can you believe that I chose St Martha's because it was particularly strong in constitutional history.' She snorted.

'Isn't it?'

'That's not the point. It's all right for what it is but it's irrelevant. Why should I waste myself on the study of male political ideology?'

'Know your enemy?'

'Well, yes, there is that,' she said grudgingly. 'But it's very hard to get Dr Windlesham to address herself to the centrality of misogyny in the development of constitutional theory. Like, you know, how the Irish constitution encourages women to stay at home and outlaws abortion, and the American constitution, by guaranteeing freedom of speech, deliberately encourages pornography.'

'Deliberately? I hardly imagine the founding fathers had that in mind.'

'They were men, weren't they? And slave owners at that.' She pushed her cereal plate away savagely, her cheeks pink with outrage.

'Well, you seem to be enjoying the course anyway, and presumably Dr Windlesham has taken some of your ideas on board.' He rather doubted it. Remembering that old harridan grimly reading her medieval constitutional documents throughout dinner, he doubted if she was likely to be much affected by changing intellectual fashion. His companion's snort confirmed his guess. 'It'll be different next year when Bridget gets the centre going.'

'What centre?'

'The Alice Toon Centre for Women's and Black Studies.'

Amiss put on his enquiring look. 'Tell me about it. I'm too new to know anything.'

'St Martha's has been left a lot of money and it's all going to go to that.'

'Really? I wouldn't have thought the Mistress would be very keen.'

'Who cares what she thinks. She and her sort have had their day.'

Amiss repressed the observation that that didn't sound like

a very sisterly pronouncement. 'But doesn't she control the way the money is spent?'

'Bridget's going to win that battle. She's got us — Sisters in Love.'

'In love with . . . ?'

'Sisterhood of course.'

'And how do you demonstrate it?'

Her mischievous smile was almost flirtatious. 'You'll see.'

There was a general pushing back of chairs and Amiss and his companions stood up along with everyone else. 'Fancy a drink sometime?' he asked.

She looked at him dubiously. 'Maybe.'

'You didn't tell me your name.'

'Pippa.'

'Nice to meet you,' he said quickly. 'See you around.'

'Was that the date-raped Pippa?' he asked the Bursar, as they went to converse with Plutarch.

'The very same. I worried for you when I saw you sitting together. You should have sought the safety of high table. Control your passionate impulses, my lad. Confine them to your cat.'

'You don't understand my cat. Plutarch accuses one of date rape if one so much as gives her the time of day, as you will shortly find out if you are intent on this mad scheme of taking her for a walk.'

'Rubbish, cats are putty in my hands. We got on famously last night. You'll see. She'll jump to my word of command.'

Plutarch in fact jumped to the Bursar's bribe — a large sausage which she extracted from her jacket pocket.

'That's a fine red-blooded cat.' She scooped the animal into her arms, receiving — to Amiss's chagrin — a loud purr.

'Open the basket,' she said, as she tickled Plutarch's ear: Amiss followed instructions. Stealthily, for a woman of such solidity, the Bursar traversed the room — distracting the cat's attention awhile with rough endearments — reached the basket, dropped her in and slammed the lid shut.

'Howzzat?'

'You do realize you betrayed her trust?'

'Nonsense, it's for her own good. She needs a bit of fresh air. Now come along. Buckle up.'

The all too familiar feline yodelling drowned all conversation as they made their way down the back staircase, out of a great oak door and into the open air. Amiss put the basket down and scratched his head. 'What's a medieval cloister doing in the middle of a neo-Gothic pile?'

'An essential part of the vision of old Jeremiah Ridley; contemplation was to be encouraged along with sewing, knitting and daily exercises.'

'You don't mean he had anything to do with that carry-on this morning?'

'Sub-section four of Clause twenty-one if I remember correctly. We have to have a quorum of half the Fellowship every morning or we're in breach of the trust. Now stop asking tedious questions and get on with releasing that animal. A meditative stroll around the cloister will do wonders for her soul. Besides, she should have some company in a moment.'

As Amiss looked suspiciously at the Bursar, Plutarch leaped out of the basket. Simultaneously the door opened and disgorged Francis Pusey, who was bearing in his arms a white Pekinese sporting a smart Fair Isle jumper. It was out of his arms and after Plutarch the second their eyes met.

'You planned this,' hissed Amiss at the Bursar.

'Shut up and watch the action. Come on Bobsy, faster, faster. Atta girl, Plutarch, go for him Tarzan-style.'

Plutarch accepted her coach's advice and leaped to the top of the bench past which Bobsy was racing; from that vantage point she emitted howls of derision.

Francis Pusey stopped squeaking and rushed over to the bench. He bent down, frantically trying to get hold of Bobsy, who was working himself into a fearful state of frustration over the inability of his tiny legs to make the necessary vault. Plutarch allowed herself to get distracted from her primary prey and leaped on Pusey's back, digging her claws in so thoroughly that when he leaped upwards, emitting cries of pain, she was able to hold on grimly. Bobsy, seeing a trailing tail, launched himself the necessary twelve inches in the air and sank his teeth into the ginger fur. The combination of the cat's and Pusey's howls of pain brought the additional noise of windows being pulled up and a babble of protesting female voices filled the air.

The Bursar shook her head. 'Stupid cat. She had him on the run. All she had to do was wear him out and then swoop.'

Emitting a gusty sigh of disappointment, she picked up a bucket from behind a nearby pillar, strode across the grass and emptied its contents over the three protagonists. The animals let go, Plutarch soared back to the top of the bench, Pusey grabbed his dog and dripped grimly back to where Amiss was standing helplessly. 'Is that thing yours?'

''Fraid so, terribly sorry. I didn't realize . . .'

'I may have to sue. My jacket is irreplaceable, made for me by the only tailor who ever understood me. My shirt, my beautiful silk batik shirt, that my friend brought me from Malaysia . . .' He seemed on the verge of tears. 'And that is even before we begin to count the cost of the damage to my psyche and my body.' As he turned towards the door with as much dignity as he could muster, the Pekinese, now filled with blood lust, broke free and the whole pantomime started all over again.

Amiss walked over to the Bursar. 'I'm going in now, you old ruffian, and I may be some little time.'

8

'How could you?' he asked as she entered his bedroom ten minutes later bearing the cat basket.

'How could I what? Pack this animal up by myself, you mean? Easy. She's a pushover. You make so much fuss.'

'How could you engineer a cat and dog fight? They might have killed each other.'

'Rubbish. I never thought there'd be any danger of anything worse than a scratch on the nose and there wasn't. Besides, I had thoughtfully provided that bucket of water for emergencies. She isn't a bit hurt.'

The Bursar appeared to be right. Plutarch showed no signs of any ailment other than the lassitude one might expect after such vigorous exercise. She headed straight for the bed and began a perfunctory wash and brush up.

'What were you trying to achieve?'

'Not sure really. It just seemed a good idea at the time. Besides, I'm generally in favour of stirring things up a bit. It does old Francis good to have his routine interrupted. And I found the whole episode diverting.'

'Did she inflict any damage on that wretched excuse for a dog?'

'Alas no, it was a draw.'

'But she did pretty well with Pusey.'

'That was an unexpected bonus. I don't suppose you'd be prepared to bring her along to the Council meeting this morning?'

'Bursar, I'm going straight to the telephone to locate a cattery. I'm not going to have this animal embroiled in your amoral activities any further.'

'You haven't time,' she said smugly. 'The meeting's in five minutes.'

'Do I have to be there?'

'Of course you have to be there. You're a Fellow, aren't you?'

'Why does nobody ever tell me anything?'

'Keeps you on your toes. Now stop lazing about and come on. "It's mainsail haul, my bully boys all". We've got man's work to do.'

'Are you going to tell me anything about what to expect?'

'Certainly not. You'll pick it up as you go along. I hope you've been reading your Clausewitz.'

'Didn't he go on about war being only an extension of diplomacy.'

'Bugger the philosophy, it's his military tips I'm interested in. He said we should keep in mind three main targets: the enemies' forces, resources and will to fight. I'm particularly concentrating on undermining the last.'

'Well, I hope it will cheer you up if I assure you that like the Duke of Wellington, although I don't know what effect you have on the enemy, my God, you frighten me.'

She simpered. 'You mustn't turn my head. Now come along, it's time we went and stirred the shit.'

As he left the room, Amiss observed that Plutarch had fallen into an exhausted sleep. He rather wished he could join her.

Accelerating down the corridor after the Bursar, Amiss wondered why he was always chasing after her. She was more than thirty years his senior, was four inches shorter than him and two stone heavier.

'Jet propulsion,' he muttered as he caught her up.

'What?'

'You. I was wondering where you get your turn of speed from. Not to speak of your energy.'

'It's not that I'm particularly energetic. It's that all you lot are anaemic. It comes from all that faddy eating and no bad habits.'

Amiss was about to deny this slur indignantly when his

attention was distracted by what sounded like loud chanting.

'What's that?'

'Another demo.'

'Who, what, where, why?'

As he approached the source of the disturbance he could make out 'What do we want?' followed by something indistinct and then by 'When do we want it? Now.'

'What *do* they want?'

'Gender and ethnic studies, "GES".'

'That's not what it sounds like.'

'That's because some of them want ethnic and gender studies. And some of them think all this too non-specific and want black and gender or even gender and black and then some would prefer women's and not gender studies because they don't think they should study men and so on. There's a bit of a row going on about priorities and they're shouting each other down.'

As they rounded the corner and began to proceed down the corridor towards the Council Chamber, the sound dropped and the demonstrators came into view. There looked to be about twenty of them, mostly clad in *de rigueur* Doc Martens and droopy black hangings and waving banners which included the legends 'DOWN WITH DWEMS', 'SISTER CENTRIC NOT PHALLO CENTRIC', 'THE SISTERHOOD OF WIMMIN', 'PENETRATION IS RAPE' and even 'RELEVANCE NOT RIGOUR'. As they spotted Amiss and the Bursar, somebody started a chant which the others swiftly picked up: 'Sexism: Out Out Out.'

'Is that directed at me?'

'Yes, but at me too. For some reason I can't quite grasp they think I'm a bit insensitive.'

'I think what you have is what our American cousins would describe as an attitude problem.'

'Nothing wrong with my attitude,' said the Bursar. 'It's good old Anglo-Saxon. Now come on, let's charge through all these ninnies.' Suiting her action to her words she cleared a path for Amiss through the mob.

*   *   *

Bridget, Sandra, Mary Lou, the Reverend Cyril and Dr Windlesham were already *in situ*, along with a dim creature who was gazing worshipfully at Bridget. Amiss was tempted to avoid conversation by sitting beside Dr Windlesham, who was intently reading a scholarly journal. Instead, he sat down at the end of the table beside Mary Lou, to whom he introduced himself and rather hesitantly offered his hand. She seemed nervous and equally hesitant, but she put out her hand and shook his.

'Have you been here long?'

'Two days.'

'Oh, just ahead of me. What do you think of it?'

'I don't know.'

'Nor do I. What's your field?'

'The interaction of lesbianism and ethno-centrism.'

'You must explain it to me sometime,' he said politely and addressed himself to the pile of papers in front of him. Before he had begun to get the hang of them, the door opened and on the dot of 9.10 the Mistress swept in, flanked by the Senior Tutor and Primrose Partridge. She had no sooner taken her seat and opened the meeting than the door opened again and Francis Pusey came in. He scurried to his seat.

'I apologize, Mistress, but I've gone through an absolutely gruelling experience this morning, and I'm all at sixes and sevens.' He shot Amiss a venomous look.

'Excuse me,' said Bridget Holdness. 'Point of order.'

'I hope it is,' said the Mistress levelly.

'I can no longer accept the use of the word "Mistress".'

Even the imperturbable holder of that title looked shocked. 'Could you elaborate?'

The Bursar broke in. 'I suppose she wants us to call you Mstress, Mistress. All that crap again.' Dame Maud gave her an admonitory look.

'Bursar, please let Dr Holdness speak for herself. She has little difficulty in doing so.'

'I shall ignore the Bursar's typically offensive and collaborationist remark,' said Bridget. 'First, may I remind you that I wish to be addressed as "Ms", not "Dr", which is a legitimization of elitism. Second, the word "Mistress" – like "Master"

– implicitly acknowledges patriarchal archetypes as well as having unacceptable overtones of a proprietorial sexual relationship. If we insist in clinging to hierarchical systems, which I don't think we should, you could be called "Head".'

'"Head Fellow"?'

'Certainly not "Fellow",' said Bridget. 'That is a masculine word used here to imply spurious inclusiveness.'

'Mistress,' bellowed the Bursar, 'are we going to waste yet another morning arguing about whether what we have for tea is a gingerbreadperson?'

'Ladies, ladies, please . . .' intervened the Reverend Cyril. As Bridget's eyes narrowed and her mouth opened, the Mistress interrupted hastily. 'Thank you, Dr Crowley, but though well-intentioned, that is not a helpful contribution. Now, Bursar, please remember that we have a tradition of tolerance in St Martha's: it is right to take note of the views of the younger generation. I am, however, inclined to agree that we are giving a disproportionate amount of time to matters which could perhaps be resolved in a different forum.'

'These are central issues,' said Bridget Holdness. 'They cannot be marginalized.'

'Might I make a suggestion?' asked Amiss.

Bridget Holdness glared at him, 'Chair, this is the second instance this morning of a male interruption.'

'I didn't interrupt,' said Crowley and Amiss simultaneously.

'There they go again, Chair.'

'Dr Holdness . . .'

'Ms.'

'I see no reason why I should change the way I refer to you when you persist in addressing me as if I were a piece of furniture,' said the Mistress. Her normal imperturbability seemed to be acquiring a tinge of irritability. 'Mr Amiss, what is your suggestion?'

'A language sub-committee?'

'We don't usually have sub-committees of the Council,' said the Mistress.

'Good time to start,' said the Bursar. 'Got to get language off the main agenda. As it is, we'll have to work like blacks to catch up with all we've got to do.' There was no response. A kind of chill had descended on the company. The Bursar looked at her colleagues in a baffled fashion and then made the connection. 'Ooops! Sorry about that, slip of the tongue. Nothing personal, Dr Denslow.'

As Mary Lou opened her mouth to respond, Bridget Holdness pushed back her chair noisily and said, 'Come on.'

'Dr Holdness, the Bursar has apologized.'

'There are some things for which no apology will suffice. A protest has to be made. Come.' She jerked her head at Sandra, Mary Lou and the dim hanger-on and the four of them exited.

Amiss settled back in his seat in relief, waiting for the constructive part of the meeting to start.

'Fellows, I regret this disruption,' said Dame Maud. 'May we reconvene tomorrow at nine-thirty? I shall see in the meantime if Dr Holdness and her friends can rejoin us.' She swept out of the room followed by her entourage.

'What happened?' Amiss asked the Bursar. 'Why didn't we go on?'

'Quorum, you idiot. The statutes are very firm on that. And since Thackaberry and Anglo-Saxon Annie again forgot to turn up, we were buggered. You can't pick your nose in this institution without a quorum. Oh shit, sometimes I think I'm a little lacking in tact.'

The demonstration outside the door was revitalized by the news that Bridget had borne out of the Council Chamber. 'Racist: Out Out Out. Racist: Out Out Out,' was clearly directed at the Bursar, with the occasional 'Sexist: out' thrown in for good measure so as not to make Amiss feel out of things. The Bursar jet-propelled herself through the throng; she and Amiss sped down the corridor with their persecutors on their tail. When they got to the Bursar's room she slammed the door behind them and locked it.

'Have a drink.'

'You're lucky you weren't lynched.'

'Huh! Lynched? Me? It would take more than that phalanx of washed-out morons to lynch me, I can tell you. We Troutbecks don't lynch easily.'

'What are you going to do now?'

'I have a plan.'

'Are you going to share it with me?'

'It's not ready yet.' She pushed his drink over to him. 'I've homework to do.'

There was a padded envelope sitting on her desk which she patted knowingly. 'And how are you going to occupy yourself today?'

'I shall seek out male company. When I've dealt with the cattery, that is.'

'You're determined to exile that splendid cat of yours? Pity. I like her.'

'She's exactly your sort.' Amiss spoke frostily. 'That's why I have no option but to exile her.'

'All right then. Drink up and get cracking. I've a lot to do.'

Amiss looked hesitantly at the door through which were coming sounds of angry slogans.

'Oh, I see. Chicken, are you?' She jerked her head towards the window. 'I should hop it out the back way if I were you. Don't suppose you can cope with them without me to protect you.' She shook her head, 'What is the modern male coming to? There were never any New Men among the Troutbecks.'

Amiss swallowed his drink and walked to the window with as much dignity as he could muster.

9

Amiss headed straight for Francis Pusey's rooms, arriving just as Miss Stamp was emerging in an advanced state of twitter.

'Oh, Mr Amiss,' she began. 'Isn't it all dreadful? Poor Dr Pusey is in such a state. Between Dr Holdness and that cat of yours . . .'

Well, thought Amiss, if nothing else, Plutarch had achieved the feat of moving from 'dear little pussy cat' to 'that cat' in a matter of a few hours. She was undoubtedly a feline delinquent of a high order.

'I do feel terrible about all that, Miss Stamp. She's very highly strung, you know and the sight of Dr Pusey's Pekinese put her in a frightful tizz. I do hope Dr Pusey will forgive me.'

Her face cleared. 'I'm sure if you just explain. He gets upset, does Dr Pusey, but he's not someone to bear a grudge. Well, not really.'

'Advise me, Miss Stamp. What should I offer as an olive branch? Should I ask him to lunch?' She looked over her shoulder at the heavy oak door behind her, tripped over to him and stood on tiptoes to whisper in his ear. 'What he likes most is a nice walk followed by a really nice afternoon tea. And he does love showing people round Cambridge.'

Amiss rapidly translated this into frightful old bore prepared to do anything for a few cream cakes and an audience. 'Thank you, Miss Stamp,' he said gravely. 'I shall act on your advice. You are a great comfort to me.'

'So you do see, don't you?' Pusey replaced the card in the box and selected another. 'In fact, it was my last visit.' He peered through his big round glasses. 'Yes, it says it here. "22 February 1990, Sprogget deceased".'

'Did it come as a shock to you?'

'A very, very great shock. Why, as I've shown you, I'd been going to him for more than twenty years. He understood me; no one else has ever quite understood me. It's a matter of compensating for the very slight difference in height between my shoulders and' – he giggled – 'what I am forced to admit is a slight touch of pigeon chest. It takes a genius, you know, to get things just so.'

'So do you have a new tailor?'

'Yes, yes, but he's hopeless; just doesn't understand about shoulders. I keep searching. You don't know anyone, I suppose?' He looked Amiss up and down. 'No, I expect you don't.'

Pusey returned the card to its box, which he replaced carefully in the corner cabinet. He turned round and threw his hands out in an expansive gesture. 'Now I hope you appreciate the extent of my loss.'

'Can anything be done to mend it?'

'Mend cashmere? At prodigious expense. And what will be the result?'

Amiss decided on a calculated risk. 'Perhaps I might be allowed to contribute, if you wouldn't mind waiting until the first instalment of my stipend. I'm very hard up at the moment.'

'My dear boy.' Pusey positively beamed at him. 'That's extremely kind of you but I wouldn't dream of it. It is quite enough that you are sending that . . . that . . .'

'Beast?' offered Amiss.

'Beast away. I don't wish to be offensive. You are no doubt attached to it.'

'Tethered rather than attached. It was,' Amiss added mendaciously, 'a legacy from my dear, late mother.' He gazed at the floor for a few moments while Pusey emitted a couple of embarrassed squeaks. Then Amiss sat up, squared his shoulders and looked brave. 'You've been most forbearing, Dr Pusey, and you are very good to forgive me. Might I ask you another favour?'

'Certainly.'

'I don't know Cambridge, and I wondered if you would be so kind as perhaps to find some time one afternoon to show me around. We might then possibly have tea somewhere nice. I need something to lift my spirits after the really rather terrifying introduction I have had to St Martha's.' He could see the gleam in Pusey's eyes.

'Show you round? Why I'd be delighted. Indeed, I think it would be unwise to postpone it. One cannot always rely on the weather. Come back to me here after lunch at two o'clock sharp.'

'How very kind.'

'What are your main fancies?' He caught Amiss's blank look and tittered. 'Architecturally, I mean.'

'Pretty catholic.'

'Medieval? Renaissance? Georgian? Victorian?'

'I'd be happy with all of them. Whatever's going. I really just want to acquire a general sense of the place.'

That was clearly the wrong answer. 'Oh, dear.' Pusey rushed over to the corner and took out another box of cards. 'Look, look.' He pointed to the title. 'You see?'

'Er, yes. The medieval tour.'

'I like to take people round chronologically, you see. So with the medieval tour I start with Peterhouse in 1284 and take you right through to Clare in 1359.'

'That sounds . . . very interesting. Does it take in most of the major colleges?'

'Oh no, no, no. You've got King's and Queens' and Jesus and so on in the Renaissance tour and then of course the Reformation and so on.'

'I'm in your hands, Dr Pusey.'

'Ah, very well then. What I suggest is that today we do the medieval period, or as much as can be done in only an afternoon – not forgetting our tea of course.' He tittered again. 'And then, when it is again clement, we can advance to the Renaissance.'

'Gosh, that's terrific. I look forward to this afternoon immensely.' As he left the room Amiss wondered whether he should be blaming the Bursar or Miss Stamp for his impending doom. He concluded reluctantly that the buck stopped with him.

'Sorry, I didn't catch that.'
   'Uncoursed clunch rubble. Can't you see?'
   Amiss gazed dully at a clump of masonry.
   'Pevsner thinks some of these windows are originals from the third quarter of the fourteenth century, but I'm not at all sure, not at all sure. I think he may have been misled by the cusped lights.' He peered down at his card. 'I hope you were moved by it, Mr Amiss. As dear, dear Spenser has said:

   ' "My mother, Cambridge, whom, as with a crowne,
   He doth adorne, and is adorn'd of it
   With many a gentle muse and many a learned wit." '

Spenser had clearly struck lucky, thought Amiss lugubriously.
   'Now I think it's time for tea. We have finished the medieval tour,' said Pusey. 'Come along now, we'll go to the Copper Kettle on King's Parade. I'm very, very partial to their chocolate cake.'

Amiss did not have a sweet tooth and forcing down rich cake was a torment to him, but it was required by the Pusey code. This Amiss resentfully summarized as: 'I'm-a-greedy-little-bugger-without-the-courage-of-my-convictions-who-requires-my-companion-to-carry-the-can-for-my-over-indulgence.' 'Oh, well, I'll have another slice if you insist, but only if you do,' Pusey kept wittering.
   The main advantage of tea, however, was that it temporarily stopped Pusey from talking any more about medieval architecture and enabled Amiss to recover from that state of catatonic despair into which merciless bores always threw him.
   But as he swallowed his last piece of goo, Pusey started to fumble in his pocket for his cards again. Amiss swiftly intervened just in time. 'Dr Pusey, please could you tell me a little about Cambridge in its wider sense; perhaps we could

make a great leap from medieval to contemporary – looking at the people this time rather than the artefacts.'

'I'd rather have artefacts any day. Give me a nice little Meissen pot or a Doulton vase rather than one of those nasty coarse creatures who abound in this uncouth world. My idea of heaven is to settle down with Bobsy in the middle of all my nice things with a new piece of knitting or a particularly tricky piece of embroidery, a little bit of chamber music, and perhaps – if I'm feeling very wicked – some cocoa and sugared biscuits.'

Amiss doubted if he and Pusey were likely to strike up a close comradeship. 'I do understand. Peace and quiet are a great joy. But still I must admit to some curiosity about people. Do tell me something about them.'

'The people. Ah, the people. Well, of course poor Rupert Brooke said it all:

'"For Cambridge people rarely smile,
Being urban, squat and packed with guile."'

Amiss hoped that he was grinding his teeth silently. 'I was thinking more about the St Martha's people, really. I'm not an academic, you know, so I find them rather odd. A man of your discernment must be able to fill in a poor novice like me. It's meant a lot to me getting this job, and I'm terrified of putting a foot wrong. How about some more tea?'

'Only if you are.'

'And this last piece of cake, go on.'

Pusey looked at it longingly, and then patted his stomach. 'No, no, I'm getting a little tum. Quite spoils the line of my jacket.' The word 'jacket' brought back unhappy memories and he looked reproachfully at Amiss, who pretended not to notice and started wheedling again. 'I need advice, and from a man.'

'I doubt if the Bursar would agree that I'm a man. I know very well that she calls me an old woman. Fat lot she'd know about being a woman, nasty old dyke.'

'Is she? A dyke, I mean.'

'She must be. My dear, haven't you noticed? Absolute

69

bulldyke. She doesn't have an ounce of femininity. Those clothes, those shoes, great horrid clumpy things, and above all, those knickers. When I think of the wispy lingerie I've created for proper women in my time, it makes me weep to be confronted by this butch apparel.'

'You don't like her, I gather.'

'Absolute savage,' said Pusey. 'Still, I grant you she's useful. The sort that gets the trains to run on time. I have to admit she's our only hope for the future.'

Amiss felt very close to the end of his tether. 'Dr Pusey, will you please, please, tell me what has brought St Martha's to this pretty pass?'

Pusey looked longingly again at the cakestand.

Amiss set his teeth. 'Would you like just a little bit more? I'll halve it with you.'

'Oh, you are a naughty boy. All right. I give in.'

10

'Thank God you were free.' Amiss was stretched out in a comfortable armchair in the flat of his friend, Detective Sergeant Ellis Pooley. 'I was going crazy for someone to talk to.'

'Are you sure you don't want something to eat?'

'No, no, please. I'm still crammed to the gills with vast amounts of cake, consumed in the quest for information. A combination of Jack Troutbeck, who communicates in a kind of oral semaphore and Francis Pusey, who has to have information bribed out of him, has left me pretty desperate. Oxford was never like this. I always knew there was something funny about Cambridge – all those gay spies and mad right-wing dons – but I didn't realize it was this bad.'

Pooley waited patiently for Amiss's tirade to cease. 'Why don't you tell me what you've found out, Robert, and then if you want to, we can talk more generally about Cambridge.'

Amiss took another cheering mouthful of his drink, wriggled more comfortably into the corner of his chair, threw his leg over its arm, collected his thoughts and began.

'The sequence as I understand it is that St Martha's was established in partial reaction against the academic success of Girton and Newnham. The founder was up to a point a realist. Although he would have preferred to see women staying submissive and attending to their family and philanthropic duties, he realized the writing was on the wall. What he decided to do was to try and contain the revolution and in particular contain his own daughter, who was making his life hell. So he conceived the notion of a college which would meet the criterion of giving women higher education while preventing them from undertaking unduly unwomanly things like maths or the sciences. He adhered to the Victorian view with which he had grown up, that the nervous system of women was liable to give way if exposed to undue strain. Now, do you have a Bible and a collected Rudyard Kipling?'

'Certainly,' said Pooley. It took him two or three minutes. 'Have you got these catalogued?' Amiss waved his hand at the shelves which lined the room.

'Yes,' said Pooley warily. 'Why?'

'By author, subject or what?'

'By author, just so I know what I haven't got so to speak. It's very simple when you've got a computer.'

'Francis Pusey's collection of books on aesthetics and the womanly arts are catalogued by hand under subject, author, years of acquisition, places of acquisition and for all I know, climatic conditions and astrological signs on the day of same.'

'He sounds like a busy little person.'

'A potty little person would be more like it. Right. Now you remember the bit in the Bible about Martha?'

'She did the housework while Mary entertained Jesus. Wasn't that more or less it?'

'Let me read it to you: "Now as they went on their way, he entered a village; and a woman named Martha received him into her house. And she had a sister called Mary, who sat at the Lord's feet and listened to his teaching. But Martha was distracted with much serving." What a boring, nasty version of the Bible you've got – what's happened to "But Martha was cumbered about much serving"?'

'Shut up and get on with it.'

'"And she went to him and said, 'Lord, do you not care that my sister has left me to serve alone? Tell her then to help me'. But the Lord answered her, 'Martha, Martha, you are anxious and troubled about many things; one thing is needful. Mary has chosen the good portion, which shall not be taken away from her.'"' He looked up. 'I must say I always thought that a bit thick. Bet you anything you like he didn't refuse on principle to eat his dinner.'

Pooley refused to be side-tracked. 'I really don't follow that. If Christ thought that Mary was right and Martha was wrong, calling a college St Martha's is sending out rather strange signals, isn't it?'

'Hah, no. The plot thickens. Just at the moment when the founder was finalizing his plans for the college, buying the property and racking his brains for a suitable role model, Kipling produced a poem called "The Sons of Martha". Do you know it?'

'No.'

'Quite long. It's jolly good, but I'll spare you most of it. The opening lines are the nub:

' "The Sons of Mary seldom bother, for they have
inherited that good part;
But the Sons of Martha favour their Mother of the careful
soul and the troubled heart.
And because she lost her temper once, and because she
was rude to the Lord her Guest,
Her Sons must wait upon Mary's Sons, world without
end, reprieve, or rest.'

'It then goes on about the Sons of Mary having a high old time being waited on hand and foot by Martha's crew who have no such expectations for themselves:

' "They do not preach that their God will rouse them a
little before the nuts work loose.
They do not teach that His Pity allows them to drop their
job when they dam'-well choose.
As in the thronged and the lighted ways, so in the dark
and the desert they stand,
Wary and watchful all their days that their brethren's
days may be long in the land." '

'That poem, would you believe, is written into the statutes of the college. It's a sort of institution of atonement. Didn't you ever hear of it while you were at Cambridge?'

'King's was a very snobby place. We only took a handful of the most important colleges seriously, and because they were mostly mixed, the single-sex women's colleges were really looked down on even more than before, I'm ashamed to say.'

'And St Martha's?'

Pooley rolled his eyes. 'Too much off the beaten track geographically and academically to matter. I mean, for heaven's sake, Robert, Girton was two miles away and I never set foot in it in three years. I once heard a don in Caius express sympathy for his opposite numbers in Peterhouse because it was so far out.'

'But they can't be more than a few hundred yards apart?'

'Yes, but Peterhouse *is* the farthest south of the Trumpington Road group of colleges.'

'Blimey. Funny people, dons. So what did you hear about St Martha's?'

Pooley knitted his brows. 'Poor, dotty and inaccessible. I never met anyone who came from there. I think they produced the occasional first in History or English or something, but search me, I don't really remember.'

'You're a fat lot of use.'

'Get on with the story.'

'So because of the founder's thoughtfulness, those in authority at St Martha's were imbued with the spirit of duty and sacrifice and womanliness.'

'They don't sound very womanly to me,' said Pooley sternly. 'Not from what you've told me so far.'

'Womanliness was defined in the statutes in terms of accomplishments of an Edwardian nature. Thus the only subjects for study were in the humanities and one could not – and still cannot – become a student there without being able to give evidence of being able to play the piano, sing, tat, crochet, embroider or do one of those things. All students have to take compulsory instruction in a second accomplishment. The Fellows – usually fourteen – between them have to have accomplishments in twenty-eight different areas.'

'Twenty-eight? How do you achieve such a high number?'

'Add in lace-making and gardening, cooking, home-management, book-binding, nursing, bee-keeping, hairdressing, painting – that sort of stuff. You get the gist?'

'Oh, I get the gist. Did you say they had to have twenty-eight accomplishments *between* them?'

'Well spotted. Yes. I think there must have been a bit of a slip-up in the drafting.'

'I'm beginning to understand Francis Pusey's role in all this.'

'You've got it, Ellis. That little creature can produce evidence of eighteen accomplishments, thus taking a heavy burden off the Fellowship and enabling them to have the occasional Fellow like Jack Troutbeck who is everything that featured in the founder's worst nightmares.'

'How did they get round Pusey being a man?'

'It was so unlikely a contingency that it didn't occur to anybody when they were framing the statutes. Now, apart from these requirements there were other duties laid on Fellows like exercising, Sunday services, regular classes in moral guidance for the young and so on and so on. That means people with options aren't exactly queuing up for the privilege of joining the Fellowship.'

'Couldn't they get the statutes amended?'

'You don't know the Mistress. She sees her main role in life as fighting the future, while Bridget Holdness and her pals see their main duty in life as reinventing the past.'

'How did this Holdness woman get in, for heaven's sake?'

'Good academic record, Oxford first in History and then a Ph.D from London where she was a bit of a dark horse. Could even throw in an ability to paint and cook.

'She was perfectly pleasant when she first arrived. She's been there a year, managed to get a pliable student representative on to the College Council as well as filling two Fellowship vacancies with Sandra Murphy and Mary Lou Denslow, both of whom are lesbian and ethnically right-on, Sandra being a rabid Irish-American of the kind who thinks the IRA are the oppressed and Mary Lou being a black agitator. Bridget was clearly planning a gradual Dyke takeover as she could reasonably expect a few more Fellows to drop off their perches through retirement or death in the next five years or so. If she'd played her cards right she could have been

Mistress pretty quickly, but the Alice Toon bequest scuppered all that.'

'I don't quite see why.'

'These are straitened times, Ellis, in the academic world, particularly for postgraduate students in the godforsaken subjects the Mistress has in mind to throw money at. So decent bursaries in obscure subjects will certainly attract good candidates. Theologians and paleographers of the first water will flock to St Martha's, swamping the Holdness crew.

'So from what I can gather she has decided on a high-risk strategy. She started making trouble about six months ago, and over the past few weeks she been escalating the dispute to the point it's now reached. Now that she's got a lot of students backing her, she's essentially trying a form of psychological terrorism.'

'It all sounds very like the late sixties — students on the rampage and all that.'

'Indeed. But while Dame Maud Theodosia Buckbarrow is a throwback, she's a throwback to a tougher age than the late sixties. Nothing spineless or trendy about her. She won't cave in like all those terrified dons who threw in the towel at the sight of a demo of stoned sociologists. Dame Maud knows what's right for scholarship and her gels and no threats are going to move her.'

'Mmm,' said Pooley, 'you've got all the ingredients for a . . .'

'Murder?'

'It does seem like that.'

'However, Ellis, I do not have your fanciful streak. I do not see the armies of the politically correct or of the land records of old Athelstan as putative murderers. I'm just going to try to enjoy the experience and make peace where I can. The Bursar is convinced the Dykes can't win. She quoted some Chinese general who pointed out that one could never successfully attack a walled city.'

'What exactly is her role in all this?'

'Preparing the vats of boiling oil to pour out the windows on the enemies' heads I should think. I rang her to say I was popping up to town and she instructed me to be back at

9.30 sharp tomorrow morning for what she termed "the counter-offensive".'

'You'd better wear your steel helmet.'

'Steel underpants would be more like it. Some of those demonstrators have a nasty glint in their eyes. Now enough of all that. Fill me in on the latest upheavals in the Met.'

11

The Bursar was declaiming Kipling:

> '"I'm the prophet of the Utterly Absurd,
>   Of the Patently Impossible and Vain –
> And when the Thing that Couldn't has occurred
>   Give me time to change my leg and go again."'

'What's that about?'
'My new stratagem: I think I'm word perfect.'
'In what?'
'Never you mind. You'll see.' She finished pinning to her ample chest a badge which she had taken from the top drawer: in large red letters it bore the legend 'DYKE POWER'.
'Bursar,' said Amiss faintly. 'What is that?'
'I couldn't get a T-shirt in my size. Can't think why, mind you. The butch dykes must have made a run on them. So this'll have to do for the moment.'
'But why are you wearing it?'
She looked surprised. 'Because I'm coming out, of course. Now come on, come on.' And she catapulted from the room with Amiss in pursuit.

The demonstrators were in good voice when they were joined by the Bursar, who planted herself in front of them and pointed at her badge: the chanting stopped abruptly. She paused, bowed to the left, bowed to the right. 'Thank you, sisters. I need your support. It has taken me until now to have the courage to declare myself' – she paused for effect and then raised her voice another decibel – 'a lover of women, spelled "w-i-m-m-i-n".

'For too long,' she said, warming to her theme, 'I have been a victim of my herstory, pandering to patriarchal stereotyping and intimidated by the collaborators into denying my wimmin-bonding.'

Amiss felt that she had used that last phrase a touch uncertainly.

Her voice dropped; the spellbound mob waited anxiously.

'Will any sisters here help me to share my pain and hurts, to grow, and to be part of wimminess?'

Two Doc Marten-shod figures rushed forward and enveloped her in a loving embrace and by the time Bridget Holdness and her Praetorian Guard arrived on the scene, the Bursar was the centre of a sobbing, cheering mob. Banners had been cast aside, all anger had fled. She broke free with some difficulty, clearly on this occasion feeling inhibited from using her usual strong-arm techniques.

'Forgive me, my sisters.' There was a trace of a sob in her voice. 'I am overwhelmed by your love. Yet I am now empowered to advance our cause.' Her voice gained in strength. 'I go into the battlefield now secure and confident that this new vision will prevail.' And with the air of a particularly self-satisfied Christian going forth to meet the Roman lions, she marched towards the Council Chamber.

Amiss was skulking quietly after her when a strapping young woman, who looked as if she had a long background in public-school sporting activities, suddenly shouted, 'Come on sisters,' and led them in a chorus of 'For she's a jolly good sister, for she's a jolly good sister, for she's a jolly good sister, and so say all of us.'

He sat across the table from the Bursar, trying and failing to catch her eye. She had adopted a pious expression and was seemingly lost in spiritual contemplation.

'What's all that about?' whispered Francis Pusey in his ear. 'What's she up to now?'

'She's come out,' whispered Amiss. 'Can't you see her badge?'

Pusey gazed, opened and closed his mouth, gazed again and then shrugged. 'Well, I did tell you.'

'Indeed you did. But I hadn't expected quite such dramatic corroboration.'

Bridget and her crew had not yet followed them in. There appeared to be quite a spirited conversation going on outside. Amiss doubted if Bridget was likely to be as easily persuaded of the Bursar's *bona fides* as had been the impressionable young, but he did not have long to tease out the problem. Two minutes later, at precisely 9.40, the Mistress entered, followed by a mixed group of Dykes and Virgins. The Council was two up on the previous morning. Not only had Miss Thackaberry turned up, but she was accompanied by a twenty-something with tangled brown curls who looked as vague as she did and whom Amiss identified as Anglo-Saxon Annie.

The Mistress sat down and looked round the table. 'Good morning, colleagues. I trust this morning will be more profitable than yesterday. May we take item one on the agenda? Admissions policy. The issue here, as you will remember, is that Dr Murphy has made a proposal that examination results should be ignored as a criterion for assessing a candidate's worth.'

'Well what are we going to do instead?' asked the Senior Tutor. 'Standards have gone to pot already. Do you know that yesterday I met a student who'd never heard of Milton and she had passed some exams? I have come across a Fellow who does not know the difference between "imply" and "infer". What happens next? Do we start accepting girls who can't even read or write?' Her voice rose to a squeal. She quivered across the table at the Dykes. 'You're trying to fill this college full of illiterate morons. I can't take any more of this.'

'Chair,' said the Bursar. The Mistress looked at her, shocked.

'Forgive me, I know you dislike that terminology, but I do not wish to give offence to my younger sisters by using words which they find insensitive. Bear with me, I beg of you, I wish to propose a peace plan.

'We are a band of wimmin – well, that is, apart from a few exceptions here – but we needn't pay any attention to them. We must stand together in our femaleness and solve our problems by seeking truly to understand each other's psyches and analyse each other's experiences.'

The Mistress's eyes had caught and read the Bursar's badge; she looked dazed.

'And sisters, we can't go on bickering and squabbling like this while society demands of us that we work together to help those who for so long have lived in the shadow. We must bring them forward, we must heal them, we must make them whole.'

'Bursar,' said the Mistress testily, 'moving though your rhetoric might be, it seems of little relevance to the item under discussion.'

'On the contrary, Mistress . . .' The Bursar clapped her hand over her mouth. 'Sisters, I deeply apologize. Chair, what I'm trying to say is that I have had a change of heart. I had a long wrestle with my soul and I decided to cease to deny my identity and my sexuality.'

It must, thought Amiss, be a first for the Council Chamber to hear a discussion on sexuality at a Fellows' meeting. He observed that she had drawn even Anglo-Saxon Annie and Miss Thackaberry out of their reveries: they were gazing at the Bursar in perplexity.

'Really, Bursar, I don't think this is the place . . .'

'You misunderstand me, Chair. It is just that I feel I now have something to offer. Having been for so long a part of the old St Martha's ethos and having just come to realize the glory that is the new, I feel I can act between both groups as an envoy. I wish therefore to propose that we continue with all non-controversial business this morning and that all contentious matters be referred to a sub-committee which will try to find a way through. We will look at sexism, racism, disabledism, ageism and so on in language, appointments, curricula and until we come up with a proper report all of us should make a self-denying ordinance to wage no such battles here. That would enable us to get on with such mundane matters as finalizing the budget, deciding on urgent maintenance priorities, making tutorial arrangements and the rest of it.'

Nobody said anything for a moment and then the Mistress rallied. 'Bursar, I have, as you may imagine, been taken a little by surprise, but I see some way forward in your proposal. Does anyone object?'

'What will be the composition of the sub-committee?' asked Bridget Holdness.

'I think it would be churlish, in view of the Bursar's really exceptional gesture, to have anyone other than her in the chair. But I would of course expect that you, Dr Holdness, and the Senior Tutor, be the other members.'

There was a squeak from the other end of the table from Francis Pusey. 'Do you mean that on a sub-committee addressing itself to discrimination there is to be no male representation? There is no minority in this college as much under threat as men.'

'If Dr Holdness . . . sorry, Ms Holdness . . . has no objection,' said the Bursar smoothly, 'I think we should take note of that minority representation and ask Mr Amiss to act as our secretary. Someone after all has to take the minutes and make the tea.'

'Any objections, Mr Amiss?' asked the Mistress crisply.

'I'm here to try to perform a useful function.' He hoped he had put enough hurt into his voice to make the Dykes feel good.

'Very well then,' said the Mistress with deep relief. 'If the Senior Tutor does not mind, she will be replaced by Mr Amiss. Now may we please address ourselves to the matter of maintenance priorities.'

What had amazed Amiss during the first half hour of the sub-committee meeting that afternoon was Jack Troutbeck's quite extraordinary patience. There were moments when he thought that the old girl really might have flipped and become a Born Again Dyke.

'Very well then,' she said. 'I think we've got the headings sorted out, Mr Amiss. Would you care to take us through them if you've got them in order?'

Amiss adopted his best impartial civil service manner. Just as he was about to address the Bursar as 'Madam Chairman', he reminded himself on which side the Dykes supposed him to be. With some difficulty, he began, 'Certainly, Chair. I think the issues at present come under four main headings. The first is, for want of a better word, to be described as in Ms Holdness's words — ''Invasions of Personal Space'', with specific reference to smoking and perfume.'

'Very well,' said the Bursar. 'I suppose, Dr Holdness,' she said wistfully, 'that you would like smoking banned from public rooms in the college?'

'Oh no, Chair. I insist it be banned from the entire college.'

'You're kidding. Are you suggesting I shouldn't be able to smoke my own pipe in my own room?'

'I most certainly am. It is bad for the health of those who visit you.'

'But they do that, do they not, at their own peril?'

'Sometimes people have to visit your office, Bursar, and I have to say it's a most unpleasant experience.'

'But no one is required to visit me in my bedroom. You can't seriously suggest that it should be banned in private quarters.'

'The smell clings to your clothes and exacerbates allergies, even more than does perfume.'

'Would you say the same to somebody who suffered from BO?' asked the Bursar. 'Like at least three students I can think of.'

'An unacceptable comparison,' said Holdness. 'Tobacco and perfume are products developed by capitalism in the pursuit of profit without any consideration of the damage done to the individual and her environment.'

'So is soap,' said the Bursar, forgetting to be meek, 'which is presumably why you don't approve of recommending it to our naturally smelly sisters.'

'Item two,' said Amiss, taking the risk of being ticked off for interrupting, 'is language. Ms Holdness has proposed a priority exercise to make the language of all documentation free of ethnic and gender bias. Item three is the introduction of training courses to sensitize the Fellowship, staff and students and item four is her proposal to democratize the college through the abolition of titles of all kinds – and indeed, the power that goes with them.'

'That's pretty comprehensive,' said the Bursar. 'Since these are so far-reaching, we should set up democratic working groups to examine each of these matters in turn.'

'No,' said Bridget. 'That's a delaying device, the academic equivalent of setting up a royal commission. I insist on prompt action now.'

'And what does that mean? We couldn't abolish titles tomorrow if we wanted to without changing the college statutes, which is a slow process.'

'You procrastinate.' We do not have to be trammelled by male law. The Council can simply agree to the *de facto* abolition of the elitist structure of this college; it can be accomplished formally in due course. Otherwise, I shall have to call on the students to apply pressure.

'Furthermore,' she ran her hands vigorously through her hair, 'on the question of language, I have here, as an interim measure, a list of words which should be banned immediately from use.'

'That sounds very democratic,' said the Bursar.

Other than 'ugh!' (offensive to Native Americans and to replaced by 'how unpleasant!'), the extensive list circulated round the three of them held few surprises for Amiss. The familiar targets were there – from the gender unacceptables (or in Bridgetspeak 'pseudogeneric') like 'brotherhood' and 'policeman'; the ethnically offensive like 'blackboard' and 'yellow' (as in 'coward'); and the section headed 'handicappism', which included 'blind' and 'idiot' (to become respectively 'visually' and 'cerebrally challenged').

'There must be three or four hundred words here,' said the Bursar. 'Are you seriously suggesting that the likes of Miss Stamp and the Senior Tutor are to be forced to learn' – she gazed down at the list – 'to say "animal companion" instead of "pet"?'

'And why not?'

'Because it's like asking them to learn Urdu.'

'A typically ethnic slur. It implies that Urdu is an unnecessary language for white people to learn.'

'It bloody does not!' shouted the Bursar. 'It implies it's difficult – which it damn well is. You know perfectly well that this would be an impossible task for that generation.'

'Not once the training courses are instituted. Which brings me to my next point. The prime object for this college now has to be to heighten sensitivity and make us all more multiculturally sensitive. We will have to seek and root out the white racism endemic in our values, attitudes and structures and ensure that no one ever uses any terminology found offensive by any other.'

'I find a great number of these substitutes offensive,' snarled the Bursar. She seemed, noted Amiss, to have temporarily forgotten her new role. 'What about me?'

'I should have said "found offensive by any other from an oppressed group". Next, I want the College made smoking- and scent-free immediately.'

'I don't detect that you are much in the mood for compromise.'

'When dealing with human rights, compromise is wrong.'

'But you can't seriously think that you can overthrow the structure, languages, habits and thought processes of almost a century just like that?'

'We'll see about that.' Bridget began to assemble her papers and put them into her case. She stood up. 'I think you will find pressure can be brought to bear to make this step towards recognition of the rights of others preferable to the chaos which is likely to ensue if you strive to retain paternalistic values.'

'I understand you,' said the Bursar grimly. 'But I have my allies too.'

'What conclusions should I report from this meeting?' asked Amiss.

'Standoff,' said the Bursar. 'Now you must excuse me. I am going to smoke a pipe in my room; it helps me to plan.' She shot at Bridget a look that would have made a rhinoceros nervous and stomped out.

12

Trapped by a prior engagement with Francis Pusey to be shown around every last nook and cranny of St Martha's with accompanying no-stone-unturned commentary, Amiss was chafing with impatience to find out what had been the fruit of Jack Troutbeck's ruminations. But Pusey insisted on keeping him by his side and giving him a glass of sherry before dinner.

'A rare treat for me, dear boy. I have to have the excuse of a visitor. Go on, have another. I will if you will.'

Amiss was happy to oblige. With the second, Pusey was moved to confidences. 'I'm depressed, Robert. The writing is on the wall, I fear. There was a stage when I felt that somehow common sense would prevail and we might see the Alice Toon money make our lives here a little less austere, but now I see no hope. Cyril and you and I are caught between these ferocious Amazons and have no power to affect matters.'

'With which side are you sympathetic?'

'Neither. Are we, Bobsy? All we can aspire to now is to avoid being drawn into any rows. Have another sherry, dear boy.' The fourth followed with considerable speed, so it was in quite a mellow mood that Amiss approached dinner. This was quickly dispelled by the combination of Jack Troutbeck's absence and the presence of the Reverend Cyril Crowley. Amiss endured the lecture on the role of the Anglican Communion in these days of changing values with as good a grace as he could muster until he got a chance to ask Miss Stamp if she knew of the Bursar's whereabouts. 'I've got a rather urgent financial problem to sort out with her,' he confided.

'She's probably gone out to see her friend.'

'What friend?'

Miss Stamp giggled. 'Ooh, there's someone in the Bursar's life you know. She slips out once or twice a week and disappears for the whole evening. Quite often for the night. We've never seen him.' She stopped and thought. 'Well, we thought it was a him. But maybe it's a her.'

Amiss could just about imagine what a female lover of the Bursar's might look like; the notion of a male was too taxing an idea for him to address. 'Oh, well, it'll just have to wait.'

As he left the dining room, he felt a pull on his arm which proved to be provided by Francis Pusey, low-voiced and conspiratorial and still rather merry from his pre-dinner debauchery.

'I wondered, Robert, if you'd like to see a film. I have quite a selection on video in my room, and if you'd like, we might even have a little port.'

Amiss wasn't very keen on port but in his present mood he would have looked kindly on an invitation to partake of turpentine. 'Why not? What a nice idea.' And off we went together, as he wrote the next day to Rachel – two chaps getting away from the women by sitting with their Pekinese amidst the chintz and needlework and trinkets of Francis's dainty little nest.

Amiss had been rather attracted by the idea of watching the kind of film he expected Francis Pusey to favour – *Arsenic and Old Lace* or an old Ealing comedy like *The Ladykillers*. In fact, when Pusey had dispensed port along with much information about origins, suppliers, vintages and so on, and had produced his index to his video collection, his visitor got a nasty shock. Ladykillers there were aplenty but they came from a genre, wrote Amiss to Rachel, that could be described most succinctly as '1990s dismembering'.

He announced in that prissy little voice and with that self-deprecating 'tee-hee' that makes my toes curl with the effort of suppressing a scream of irritation, that he and Bobsy liked nothing more than to curl up at night with some choccies and a good film. I was not, he sniggered, to think he was some horrid old sadist because he liked a bit of gore in his films. 'Just a bit of escapism, Robert. Helps me wind down after a hard day.'

Hard day my arse. I've yet to discover anything he does that a normal person would classify as work, since the young breed of gel is about as interested as I am in learning to tat, knit, sew, dry flowers or turn last year's skirt into a spring hat. For their accomplishments they mostly these days go to Sandra's course on 'Getting in Touch with your Feelings Through Tree-Hugging and Dance Movement Therapy' or some other similar kind of crap which in these days passes muster as a female accomplishment. (This is not an area in which the Mistress takes much interest.) So he has a negligible amount of teaching.

You know how squeamish I am. So you can imagine how thrilled I was to be faced with making it a choice between films with names like *Eviscerate 3* or *The Gouger Stalks*. So I simpered and said I wasn't macho enough for the really horrid stuff. That made him – and no doubt Bobsy – feel very tough, but fortunately left him protective enough to expose me only to some drama that involved a muscley chap avenging some insult by rushing round the place waving an AK47 and knocking off thousands. I found if I shut my eyes during the worst bits and thought about tatting I could get through without too much pain.

The pain came later. Just as the moronic machine-gunner espied someone who had made fun of him in nursery school and decided terminally to assuage his hurt feelings, Miss Stamp knocked on the door perfunctorily and came rushing in squawking. 'Oh, I'm sorry, I'm sorry to interrupt, but she said I had to come and get you. She won't let me get a doctor or anything.'

'Who wants whom?' asked Amiss.

'The Bursar. She's been injured by the blunderbuss.' The images that this information set coursing through Amiss's imagination would have done credit to the most deranged product of Hollywood.

'She's been shot with the blunderbuss? And survived?' squeaked Pusey. 'I know she's got the hide of a bison, but . . .' He tailed off, evidently appreciating that this comment was hardly suitable to the crisis in hand.

'Not shot. Hit over the head. Come on, come on. She wants you.'

'Me?' asked Pusey incredulously.

'No, not you. Mr Amiss.'

As Amiss – followed by an excited Pusey – ran after his nimble-footed guide, he realized to his dismay how attached he had become to Jack Troutbeck.

She was sitting in her customary leather armchair taking a copious draught of what looked like neat Scotch. Around her stood a small group of protesting colleagues.

'Nonsense,' she was saying. 'A bit of blood never did anyone any harm. Ah, here he is. Talk sense to this crew, will you, Robert? Everyone's making such a fuss. Nothing wrong with me that won't be cured by a couple of stiff drinks and an early night.'

Observing the bloodstains on her jumper and the greyish tinge of her complexion, Amiss's initial relief turned to crossness. 'Do I understand that you're trying to avoid having proper medical attention?'

'Stuff and nonsense. Proper medical attention is one thing, sending for ambulances is another. I won't have it.'

'Jack, how long have you been unconscious?'

'Not long.'

'The Bursar,' said the Mistress icily, 'appears to have been concussed since about six o'clock. That is, about four hours ago. She is extremely fortunate not to be dead.'

'I haven't been unconscious. I've been asleep.'

Dr Windlesham let out a hoot of derision. 'Being assaulted with about half a ton of wood and iron sent you to sleep, did it?'

'No, Deborah, I fell asleep first. I distinctly remember sitting here having a pre-prandial gin and feeling very sleepy. I must just have been over-tired and needed a nap. So that, combined with somebody hitting me, does knock a girl out for the count a bit.'

'Bursar,' said the Mistress, 'you've probably got a fractured skull.'

'Feel this,' said the Bursar pointing at her forehead. 'Hard as a rock.'

Curiosity drove Amiss to press his fingers gingerly to her head.

'Not like that,' she said impatiently. She grabbed his hand, forced it into a fist and rapped hard with his knuckles on her forehead. 'Ebony,' she said. As he sucked his bruised knuckles, he felt inclined to agree.

'All the Troutbecks were like that. It would take more than a few bashes on the head to make any impact.'

'Have you called for an ambulance?' Amiss asked the Mistress.

'No,' she said wearily. 'We've been arguing for the last half an hour. Any sane person would have an X-ray but since we're dealing with the Bursar, normal rules do not apply.'

The Senior Tutor, Miss Stamp, Pusey and Miss Thackaberry together embarked on various squealing imprecations: the Bursar took another defiant swig.

'Compromise, Bursar, please,' said Amiss. 'Come upstairs to bed and receive a doctor – just to clean you up and make sure everything's hunkery-dory.'

'Oh, all right.' Her voice sounded exhausted.

'Let me give you my arm.'

'*Festina lente*,' warned Miss Partridge.

'Oh, stop fussing,' said the Bursar weakly, as she accepted Amiss's offer. And leading a small procession of worried scholars and against a background of agitated chatter, they proceeded towards her sleeping quarters.

It was an hour later when Dr Scott reported back to the group. He was a man who was economical with his words. 'She should be dead. Abnormally thick skull, so the wound's only superficial. Try and persuade her to have an X-ray, but it's my guess there's no damage done. She should have a few days in bed.

'I'll drop by tomorrow. Have you called the police yet?'

'Should we?' The Mistress seemed surprised at the suggestion.

'Unless you actively enjoy the idea of consorting with a would-be murderer, I should.' He raised his eyes to heaven at the daftness of intellectuals and left.

'There's no need to do anything till the morning,' said the Mistress firmly. 'We all need a good night's sleep. I'll ring the police after drill.'

Amiss looked at her incredulously. 'It doesn't worry you that somebody might try again?'

'Certainly not. This is nothing to do with any of us. It was a burglar and he will have escaped by now anyway.'

'Supposing it wasn't? Supposing it's somebody within who might try again? Shouldn't the Bursar have police protection?'

'Oh really, Mr Amiss. You're being a little alarmist, surely.'

'Nonetheless.' He adopted his firmest tone. 'I'm going to spend the night on the sofa in her room.'

'Mr Amiss,' said Dr Windlesham, 'that would be not only improper but contrary to the statutes.'

Amiss felt his temper rise. 'Madam, I am aware that there are persons in this institution who believe that all men are potential rapists, but I assure you that the Bursar's virtue is safe with me.'

'But the statutes . . .'

'Say what? "There shall be no shacking up in this establishment?"'

'There's no need to be coarse. The Founder made it very clear that no man was ever to be permitted within the sleeping quarters of either staff or students except for tea and under the supervision of a chaperone.'

'I'm quite happy with that,' said Amiss heading for the door. 'Feel free to join us with a tea-tray. And remember to make the cucumber sandwiches with very thinly-sliced bread.'

13

Throughout the long night, Amiss had frequent cause to regret his gallantry. While the Bursar's lusty snorings were a reassuring indication that the life force coursed vigorously around her veins, they took their toll on her guardian's jangling nerves. At about 3.00 a.m. he could stand no more. He climbed off his sofa and found his way across the room to the bed.

'Jack,' he hissed – gently, so as not to alarm her – 'please stop snoring.' There was no response other than a particularly rich explosion of sound. He raised his voice progressively for the second, the third and the fourth attempts, rousing her finally only by shaking her.

'What's wrong?' she muttered. 'What is it? Is the joint on fire?'

'No, Jack. But you're snoring so loudly I can't get a wink of sleep. Can you please try turning over?'

'Nothing wrong with a good snore. Clears the tubes. I like snoring. You should try it.' She fell asleep as she finished the sentence.

Miserably, Amiss crept back to his uncomfortable sofa and fell into a sleepless gloom.

Just before 7.00 came a commanding rap on the door, which he found had been inflicted by Deborah Windlesham. Amiss closed the door quietly and joined her in the corridor. She threw a disparaging glare at his crumpled appearance. 'You look as if you've slept in your clothes.'

'I have. I had little option.'

She sniffed one of those sniffs that substitutes for whole

paragraphs of criticism. 'No alarms in the middle of the night? No interruptions by assassins?'

Amiss opened his mouth to sympathize with her on her disappointment and closed it again. New Men didn't cheek women: he had stepped out of character quite enough the previous night. 'Thank you,' he said. 'We have been quite undisturbed.'

'You'd better hurry up or you'll be late for drill.'

'I'm not going to drill.'

'You must. We won't have a quorum otherwise. I don't expect the Bursar's going to be up to it.'

'Dr Windlesham.' Amiss spoke with as much patience as he could muster. 'I'm not leaving the Bursar alone until the police are with her.'

'That's melodramatic stuff and nonsense, as I'm sure Miss Troutbeck would be the first to agree.' She threw open the door and marched over to the recumbent – now just slightly snorting – Bursar and gazed on her with evident irritation. 'Can't think why you're so solicitous,' she said over her shoulder to Amiss. 'What is she? Your long-lost mother?'

'Got it in one.' Amiss's temper suddenly got the better of him. 'Now will you leave us together to celebrate our reunion?'

This time Dr Windlesham's sniff penetrated the Bursar's slumber. She opened her eyes slowly and then sat bolt upright. 'What a damn disinheriting countenance, Deborah. To what do I owe the honour of this visit?'

'I was just checking that you'd been looked after properly by your poodle.'

The Bursar's eyes flickered over towards Amiss, who was leaning against the door trying to look *soigné*. 'Push off, Deborah, will you? Go and be unpleasant to someone else for a change.'

Dr Windlesham marched out. Amiss applauded. 'That's what I like about you, Jack. Never use a stiletto when there is an axe to hand.'

'An axe isn't a bad weapon, but we Troutbecks rather favour the flail. That iron-spiked ball on the end of a chain saw off large numbers of infidels in short order during the

Crusades, I can tell you. Now, what's going on? Fill me in. My memories of last night are as hazy as if I'd been doing the Freshers' pub crawl.'

Amiss told the story rapidly. 'So,' he ended, 'a couple of days in bed and you'll be back to normal, if that's the right way to describe you.'

'Rubbish!'

She clambered out of bed and stood there arms akimbo. Despite his irritation, Amiss thought her a rather magnificent picture of defiance. Even her lavender-sprigged flannelette nightdress could not detract from her presence. 'I'm carrying on,' she announced. 'Business as usual.'

'God preserve me,' yelled Amiss, 'from stubborn old cows who can't get it into their thick heads that they're going to get murdered if they don't take some elementary fucking precautions!'

She looked at him in a mildly surprised way. 'I thought it was a good thing that I had a thick head.' Then, observing his expression, she grinned. 'Oh, all right. I'll be careful and I will see the police. In fact, I'll permit you to stand guard outside the bathroom door while I ablute.'

'And then you'll lock yourself in the bedroom while I go and get changed until I come and collect you.'

'Yes.' She shook her head. 'I don't know what old Major-General Bozo Troutbeck would make of this. He didn't single-handedly take out a platoon of Zulus by hiding in his bedroom.'

'Zulus don't have platoons.'

'These ones did.' She picked up a towel. 'Come on, then.' As he trailed wearily after her he wondered by what process she had absorbed all the vitality he had lost.

They caused rather a stir when they arrived at breakfast. The Mistress was positively solicitous, Miss Stamp went into an orgy of wittering and even Bridget Holdness managed a civil if terse enquiry.

The Bursar blossomed under all this attention. On hearing her launch into her 'a-little-tap-on-the-head-never-damaged-a-Troutbeck' routine, Amiss sloped off to the other

94

end of the table and left them to it. He was rewarded by finding himself sitting between Sandra and Mary Lou and having to listen to an interminable moan from Sandra about the permanent peril in which women lived. 'Atmosphere of male violence/no women safe walking the streets/intimidation/male resentment at women's self-empowering/meaningful coincidence that the attack had followed the Bursar's coming out/heterosexism leading to anti-lesbian violence/ reclaim the night/curfews on men . . .' On it went remorselessly, delivered in that high-pitched mewl that he found particularly hard to bear. As his attention drifted, he glanced at Mary Lou and their eyes met. Convinced that he had seen her lip twitch covertly, he winked at her. Her lip twitched again. In better heart, he resumed listening respectfully to Sandra.

14

It was 8.45 when Amiss heard the Senior Tutor's squeak of 'Where's the Mistress?' Only he – bored out of his mind by Sandra's maunderings, and nervy with sleeplessness and worry – paid her any attention. Almost everyone was listening bemusedly to the Bursar, who was celebrating her survival by engaging in family reminiscences of a kind that unsurprisingly caused her to be accused by Bridget Holdness of colluding with colonial exploiters.

His compassion aroused by the Senior Tutor's close resemblance to a squirrel with a nervous tic, Amiss left his seat, warily circled the adversaries and went round to try to soothe her. 'What's the matter, Senior Tutor?'

'She's seven minutes late. It's never ever happened before. You know what she's like.'

Amiss was too new to have fully grasped the Mistress's complicated timetable but he did know that it was set in stone.

'She's always in at twenty to nine.'

'What does she do between drill and breakfast, then?'

'Well, after drill she showers and dresses. You know, all that sort of thing.' The Senior Tutor went slightly pink, alarmed perhaps lest Amiss's erotic urges might be awakened by the notion of Dame Maud Theodosia Buckbarrow in the shower.

'And then?' He smiled encouragingly.

'Why at 8.10, she takes a list of references to the library to check, then it's back here promptly to breakfast at 8.40.'

'She's never late?'

She looked shocked. ' "To choose time is to save time" is

her guiding principle. And she chose it many years ago.'

'I'm sure there's a simple explanation, Senior Tutor. Perhaps she's dealing with the police over that unfortunate business last night.'

The little features relaxed. 'Oh, that must be it.'

Her happiness was short-lived. It was only two minutes later that the gathering was electrified by an eruption from the kitchen. Greasy Joan came in squealing, her face a compound of terror and self-importance. She seemed to have got herself spectacularly bedraggled for this occasion. Her dank pepper-and-salt hair was all over the place, her apron sported generations of bacon fat and a long smear of egg and her stockings were mucky and bloody from where she had injured herself in her flight to bring her bad news. The gathering gazed at her open-mouthed as she wailed at top volume: 'She's gone and flung 'erself owt the winder.'

'Who has?' boomed the Bursar.

'Our blessed Daime.' And Greasy Joan set up an ululation that would have done credit to a banshee.

'Stop wailing, woman,' said the Bursar. 'Where is she?'

'On the front lorn, she is, boi the nettle bed.'

'How could she have jumped out of a window on to the front lawn?' asked Deborah Windlesham testily. 'She isn't an Olympic long-distance jump champion.'

Greasy Joan wailed louder. 'Well she 'as done. She's all over glarse.'

Rightly giving up on any idea of extracting any more useful information, the Bursar leaped to her feet. 'Show us.' Greasy Joan fled at the head of a stampede of dons through the kitchen to the back door, and so it was that the Mistress's corpse was displayed simultaneously to the vast majority of her colleagues. The sight was not one on which many of them chose to linger, for not only was her body sprawled at an unhappy angle, but there was an awful lot of blood.

It was the Bursar who got to her first, felt for her heart and then her pulse. After a minute or so she gently laid down the limp hand. 'Here,' she said, clicking her fingers at Amiss. 'Give me your jacket.'

As he handed it over, Amiss tried to repress as unworthy

his resentment that the fate of his only decent article of clothing should be to become a shroud.

The Bursar had dispatched Miss Stamp to phone the police and Dr Windlesham, who turned out to be Deputy Mistress, led the rest of the staff back to the dining room to acquaint the students with the news. Only Amiss, the Bursar and Greasy Joan remained.

'Are you sure you shouldn't call an ambulance as well?' asked Amiss. 'Can you be absolutely certain she's dead?'

'She's broken her neck and severed an artery. There's no pulse, no heartbeat, no breath. What do you think she's running on, abstract intelligence?'

Greasy Joan's lamentations increased in volume. 'Oh, shut up, Joan, for Christ's sake. You'd wake the dead.'

The tactlessness of this remark did nothing for Greasy Joan's composure: it took Amiss a couple of minutes to soothe her into silent weeping. He turned back to the Bursar, who was moodily kicking the gravel. 'I didn't know you were an expert on first aid.'

'I wasn't a girl guide for nothing,' she said absently. 'Reef-knots, path-finding, making a fire with a couple of sticks. I could survive in any jungle.'

Amiss detected a catch in her voice. 'This must be very upsetting for you, Jack.'

'She was all right, old Maud. Never did any harm to anyone unless they crossed her path with sloppy scholarship. This isn't right.'

He could see tears on her cheek. She reached into the pocket of her skirt, took out an enormous cotton handkerchief and blew her nose thunderously. 'That's better. Crying's good for you. Just like old Winston, Troutbecks have never been ashamed to cry. Now, let's get on with it.'

'What?'

'Whatever it is.'

Hearing the sound of a car on the drive she put on a burst of speed that had Amiss panting, as ever, to keep up. They had reached the front door by the time the car drew up.

'Blimey,' said the Bursar, 'it's the fuzz. How can they be here already?'

The car disgorged a middle-aged man of solid appearance and a pimply youth with an Adam's apple who, even to Amiss, seemed ludicrously young.

'Good morning, madam. Good morning, sir,' said the older of the two.

'You the coppers?' asked the Bursar.

He looked taken aback. 'Yes.'

'Right. Follow me.'

She turned on her heel and began to charge around the building. The senior policeman looked at Amiss in perplexity.

'We're here to see Dame Maud Buckbarrow.'

'The Bursar is leading you to her.'

Obediently, the policemen walked beside Amiss in pursuit.

'How did you get here so quickly? It can't have been more than three minutes since Miss Stamp rang.'

'Not with you, sir. It's almost an hour since the request came into the station from the lady.'

'Which lady?'

'Like I said,' said the sergeant patiently, 'Dame Maud Buckbarrow.'

'Oh Christ, you've come to investigate the attack of last night. Not what's happened this morning.'

'What happened this morning?'

'This,' said Amiss as they rounded the corner to see the improbable tableau of corpse, sobbing Greasy Joan and the Bursar bellowing, 'Pull yourself together woman. The fuzz'll will be wanting to get some sense out of you.'

Amiss didn't rate their chances highly.

The sergeant was a man of the old school. Faced with noisy women, he knew that a firm masculine intervention was called for. 'Now, now, ladies, let's not get hysterical. Dry your eyes and leave it to us.'

'I would be obliged, Constable,' said the Bursar, 'if you would refrain from addressing me and my colleagues here in such a . . .' She paused to find the right word.

'Paternalistic manner?' suggested Amiss. She glared at

99

him. 'Such an egregiously patronizing manner,' she substituted.

These linguistic niceties were lost on the sergeant, whose feelings had been outraged by the blow to his professional self-esteem. 'Madam, I am not a constable. I am Sergeant Stephen Bunter and this is Constable Atkins.'

'Well, we can't all stand around swapping our names and telephone numbers,' said the Bursar. 'You'd better get on with it.'

'What?'

'Well whatever you rozzers do in circumstances like this. Are there only two of you?'

'The others will be on the way, Bursar,' said Amiss. 'These gentlemen came at the request of the Mistress to investigate the attack on you.'

Sergeant Bunter's face cleared. 'You, then, madam, would be the unfortunate lady who was the victim of a vicious assault yesterday evening. Am I correct?'

'Yes, yes. But that's ancient history. You've got a stiff to deal with now.'

Her unladylike language drew a gulp from Bunter. He stood there irresolute. 'Well, ma'am, me and my colleague are here to investigate that. This other regrettable event is a matter for those of my colleagues who will be following on. I would be grateful if you would accompany me to a location where I can note down the appropriate particulars. In the meantime, P.C. Atkins here can stand guard over the late Dame, and this other lady here, after giving him her name, can depart somewhere to recover her composure. Indeed, madam, if you would like yourself to visit the powder room and freshen up before we discuss the upsetting events of the past evening, that will be quite understood.'

'Sergeant Bunter,' said the Bursar in that tone of voice which normally presaged heavy irony, 'it is kind of you to be so sensitive to our womanly feelings.' He smirked. 'But I think I have succeeded in conquering any remaining girlish squeamishness, so I'm staying here and I suggest you do the same. Why don't you scrabble around a bit and look for clues.'

She plonked herself down and stretched out her legs. Looking covertly at Bunter, Amiss observed the fascinated stare elicited by the sight of the elasticized knicker legs that peeped out from below the tweed skirt and then incongruously gave way to thick woollen patterned stockings and heavy brogues, the tongue of one of which was standing upright and thus giving a startled look to the whole ensemble. This still life was broken by a shout from the young constable. 'Sir, look, look!'

The Bursar scrambled to her feet with more vigour than elegance and the three of them raced around the vast bush to where the constable stood excitedly pointing at a ladder.

'Look, sir. Burglars must have been trying to get in.'

'I thought the problem we were concentrating on,' said the Bursar, 'was of someone getting out rather than someone getting in. What's preoccupying me is how an eleven-stone woman could go through a window with sufficient force to carry her beyond normal jumping distance.'

'The burglar might have thrown her,' observed the sergeant sagely. 'You'd be surprised at the sort of things villains do.'

'Well, we'd better look for the world champion at caber-tossing then.' She paused and took a second look at the ladder. 'That's ours. From the library. Now why would she go out the library window with a ladder?'

'Maybe she was on it,' suggested Amiss.

As they pondered this possibility, Miss Stamp came squeaking round the corner accompanied by a collection of uniformed and plain clothes policemen. The leader of the pack hurried forward. 'Good morning, ma'am, Inspector Michael Romford.'

The Bursar bowed. 'Jack Troutbeck,' she said. 'Bursar.'

'The lady that was hit on the head with the gun last night,' said Bunter helpfully.

'Good heavens,' said Romford. 'You must still be in a state of shock. I think you'd better go in and lie down while we attend to matters here.'

She glowered at him. 'Inspector, let me give you one word of advice. This may look like an establishment for the education of docile young ladies, but it is packed for the most part with battleaxes, harpies and thought police. It would be better for all of you if you gear yourselves up to expect Bette Davis on a bad night rather than Doris Day.'

She surveyed the gathering. 'I am now going inside to have a large drink. Would you care to accompany me, Robert?'

As she strode off, Amiss began to sidle after her, hoping to escape notice. He was halted by Romford. 'Well, well, if it isn't Mr Amiss. What a surprise to see you yet again, sir.'

'My pleasure, Inspector Romford. Now if you'll excuse me, I must look after the Bursar. As you can see, she's not very well.' And he galloped away in pursuit.

15

Can you believe it? Amiss wrote to Rachel. I'm lumbered with Inspector bloody Romford, the half-wit that fingered me as a murderer at the time I was actually acting as a copper's nark and then turned up on a later occasion to screw up things at the Knightsbridge school. He's the Bible-thumping, family values, moral majority asshole who made Ellis's life a misery for ages. Fortunately, he got up Jim's nose so much with his sanctimonious clucking and tut-tutting, not to speak of the way he used to draw in his breath with a shocked hiss any time anyone said anything that would not have passed muster in a roomful of Mormons, that he ruthlessly dispatched him to Stolen Vehicles, leading the whole of the division to celebrate mightily.

Unfortunately, he didn't enjoy his new job. I learn from Ellis that in the true tradition of a hellfire-and-brimstone preacher, old Romford pined for the days of investigating exotic vice and grisly murders and eventually got himself transferred to the Cambridgeshire constabulary.

He is, you can imagine, going down big with Jack Troutbeck and Bridget Holdness. Indeed, if he stays around much longer, he may succeed in uniting the whole college against him. Being one of the boys, Jack doesn't take very well to being treated like something out of a 1950s advertisement for washing powder; Romford is firmly of the 'Ladies-God-bless-'em' school of chauvinists.

Mind you, he's had such a rough ride here already that he shows signs of moving to the 'woman-as-sin' position. Ever since Jack sported her 'DYKE POWER' badge, he has viewed her with salacious horror. He even had his young

WPC transferred to other duties, presumably lest she become a victim of gang rape by the Fellows of St Martha's.

There seems to be no one to control him. The local superintendent has rushed in and out a few times looking harassed, but he's got a frightful double murder to deal with of the kind in which the Fens specialize. You must have read about the sort of thing often: swirling mists, severed heads, inarticulate locals and a lot of incest thrown in here and there. Romford's chief inspector isn't around either; apparently he's off on some kind of course. Anyway, initially St Martha's wasn't given much priority because it wasn't clearly a murder case, but it clearly is now.

Dame Maud, it emerges, was in the habit of 'scooting' on a ladder along the library shelves, sometimes at some speed, since the two books she most frequently consulted when checking references were the *Dictionary of National Biography* which was at the end nearest to the entrance and a book on Anglo-Saxon place names which was just beside the window. You know the kind of ladder I mean — one that is attached to grooves at strategic places on the bookshelves.

Where more cautious scholars used to push the ladder from one spot to another, the Mistress had the unexpectedly skittish habit of scooting it along at top speed, steadying it at the end with a combination of her foot and the force of the stoppers that prevent ladders from falling out of the grooves. This time there were no stoppers and Mistress and ladder sailed on through the window.

The key question is why were there no stoppers? It could hardly have been an accident that three vanished simultaneously without leaving a trace and it seems pretty unlikely that she removed them herself in order to commit suicide. If so, why wouldn't they be in the library? Nor did she have a perverse or convoluted mind.

It could, of course, have been a practical joke that went badly wrong, but St Martha's isn't a practical-jokey sort of place and it would have taken an absolute cretin not to realize how dangerous it would be. No, it's obvious to the meanest intelligence, even Romford's, that someone was out to get Dame Maud.

Romford's main problem is that the motives are completely beyond him. Trying to explain to him how passions could run high over theology lectureships as opposed to women's studies is like trying to explain to a witch doctor the difference between penicillin and aspirin. Once he had grasped that women's studies were not – as he thought – accomplishments of the kind possessed by old Francis Pusey (and you should have seen his face when he discovered that the Womanly Arts Fellow was male) but were somehow academic, he was lost.

He picked up from someone that there was tension over something called political correctness and asked Jack to explain what that meant. She defined it as: 'an American fashion or indeed species of intimidation, to make us change our ways of speaking about people so that all savour is taken out of life'. She reported to me gleefully that this had not appeared to clarify matters.

Summoned in my turn and also not feeling particularly well-disposed towards Romford, I proffered the definition: "intellectual fascism applied to language". He looked really miserable after that, but instead of having the sense to throw himself on my mercy, in which case I would have yielded and explained it all to him in pidgin (oops!) English, he started getting aggressive about what I was doing in the place anyway. Insofar as I can understand, the reason for Romford's hostility to me is to do with notions of no smoke without fire: I've been in the proximity of a suspicious number of murders.

I have to admit to rather enjoying myself at present. I am, of course, sorry about poor old Maud Buckbarrow, but it was, after all, an absolutely splendid way for her to go. I have no idea at the moment what its effect on college politics is going to be, but I don't think there'll be a long remission in the war. Bridget Holdness has a nasty glint in her eye and Jack is going about the place with that preoccupied expression that means she's thinking of further ways to scupper enemy plans. When she's in that mood she's totally uncommunicative, so, between coppers who won't talk to me and a chief conspirator who keeps everything close to her formidable chest, I'm feeling at a bit of a loose end: I may have to seek solace again with

Francis. I'm still worried about Jack but she stoutly refuses to believe she's in any danger with a posse of policemen clumping around the place. I suppose she's right; anyway you can't guard someone against their will.

Now to the really important matters. What's the news from Personnel? Are you being released back to London or am I fated to be a Foreign Office common-law widower for the rest of the year . . . ?

'Excuse me, sir, do you have a moment?'

'Come in, Ellis.'

Chief Superintendent Jim Milton disentangled himself with relief from his snowstorm of paperwork and smiled welcomingly. 'Sit down. I hope it's about something more interesting than budgets.' He felt pretty confident that it was; promotion had not removed from Pooley the look of quivering eagerness that overcame him when his imagination was aroused.

'It's Robert, sir. He's been on from Cambridge.'

'Cambridge?'

'Don't you remember? I told you the other night about what he was up to in that peculiar female college.'

'Oh yes. Sorry, Ellis. Of course – the PC battleground. What's happened?'

'There's been a murder of the Mistress and an attempted murder of the Bursar.'

'How does Robert get himself involved in these things? It's looking too much like coincidence. Maybe we were wrong about him and he really is a serial killer.'

'He thinks that's what Romford thinks.'

'What do you mean, Romford?'

'He's in charge of the case.'

A smile of pure pleasure spread over Milton's face as he remembered Romford's many frightfulnesses. 'Excellent casting. Just the man for this. Thanks, Ellis, you've brightened my morning.'

'But, sir, what I was wondering was if there's any way we can get involved?'

'Of course there isn't.'

'But I wondered if I mightn't be useful to them. As a Cambridge graduate, I mean.'

'Ellis, we do not lend people round to other forces on flimsy pretexts like that.'

Milton always hated it when Pooley's eager look gave way to disappointment. 'I'm sorry, Ellis, but bureaucracies are bureaucracies and this is a bureaucracy. You're going to have to get your kicks on this one vicariously from Robert, I'm afraid. Keep in touch with him and we'll have a drink one night and you can fill me in. Now, we'd better both get back to whatever it is we're being paid to do.'

He averted his eyes as Pooley trailed dejectedly out of the room.

It was at around five o'clock that afternoon that Milton's curiosity got the better of him. On an impulse – and pausing only to fabricate a suitable enquiry – he rang his friend Superintendent Hardiman of the Cambridgeshire police.

'I was just this very moment thinking of ringing you,' said Hardiman. 'First chance I've had all day. What did you want?' He did not sound friendly.

'Just a quick word about the drug ring that's impinging on both our territories.'

'Bugger that, I've no time at present to think of anything less serious than murder.'

'Things bad?'

'Fucking awful.'

'Are you looking for help?'

'I wasn't going to ask for help. I was about to enquire what I had ever done to you that you should have unleashed on to me that buffoon Romford.'

'Oh, he's not so bad.'

'Not so bad as what? I don't mind him having no brains: I'm used to that. It's the Holy Joe carry-on combined with his absolute misreading of everyone around him that drives me wild. You can completely rely on Romford to be wrong about colleagues, suspects and the lot. What I want to know is how the hell he got promoted. Was he a fucking freemason or something?'

107

'Search me, Gordon. I always found that mysterious myself. He was already an inspector when I acquired him. And it's no good blaming me. I didn't know he was trying to transfer to Cambridgeshire.'

'Well, he had good reports from you as well as from Stolen Vehicles.'

'Not exactly good,' said Milton rather guiltily. 'More a case of being economical with the truth. How the hell else do you ever get anyone transferred? Anyway, what's he doing at the moment?'

'Making a total bollocks of a murder in some daft local women's college. Mind you,' said Hardiman grudgingly, 'it's not easy. I've been in there a couple of times to see those birds and all I've grasped is that lots of them hate each other like poison.'

'Why?'

'Well, as far as I can see, there's a lot of lefty lezzies in there who are trying to turn everything upside down and some right-wing lezzies that don't like it.'

'Sounds confusing.'

'Let me give you an example. I'm introduced to some beefy dame who claims to be called Jack and who is wearing a badge announcing that she's a dyke and she smiles sweetly and says, "Ah, Superintendent, I fear that in this establishment yours will be regarded as an unacceptable surname. Dr Holdness here," she says, indicating a frizzy-headed bint standing nearby, "will wish no doubt to alter it forthwith to Hardiperson." At this stage the frizzy-headed bint storms out of room followed by a couple of droopy-looking birds in stout boots and a tasty black.'

'Hmm,' said Milton. 'Challenging.'

'Challenging? I don't need fucking challenges. Got my hands full of decapitated corpses as it is and the most senior person I've got to put on this is a moron who doesn't know a Cambridge college from a garden shed. For Christ's sake, when he was told that the corpse was the college Mistress, he was initially under the impression that she was a lady of ill-repute.'

'Haven't you got some bright youngster who knows his way around academia?'

'I have not,' said Hardiman bitterly. 'Joining the local police force is not what Cambridge graduates think of doing. And all that any of my lot know is how to charge a few drunken undergraduates after a May Ball.'

'Tough luck. It's a shame really. I've got the very man here. Young sergeant, graduate of King's, well read, up to date with political fashions, even knows how to handle Romford.'

'Are you offering me this guy, and if so, why?'

'Well, since you're in such dire need and we're old friends I could let you have him on secondment for a week. There will, of course, be a price.'

'Ah, I thought as much.' Hardiman no longer sounded suspicious. 'There's no such thing as a free detective sergeant, eh? All right, let's have it.'

'Actually,' said Milton to Pooley, 'I got quite a good price for you. He's taking on quite a lot of boring leg work on this drug business.'

'Oh, Jim. Sorry, sir,' said Pooley, who occasionally got confused in his twin roles as friend and subordinate. 'I can't thank you enough.'

'Quite so. But remember that I want you back after a week. There will be no extensions, so you and Robert had better get your skates on. Mind you, what I don't understand is how you can be dancing with happiness over working with Romford in view of what you think of him.'

'Oh, he's just a minor irritant. A murder in Cambridge. It's what I always wanted. When I think of all those Oxbridge murder stories I've read, Dorothy Sayers and Michael Innes and Edmund Crispin and . . .'

'Yes, yes,' said Milton hastily. 'OK then. Off you go and enjoy yourself, bearing in mind that you're looking for a real live murderer and that I want you to bring Robert out safely.'

As Pooley rushed out, panting with impatience to tell Amiss the good news, Milton felt a great stab of regret at not being able to go too.

16

Over the next few days, Pooley was frequently to forget his optimistic prediction that Romford would be only an irritant, but these moments were more than balanced by the pure enjoyment of his boss's frequent discomfiture. His favourite moment of all occurred on the very first morning.

They were ten minutes into Romford's second cross-examination of the Bursar and it had become patently obvious that she had taken a rooted objection to him. She attacked on two flanks. On the one hand, she lost no opportunity to use a blasphemy here, a four-letter word there: on the other, when she wasn't being monosyllabic, she was even more elliptical than usual – dropping, as far as Romford was concerned, impenetrable references at every turn. As Pooley painstakingly wrote down her observation that 'Christ only knows the mysteries of Sappho' in answer to a question about the Mistress's personal life, he caught a glimpse of Romford's face and almost laughed out loud.

'So who do you think might have wanted to kill her?' asked Romford.

'Fucked if I know,' said the Bursar happily.

'Please, Miss Troutbeck,' Romford was goaded too far. 'I must ask you to watch your language.'

'Ask away,' said the Bursar breezily, 'but will anyone answer? You have to understand that the argot of rough tough dykes is rough and tough.'

It was at that moment that the door crashed open to reveal a dapper little man in a check tweed suit, plum-coloured waistcoat and trilby. She jumped up.

'Ida,' he shouted, 'are you all right?' He rushed to her side, clasped as much of her as he could in his little arms and implanted a great kiss on her lips. 'Why didn't you tell me, you silly girl? I was frantic when I saw the paper this morning. Let me look, where did she hit you?'

The Bursar indicated the offending spot, which the little man promptly kissed. Then, clearly relieved at the obviously vigorous health of his beloved, he looked around and addressed the startled police. 'My apologies, gentlemen, for interrupting. My name is Myles Cavendish. I had to come to see that Ida was all right.'

Romford felt it time he took control.

'Excuse me, sir, but are you a relative of Miss Troutbeck?'

'A relative? Certainly not. I am her lover. Now have you finished with her? I want to take her away for a romantic stroll on the Backs.'

'I suppose so,' said Romford, wriggling with embarrassment. The Bursar got up, took Myles's hand and smiled.

'Who can predict where Eros will strike?' she observed airily. 'I shall see you anon, gentlemen. In the meantime, Inspector, I suggest that you pray to God. She will help you.' And with the guffaw that always accompanied her own sallies, she pranced out of the room arm in arm with Myles; — with his hat on he reached her chin. There was a silence, broken by Romford.

'But she's supposed to be one of those perverts. In fact, she wears a badge which says it.'

'Says what?'

'Says she's a pervert.' Romford was unable to bring himself to let the word 'dyke' cross his lips.

'Perhaps it's a joke.'

'I don't like jokes. "As a jewel of gold in a swine's snout, so is a fair woman when she is without discretion."' He brooded further. 'Not that she's what I'd call a "fair woman".'

The silence grew oppressive. Finally Pooley spoke. 'What are we going to do now, sir?'

'I don't know. I don't know where to start.'

'If I might make a suggestion, sir?' Pooley put into his voice every last ounce of obsequiousness he could muster.

'Yes?'

'Perhaps we might find it easier to sort out the basics if we got help from an outsider?'

Romford looked at him suspiciously. 'Are you talking about Robert Amiss?'

'Well, yes, sir. When you told me he was here, I confess I thought it a stroke of luck.'

'Seems very suspicious to me. Always changing jobs; always in funny company.'

Pooley said nothing. Romford gazed down at his list.

'What's a Senior Tutor?' he asked.

'The person most in charge of undergraduates.'

'Oh, so she's quite important then.'

'Yes indeed,' said Pooley.

'Dr Emily Twigg,' said Romford. 'She's got to be an improvement. Sounds a respectable sort of person.'

Pooley could see the relief evinced by Romford as he shepherded the Senior Tutor into the room. Although the hairnet remained incapable of performing much of its function, the general grey effect of the woolly ensemble spoke of spinsterhood, celibacy, modesty and other traits that Romford found particularly attractive.

His relief was short-lived. When he sought enlightenment on what motive anyone might have had to murder Dame Maud the dam broke and a torrent of impassioned words spewed forth, with 'rigour', 'excellence', 'honour', 'integrity', 'truth', 'scholarship', 'Beowulf' giving way to 'vixens', 'minxes', 'sloppiness', 'lack of standards', 'unknown American tenth-rate writers', 'destruction of all that St Martha's stood for' and much, much more.

'Excuse me,' interrupted a desperate Romford five minutes into the monologue. 'Can you be more specific? I'm new to all this you see. I'm just a policeman.'

The Senior Tutor gazed at him and – conscientious teacher that she was – cocked her little ear the better to understand his question.

'What I'm trying to understand is the big difference between them, these two sides you're talking about. You thought you should be teaching different things, is that it?'

She nodded.

'Could you maybe give me a simple example?'

'Well, if I tell you,' she said, struggling desperately to be helpful, 'that the only English playwright they wanted to study was Aphra Benn, that George Eliot wouldn't be acceptable at all if she hadn't been a woman and that you're not supposed to be allowed to think that F.R. Leavis had anything to say. No, no, no, even though they didn't like anything he said, it all had to have been said by Queenie; he was supposed to have been a parasite on her superior intellect.' Her whiskers quivering, she waited for his reaction.

'Thank you, Dr Twigg,' Romford said heavily. 'I'll be in touch later if I have any more questions.' He watched her dully as she scuttled from the room. 'We'll go back to the station,' he said to Pooley, 'and see what forensic has come up with. You'd better arrange to have that fellow Amiss in this afternoon.'

'Try and win him over, Robert.'

'How am I supposed to do that? Let a Bible fall out of my pocket?'

'Don't say anything that shocks him.'

'I thought everything shocked him.' Amiss sounded grumpy.

'What's the matter?'

'Bored and restless. There's no one to plot with. Jack Troutbeck hasn't been seen since she disappeared off on the arm of that little bookie and you're hardly available at all. And I don't even have a proper job to do in this establishment.'

'Go and make friends with somebody. Snoop.'

'I can see you haven't been listening to me, Ellis. You might as well tell a smoker to make friends in a Californian gym. As far as the Virgins are concerned, I'm something in short pants from another planet and it suits the Dykes to believe I'm Jack the Ripper. Anyway, you never catch them singly.' He sighed. 'Sorry. I'll stop whinging and look forward to tonight. Where will we meet to chew it all over?'

Pooley looked embarrassed. 'I can't make it tonight.'

Amiss's wail was desperate. 'You can't mean it.'

'No option, I'm afraid. Romford's asked me to come home and have tea with his wife. He said he didn't want me at a loose end on my first evening here.'

It was unfortunate that Amiss's cry of 'fucking hell' coincided with Romford's entry into the interview room. He pursed his lips so hard that they disappeared into a thin line. 'You are upset about something,' he observed frostily.

'I am, Inspector Romford. I must apologize for using that expletive, but I fear my nerves have been frayed by the happenings of the last twenty-four hours – particularly by the callous murder of that fine woman.'

Romford visibly softened.

'I did not know her long,' went on Amiss, 'but long enough to know her to be a gallant and gracious lady.'

As ever, when Amiss began to perform, Pooley was gripped by the fear that he would overact and blow it. Romford, however, was looking a little less acidulous.

'It would have been her then that gave you the job, would it?'

'Er, no, not exactly. I was appointed by an interview panel that included the Bursar and the Senior Tutor.'

'Oh, them. I hope they were better at interviewing than at being interviewed. What do you make of them then?'

'Well,' Amiss said cautiously, 'Dr Twigg is a woman who is most dedicated to her profession, but I have to admit that she's not always the easiest person to have a conversation with.'

'And the other one?'

'Bit of a rough diamond?'

'You can say that again. Except I don't know about the diamond. I wouldn't want her near my daughter. No manners, filthy tongue and no morals as far as I can see.'

'Heart of gold though, I've heard it said,' added Amiss in a sudden rush of loyalty to his friend.

'Who says?'

Amiss was only briefly foxed. 'The late Dame Maud, oddly enough. They and the Senior Tutor were old friends – undergraduate rowing companions.'

114

'Rowing? I don't hold with rowing for young women. It's unladylike.'

'Ah, but Inspector, we are mere men. Who are we to block the progress of the ladies?'

He caught Pooley's eye and stifled the temptation to take the rhetoric further. Instead, he brushed up his pious expression and listened intently to Romford. 'In the course of the next few days, we will be taking details about when the library stairs were last used and narrowing down the time in which the outrage could have been planned, but that is a matter for more junior officers, Mr Amiss. It is my job to ascertain any possible reasons why anyone could have wished to do this disgraceful thing.'

'Inspector, I don't wish to be presumptuous and I am, of course, very new here, but might it help if I sketched in the background a little? It might perhaps save you some valuable time?'

Romford's acquiescence sounded positively friendly.

17

After an hour or so, Amiss was let go. Romford, who had been crouched on the edge of his chair, shoulders hunched and with the misery of his expression deepening as the complications mounted, threw down his pen and sighed heavily. '"Silly women laden with sins, led away with diverse lusts." This is no place for an honest man, Pooley.'

'But, sir, surely your experiences on the Vice and Murder Squads must have brought you into contact with much worse people than this?'

'I have been in dens of iniquity in my time, Pooley, but at least with ordinary villains you know where you are. All this filth and loose talk and unnatural sexual practices from so-called educated people is a different business. Especially when it comes out of my taxes. Subsidized degenerates, that's what they are here. Trying to poison the minds of the young.'

He appeared lost in thought for several minutes; Pooley wondered if he were praying. At length he roused himself and looked at his watch.

'Six o'clock. We'd better be getting home to Mother.'

'Mother?'

Romford smiled. 'That's what I call Mrs Romford.'

Pooley felt it didn't augur very well.

Pooley never was to find out Mrs Romford's first name, for Inspector Romford had firm notions about keeping a proper social distance with subordinates. It was one thing to let them into your house; it was quite another to let hierarchical standards slip. Mrs Romford herself was more friendly.

' "Ellis",' she said, 'that's a funny name. I never heard that before.'

'It's been in the family a long time.'

'Oh, how nice, dear,' she said vaguely. 'I like a nice historical name. Now, would you excuse me a minute while I ask my husband about something?'

'Can't it wait, Mother?'

'It'll only take a minute, Michael.' She seemed excited. 'I'm sure Ellis won't mind.'

'Of course not, Mrs Romford.'

They left him in the living room. Unexpectedly for a man of Romford's known austerity, like the frock Mrs Romford was wearing, the decor was big on flounces and patterns. The pink curtains with their ruffles and loops picked out one of the more overwhelming colours in the garishly-patterned carpet, the fabric of the loose covers of the three-piece suite picked up the purple, the green and the orange, and had deep frills at the hems, elaborately-worked antimacassars at the back and on the arms and a large number of tapestry scatter cushions of a quite remarkable banality. Pooley could not decide which one was the worst: the swan, the doe-eyed deer, the white fluffy kitten or the soulful labrador.

Having taken in as much of this as he could, he proceeded to the photographs – all in velvet or gilt frames – which hung on the wall or – along with crocheted coasters and embroidered mats – cluttered up the occasional tables. There was the usual clutch of sepia grannies and grandads and black-and-white mums and dads and a wedding photograph of a stern-faced young Romford, stiffly arm in arm with a pretty little woman with a big trusting smile. Though not immediately identifiable as Mrs Romford, it was undoubtedly her, for her little pill-box hat had a vast cabbage rose and sprayed veils in all directions, the nipped-in costume was enlivened by cascading ruffs at the neck and at the wrists, there were rosettes at the front of the shoes and the bridal bouquet had an elaborate muslin and lace surround.

There were three photographs of Romford in uniform, recording his progress from constable through sergeant to inspector, two of christenings of baby Romfords (at which

Mrs Romford had done things with cartwheel hats), the graduation photograph of a stiff youth who took after his father and wedding pictures of both him and what must be his sister; certainly her wedding dress bore all the signs of her mother's loving hand.

The only reading material in the room was the current copy of *Reader's Digest*, a leatherbound Bible and a copy of a women's magazine containing advice on making marmalade economically, knitting cuddly toys, making him a waistcoat for that very special occasion and many other explorations into the world of feminine crafts.

His host and hostess came within earshot. 'I'm sorry, Mother.' Romford had that tone of finality he adopted to refuse reasonable requests from subordinates. 'You just have to remember where your duty lies.'

When they opened the door they saw Pooley gazing fixedly at a *Reader's Digest* article on the Andes.

'Sorry to have left you for so long.' Romford was affable. 'Mother and I had a little domestic matter to sort out. Now, can I get you something to drink?'

Pooley was all too aware of Romford's views on alcohol to have any false optimism. 'Orange squash or lemonade?' urged Romford hospitably.

'I think just a glass of water, thank you.'

A depressed-looking Mrs Romford bustled off and Romford and Pooley sat down. 'Now, Pooley, I should tell you that I don't bring my work home. There are a lot of things that go on in our job, as you know, that are not fit to talk to women about. Their minds aren't as strong as ours and they're easily corrupted. So we'll keep off all that over tea. Just keep the conversation general.'

'I quite understand, sir. But won't Mrs Romford have seen something about St Martha's in the newspaper?'

'My wife doesn't read newspapers. I'm pleased to say she's far too busy being a homemaker.'

Pooley's culinary taste tended towards the austere and health-giving: though in content traditional, Mrs Romford's cuisine looked like everything else about her. There were fairy cakes with cherries on top, iced cakes with multi-coloured decorations, the tomatoes and radishes were sculpted, the hard-boiled eggs were quartered and symmetrically arranged and the tinned salmon was festooned with chopped beetroot.

'Mr Romford likes his food ordinary,' she said rather sadly. 'He's never been keen on experimenting.'

'There's enough foreign influences in this country, Pooley, without letting it affect what we eat. What my mother gave me is good enough for me.' His tone softened and became indulgent. 'However, I don't mind if Mother likes to pretty it up a bit the way she does.'

Mrs Romford cheered up a little after that accolade and further still when Pooley complimented her on the matching embroidered napkins and tablecloth.

'I like to keep myself busy,' she said modestly. 'My job doesn't take up much time.' She threw at Romford what looked like a rather mutinous glance.

'Mother has a little job, Pooley. Very suitable for a married woman.'

'And that is?'

'I work part time in a curtain shop.' Her eyes gleamed. 'I really enjoy it. Lots of the people that come in, they don't know what they're looking for; they just want help. And I know the difference between all the nets and I help them make all those decisions about whether you should have a valance on your soft furnishings, or if it's curtains, what to do about pelmets and swags, how to arrange the tags and the loops and the ruffles and about the curtain rods and the rails and the automatic closings and which fabrics for direct sunlight and how to keep them clean and . . .'

'Mother's quite a little expert.'

'You certainly are,' said Pooley. 'I'm very impressed. I hardly know the difference between a curtain and a blind myself.'

'They want me to be the manageress,' Mrs Romford blurted out suddenly. 'They just asked me today.'

'Now, Mother, we won't talk about that.'

'But I'd have to work full time and Mr Romford's against it. What do you think, Ellis?'

'An unmarried lad like that isn't going to have anything to say about something like this,' said Romford, much to Pooley's relief. 'Although I'd say he's seen enough to know that no good comes of women moving out of their sacred sphere as guardians of the home.'

'Are you talking about what's going on at that college, St Martha's?'

'What do you know about that?'

'One of the girls told me at work. She knows someone who works there and says there's been a lot of carry-on, even before this murder.'

Seeing the expression on Romford's face, Pooley cut in with, 'I was admiring your photographs, Mrs Romford,' and the rest of tea passed in a welter of harmless maternal boasting. That very month, it turned out, Mrs Romford was preparing to welcome the first grandchild with a trunkload of woolly hats, booties and cardies. Pooley expressed so much interest that when they went into the living room, she brought in a christening frock which seemed to be composed of about seventeen layers. Pooley wondered how they would ever find the baby in the middle of it. 'What beautiful workmanship. Your daughter will be very pleased.'

'Oh, she will. The day she got married I said to her: "I made your wedding dress and now I'll begin on the robe for the first grandchild." Would you like to see a video of the wedding?'

Pooley had long ago adopted the line of least resistance. 'That would be delightful.'

'You'll be able to hear Dad preaching. It was very powerful what he said.'

'I'm sure it was.' Pooley prayed the event would be sufficiently awful to be more horrifying than boring.

18

Amiss was having a far better time. Loneliness had led him to prowl the corridors and the gardens in the hope of meeting someone he could ask out for dinner. In the absence of the Bursar, there were no obvious candidates but he had some vague lingering hope that someone appropriate would turn up. He thought he might even take a risk on Pippa; her record would keep him safely celibate. In the end, having discovered from a passing policeman that the library was now open again, he drifted in and found Mary Lou there alone reading in an out-of-the-way corner. When she saw him, she jumped.

'Hello, Mary Lou. What are you reading?'

'Nothing in particular.' She closed her book and put it in the middle of a pile where he could not read the title. She waved vaguely at the books on the table. 'Just browsing.'

The visible titles were boringly predictable: a compendium of lesbian and gay short stories and Mary Daly's *Wickedary*, which the Bursar had told him was the worst of all the pieces of pretentious crap the sisterhood were trying to force on to the curriculum.

'Mind if I look at this?' He picked it up. The cover, adorned with mystic signs and cobwebs, set his teeth on edge. Matters were made no better by the promise on the back to free language 'from the "academic fraternities of Bearded Brother No-it-alls"', by defining words 'Naming Elemental Realities, the Inhabitants of the Background, and the fatuous foreground world of patriarchy'. He flicked through with increasing irritation. It was a paen of praise to feminist 'Nag'Gnostic scholars' who chose the 'Ecstatic Spinning Process over the accumulation of dead bodies of knowledge', that caused him to hurl the book so violently on to the table that it shot off the end and crashed against the wall.

There was a long silence. He walked around the table, picked up the volume between finger and thumb and presented it to Mary Lou. 'I'm sorry,' he said. 'I don't mean to be offensive, but quite apart from the cosmic New Age blither Ms Daly is spouting, her man-hating is a bit hard for a bloke to take.'

'Even a gay bloke?'

'I don't think one's sexuality has much to do with it,' said Amiss stiffly. 'Being gay doesn't mean you've lost your marbles. Anyway, are we not men? And if you prick us do we not bleed?'

'Is there an esoteric pun in there somewhere?'

'If there is, it's accidental.'

There was another silence. He gazed disconsolately at another couple of Daly's mad entries. 'I'm fed up wandering around this dank, depressing building,' he suddenly said violently. 'What's more, I don't think I'm going to be cheered up by sitting at high table with the mourners. How would you feel about coming out to dinner?'

Mary Lou smiled. 'Positive. Are you asking any of the others?'

'I rather thought as the two newest Fellows we might get to know each other first.'

She raised an eyebrow and then nodded. 'OK, but I'd rather not advertise it unnecessarily. I don't want to hurt anyone's feelings.'

Amiss became suddenly decisive. 'Look, neither of us knows Cambridge but we can find our way to the University Arms on Parker's Piece. I'll see you in the bar at seven and I'll have booked us a restaurant by then.'

'OK,' she said equably, 'as long as you don't expect me to dress.'

'Not at all,' he said, looking at her boiler suit and trainers. 'By all means come as you are.'

*   *   *

122

In deference perhaps to the likely paternalistic impulses of the University Arms proprietors, Mary Lou had after all changed and was looking extremely fetching in tight, white high-necked jumper, black trousers and knee-high boots. Amiss had become far too conditioned after only a few days in St Martha's to say anything at all about her appearance, but it was certainly hard to repress the decidedly sexist thoughts that were arising in him. 'Luscious' was the word that kept running through his head as his eyes flickered towards her body. He remembered the instructions given to academics on American campuses never to look at a woman below the chin lest she feels sexually abused and concentrated instead on Mary Lou's attractive face.

'Can I get you a drink?'

'Yes, please. Bourbon on the rocks.' She noticed the look of pleased surprise on his face. 'Well, what did you expect me to say. Carrot juice?'

'Well you are American; I thought you were all health freaks.'

'Haven't you been warned at St Martha's about offensive stereotyping?'

'We haven't got as far as Americans yet.'

'OK, I'll see what I can do to help.'

By the time they reached the restaurant, Amiss had learned that Mary Lou was twenty-five, that she came from Minneapolis, that she had won a scholarship to a second-rate Boston university where she'd got a first in English in her BA and MA and then a Ph.D, that she'd always wanted to go to Oxford or Cambridge and so had applied for the St Martha's Research Fellowship. She had learned that Amiss was twenty-eight, that his father, like hers, was a middle-income, white-collar worker, that he'd got an upper second at Oxford in History, that he was an ex-civil servant and that he was uncertain about his future. By the time they had finished their first bottle of wine, Amiss knew that Minneapolis was the most godforsaken hole in the US, where the locals' idea of a night life was a hamburger joint with neon lighting where the waitresses went round on roller skates and that her parents were stultifyingly respectable.

'I think they always saw themselves as playing out the role of the idealized black family. You know, Mr and Mrs Black Middle America. Mom baked cookies and worked part time as a cashier in the local department store, Dad played golf and on Sundays we went to church, a nice respectable church, not one of those tambourine-playing, dancing, black churches. My older sister became a nurse and got engaged to a doctor.'

Amiss raised an interrogative eyebrow.

'Yep,' she said. 'A white doctor. However, my brother, when he got through accountancy school, married a black, so we're not racially prejudiced.'

She chased a piece of meat round her plate with her chopsticks. 'Every day of my life I was bored and dreamt of getting away from Minnesota. What could I become but a lesbian-feminist activist? And you?'

'Mr and Mrs Middle England. Mum has a part-time job as an office clerk. They play bowls.'

'Is that English for bowling?'

'Sort of, except you do it in the open air.'

'Oh, I know it, I know it. I've seen pictures. You mean when they all dress up in white with funny hats and roll balls down a village green?'

'That's it.'

'God, I didn't think real people did that. I thought it was only actors. It's really great.'

'It's a bit lacking as a spectator sport when you're a kid.'

'You were bored too, huh?'

'I was bored too. They worried a lot about my getting a proper education so as to go into a really secure profession, so they were as thrilled as I was when I got into Oxford. The idea was for me to become a lawyer or an accountant after university. They weren't too disappointed about the civil service – job security, good pension and all that. So with that pressure from home what could I do but end up as a drifter taking odd jobs here and there while my beloved scrambles up the career ladder.' He cursed himself silently for having mentioned Rachel, even so obliquely.

She looked him straight in the eye. 'Your beloved is a bloke?'

'Er . . .'

'I knew damn well you weren't gay. Why did you pretend to be?'

'To get the job at St Martha's.'

'Not very scrupulous.'

'But expedient.'

She laughed. 'I'll buy the next bottle.'

By the time they finished Mary Lou's bottle, they had discovered they liked the same writers.

'My God,' she said. 'One reason I always had my heart set on England was that I thought I'd get away from all this American radical feminist crap about books. I bought it in Boston in the first year or two, then I realized I'd read more good literature in my bedroom in Minnesota than in a whole year as a freshman at university.

'Don't get me wrong. It's not that there aren't some great women writers but I'd already read most of them. I knew about Edith Wharton and Jane Austen and George Eliot and I thought Maya Angelou was a good writer, but not because she was a woman and black.' She knocked back the remains of her glass and held it out to be refilled. 'What's more, I became convinced that positive discrimination had done far more harm than good to American blacks. It's made it possible for racists to argue that no black ever gets anywhere on his or her own merits.

'Actually, a black woman is in a very good position to see this gender and ethnic garbage for what it is, because on the one hand you've got the women attacking macho values, yet black men are the biggest sexual chauvinists around. How do you simultaneously preach that women are superior to men and black culture superior to white and that any criticism of blacks is racism when you've got black rappers saying women are useful for nothing but fucking and breeding? And how is non-white culture automatically better if it's got female circumcision? And where's the logic in saying no literature is better than any other because judgementalism is out but still insisting on banning the DWEMs? I reckon black and female studies is for the self-indulgent wanting an easy ride. Can't wait for civil war on the campuses between the two.'

'So you're not a supporter of Bridget Holdness's proposed centre then?'

'What do you think?'

'What does she think?'

Mary Lou paused. 'I've drunk too much. I'm being indiscreet. But then you know what Americans are like.'

'Well, I'm unlikely to confide any of your secrets to your sisters. Go on.'

'Well, it's tricky, because I have to admit I'm here under even falser pretences than you.' She put her elbows on the table, leaned her head on her hands and settled in comfortably. 'I saw the ad for the St Martha's Research Fellowship in a radical women's studies magazine so I reckoned this particular Cambridge college was going in for a bit of radical chic. I knew that if I was up against competition from Yale or Harvard I wouldn't stand much of a chance academically, so I took a risk and went for broke. I'd be too embarrassed to show you my letter of application quoting the seminal influences on me of Mary Daly; she's always very useful cover. When you saw me in the library today I was secretly reading John Donne.'

'But aren't you tied to studying lesbian-ethnic stuff?'

'I'm just not going to. They can't make me.'

Amiss drained his coffee and drank some more wine. 'Let's go back a bit. I can see why your application appealed to Sandra and Bridget but how did it get past the Senior Tutor?'

'Sandra explained that to me yesterday. There was a sub-committee of three, them and poor old Dr Twigg, who was desperate to get a Research Fellowship for her protégée.'

'You mean the permanently preoccupied bird the Bursar calls Anglo-Saxon Annie?'

'Yes. She'd got a terrific first apparently and was the best scholar poor old Twigg had had in years, but they said they'd vote her down if I didn't get the other one. She succumbed, so here I am – Miss Affirmative Action 1994. I should feel a bit ashamed but I don't, not one bit. I feel I've pulled a fast one that they well deserve.' She took another healthy swig. 'Mind you, they don't know any of this yet.'

'When are you going to come out?'

'You mean come out as sane although black and a lesbian? Gradually, gradually. I'm going to tread very carefully until I know what's going on here. It's far too early to spurn my mentors. Mind you, I've already got a little problem with young Sandra.'

'What's that?'

'She wants to seal our sisterhood in bed.'

'Not your type?'

'No, I don't like wimps. Bridget would be much more my type if she weren't so nasty. Besides, presumably it was her who knocked off poor old Dame Maud.'

'I'd like it to be,' said Amiss. 'But if it was her, she's probably too clever to catch.'

'Certainly I'd say that even if Sandra does crave my body, she's sold her soul to Bridget. She'd give her an alibi anytime.' She finished her wine and looked at Amiss.

'Would you like a *digestif*?' he asked.

'Not till I've walked some of this off. Have you anything in your room?'

'Whisky.'

'Good. Let's go.'

They held hands on the way back. The moon was full, the stars were out, the night was warm and the Backs were more beautiful than they had any right to be.

'Now this is what I thought it would be all about,' said Mary Lou dreamily. 'I was a mite disappointed when I discovered I would be living in a mouldering neo-Gothic heap instead of in something off a picture postcard.'

'It might cheer you up to know that even the picture postcard colleges aren't very comfortable. I had to go down two flights of stairs to the loo when I was at Oxford and I was always freezing in my room in winter.'

'Stop being so prosaic. I'm an American. I want to believe in fairyland.'

'And toasting crumpets at the fire.'

'And funny old dons in gowns and mortar boards.'

'And aristocratic students.'

'And punting.'

'And Grantchester.' She stopped. 'Will you take me there to see the vicarage Rupert Brooke wrote about, "Where stands the clock at ten to three?"'

'Would it take away the magic if I told you that Jeffrey Archer lives there now?'

'Yes.'

'Sorry. Still, he is a lord.'

'Vicarages should have vicars.' They reached the gates of St Martha's and Mary Lou pulled away.

'I don't think I'd better be seen with the enemy,' she said. 'I'll follow on in a couple of minutes. I know where your room is.'

He had just poured out the whisky when she arrived. She walked over to him. 'Kiss me.'

When they disentangled, Amiss said, 'But . . . ?'

'I never said I was exclusively a lesbian, did I? You're very stuffy and hidebound, you British.'

As he put his arms around her again the still small voice of his conscience whispered 'Rachel'; it was answered by the robust voice of the Old Adam pointing out that he had never claimed to be a saint. It was at that moment that he heard tripping footsteps; there was a tap on the door and Miss Stamp called. 'Oh, Mr Amiss, Mr Amiss, I just saw you come in. Sergeant Pooley is here and wants to see you.'

Mary Lou flattened herself against the wall behind the door, which Amiss opened a few inches.

'Did you say he was here?'

'Yes, he said it was urgent, something official. He's in the parlour.'

'I'll be down in a moment.' Amiss shut the door. 'Shit,' he said, 'but I think we'll take it as an omen that I should go on staying faithful to Rachel.'

'My goodness. English gentlemen still exist.'

'Only just.'

She laughed. 'A miss is as good as a mile. See you tomorrow and thanks for dinner.'

She kissed him on the cheek and left.

19

'I didn't get you out of bed, did I?'

'No. Five minutes later and you would have. What's up?'

'Nothing much, but I just had the most ghastly evening and I wanted some human company. You wouldn't have anything to drink, by any chance?'

'Sergeant Pooley arriving late and demanding alcohol. You must have been suffering. Sure, in my room. Come on.'

They reached Amiss's bedroom without incident. 'You must be psychic, Robert, to have poured out my drink before I even arrived. Or were you waiting for somebody else.'

'I might tell you some other time, Ellis. For now I'll only say that I'm both glad and sorry that you turned up at that precise moment. I should also mention I've had rather a lot to drink already, so don't tell me anything too complicated. Tales of life *chez* Romford should be just about right.'

'My heart bleeds for you.' Amiss poured some more whisky into Pooley's glass. 'So what was the home video like?'

'Have you ever seen one?'

'Thank God, no. Presumably it's like an animated version of somebody's wedding snaps except you don't get to miss a single moment.'

'We had everything from the time the bride left the house through to the end of the speeches at the reception. You'd have particularly loved the reception; it was held in a temperance hall.'

'Naturally. What were the highlights?'

Pooley did not hesitate. 'Undoubtedly the Romford oration

from the pulpit, which was based around the biblical injunction that the wife should obey her husband.'

'Wouldn't have gone down big with Bridget then.'

'Well, let's say that John Knox would have been happy with it. It lasted twenty minutes, went on a lot about sacred duties, home-making, nest-building, nurturing, emotionally supporting, understanding that God had placed man and woman in their respective spheres and no man should mess around with that and then touched quite a lot on wicked secular ideas that were turning our womenfolk into fit candidates for Sodom and Gomorrah along with all the emasculated perverts that are today's menfolk.'

'Did he get the word "abomination" in?'

'Half a dozen times, I'd say.'

'Maybe you could persuade him to lend you a copy of his video. We could circulate it round St Martha's in plain brown wrappers.'

'Then there were the wedding speeches.'

'How were they?'

'Long.'

'Gist?'

'The bridegroom was thrilled to be marrying a woman schooled in the ways of the Lord and Romford talked a lot about his wife and the virtues of a happy home and was generally light-hearted. He even made jokes.'

'Romford?'

'Yes, but they were Romford-like jokes.'

'Ah! Anything else I should know?'

'There was the cake. It was as elaborate and highly-decorated as you would expect from the kitchen of Mrs Romford, but I suspect the wording on it was provided by Dad, to wit, "Whom God hath joined let no man put asunder."'

'Well, you can't say Romford doesn't make his position clear. Was that it?'

'Give me some more whisky.'

'It must have been bad. I've never known you drink so enthusiastically.'

Pooley spoke tonelessly. 'I wanted to go at that stage but Mrs Romford was determined to give me more food so we

131

had tea and cake and talked about the wedding. Then I said I should be going and Romford said nonsense, it was only nine o'clock and it would be very dull for a young man to be on his own so I must stay for another while and see the video of his son's wedding.'

'You're joking.'

'I'm not joking.'

Amiss shook his head compassionately. 'More of the same?'

'Cast slightly different, content roughly the same, though the speech by the bride's father was enlivened by golfing metaphors.'

'E.g.?'

'"Marriage is like a game of golf. You need God's help to get out of the bunkers."'

'Oh dear. When did it stop?'

'I got away at half past ten. They want me to come again and look at their holiday snaps.'

'You'd better find some friends in Cambridge fast.'

'I've invented six already. Now, that's enough of my torments. How was your evening? You obviously didn't spend it in a temperance hall.'

'No,' said Amiss thoughtfully. 'It would be fair to say that alcohol featured this evening. *Inter alia* it brought about an entente cordiale between me and Mary Lou.'

'I thought she was one of the Dykes?'

'Well she is and she isn't. It's all a bit complicated now. It was the Bursar that called them the Dykes, but she turned out to be one though now it seems she isn't. Mary Lou you might say is a Dyke on the outside and a Virgin on the inside.'

'Robert, you're not making yourself very clear.'

'I'm not feeling very clear. Just take my word for it, Mary Lou is a closet scholar and one of these days that cow Bridget Holdness is going to get a nasty shock. So with a bit of luck the Gender and Ethnic Studies Centre is scuppered despite the Mistress's death. We'll know more tomorrow.'

'What's happening?'

'There's a meeting of the College Council to decide who's in charge now the Mistress is dead.'

'It rather smacks of indecent haste, doesn't it?'

'You're telling me, but somehow or other Bridget persuaded the Deputy Mistress to call it. My guess is she's hoping the Bursar won't be back for it in time.'

'You don't know where she is?'

'Enjoying a night of passion with Myles Cavendish, presumably, but I'll be very surprised if she isn't here early tomorrow. She'll know bloody well that they will get up to no good in her absence and contrary to appearances, Jack has a very highly developed sense of duty. More whisky?'

'No, thank you. I've had more than enough.'

'Ah, good. You've recovered. So what does tomorrow hold for you?'

'Well, we'll spend tomorrow morning sorting out timings and alibis and all that kind of thing, so with a bit of luck we'll end up with a shortlist of suspects.' He stood up. 'Thanks, Robert. I'd better be off. How are you fixed tomorrow night?'

'I can be free if you want me.'

'I'll pick you up at the gate at eight in a taxi. I know a restaurant in Grantchester where we're unlikely to run into anyone.'

'Good night. Watch yourself tomorrow.'

'Why?'

'You know what he's trying to do, don't you?'

'Who?'

'Romford. He's trying to save you. He was just softening you up tonight.'

'Well, he can't do it while on duty and the only way he's going to see me off duty again is if he kidnaps me. Anyway, we Pooleys have been pillars of the Church of England since the Reformation and we're not going to break the tradition now.'

He closed the door behind him with a decisive bang.

Amiss's prediction about the Bursar was right. A quarter of an hour before the time fixed for the College Council, he sneaked down to her office on the off-chance she was back and found her there, pink-cheeked, full of beans and with the light of battle in her eye.

'Have you had a nice break, Bursar? You certainly chose your moment.'

'One must always seize the moment, Robert – grab the opportunity. That's what distinguishes the men from the boys.'

'What about distinguishing the dykes from the straights?' he said testily. 'It's a bit baffling for us simple-minded folk when a knight on a white charger makes off with an elderly maiden wearing the logo "DYKE POWER".'

'I like to keep people guessing.'

'You do a very good job of that, Jack, or should I call you Ida?'

'Young Pooley blabbed, I see. Well if I were you, young Robert, I would not be too free with this knowledge. We Troutbecks do not easily forgive or forget. Now, have you anything worth telling me?'

'I've discovered Mary Lou isn't what she seems.'

'Well that was blindingly obvious. I always knew it from the glint in her eye.'

'Knew what?'

'A bit of a goer and bored with the company of Sandra. She's a potential recruit for the Virgins. I'll give it my attention.'

She fished her badge out of her pocket and pinned it to her lapel.

'Why are you persisting in wearing that? It's hardly going to cut much ice with the Dykes since you reverted to your old ways.'

'Rubbish. This is for the benefit of the students, nipping any revolution in the bud. They're so muddled now, poor little dears, they wouldn't know which of us to follow. I have taken out the main enemy ammunition dump; now it's time to deal with the generals.'

'It's lucky you came back. I think they were trying to hold the meeting without you.'

'I thought they'd do something like that. That's why I rang Emily last night and got the low-down. There seems to be an unholy alliance between the ghastly Bridget and the different but equally ghastly Deborah.'

'What's our strategy?'

'You keep mum and leave it to me.'

20

There was a full turn out at the College Council. Sitting in the Mistress's chair, Dr Windlesham was brief.

'We are here to express our collective sadness at the death of our friend and colleague and to elect her successor.'

The Bursar broke in. 'You are not proposing that we do that today?'

'It is of the essence, Bursar. The college is in a state of crisis; it must not remain leaderless.'

'I agree,' said Bridget.

'So do I,' said Sandra.

Carol Carter, the dim Student Representative, nodded vigorously.

'Oh dear, well I suppose so,' squeaked the Senior Tutor.

The Bursar looked around, visibly calculated numbers, shrugged and sat back in her chair.

'I should like to propose the Deputy Mistress,' said Bridget Holdness. She ignored the baffled expressions of most of those present. 'At a time like this I think continuity is all; we must present a united face to the world.'

'I second that,' said Cyril Crowley.

'Any other nominations?' asked Dr Windlesham.

There was silence. 'In that case, I must declare myself appointed. I am honoured by your trust in me and will try to live up to it. Now . . .'

'I propose Dr Twigg as Deputy Mistress,' cut in the Bursar quickly.

'I second that,' said Primrose Partridge.

The Senior Tutor went pink with pleasure – a squirrel who had just been given a particularly tasty peanut.

'I propose Ms Holdness,' said Sandra.

'Seconded,' said Francis Pusey.

Amiss couldn't believe it. He tried to remember what Pusey had ever said to him about Bridget and the only words that came to mind were 'horrid' and 'bullying'. He wondered why the little bastard was currying favour, but inspiration eluded him.

'I have two valid nominations here,' said Dr Windlesham. 'Hands up those voting for the Senior Tutor.'

The Bursar, Primrose Partridge, Anglo-Saxon Annie, Miss Thackaberry and Amiss raised their hands.

'And for Dr Holdness?'

Sandra, Francis Pusey, Crowley and Carol Carter put their hands up, followed, to Amiss's disappointment, by Mary Lou. Then Bridget raised her hand.

'Six-five,' said the new Mistress. 'I declare Dr Holdness elected.'

Tears came into the Senior Tutor's eyes. 'But we never vote for ourselves, never, ever. It's a tradition.'

'Traditions,' said Bridget, 'are there to be broken with.'

'Mistress,' said the Bursar. 'I cannot believe that you want to start your period in office condoning such a betrayal of trust.'

'You are overreacting, Bursar.'

'As you well know, Mistress, when I overreact I overreact. I should point out that our press is bad enough at the moment without giving it further ammunition in the shape of accusations of skulduggery.'

'Colleagues, colleagues,' piped up the Reverend Cyril. 'I think we should try to resolve this amicably.'

There was a general murmur of agreement.

'Oh, very well,' said the Mistress. 'We'll take the vote again.'

This time, predictably, the vote was six-all. The Fellows looked expectantly at Dr Windlesham.

'Very well,' she said. 'This has now come down to my casting vote. It is not an easy decision to take. On the one hand I have my old friend and colleague, Dr Twigg, whose dedication to this institution has been unparalleled. On the other we have Dr Holdness, a comparative newcomer, and, I acknowledge, felt by some to be over-zealous in the pursuit of reform.'

She cleared her throat and took a sip of water. 'What I want is a college in which the Fellows, working in concert, lead the students to achieve ever more for the greater glory of academe. We must eschew divisiveness, we must practise tolerance, we must encourage harmony and we must remember also that age must give way to youth. So my dear friend Dr Twigg will understand that in voting for Dr Holdness I am putting the interests of the college before friendship and sentiment, as I know she would be the first to do.

'I declare Dr Holdness elected to the position of Deputy Mistress. Now to item two on the agenda. "Funeral arrangements".'

'Certainly not,' said the Bursar, 'I want chips and plenty of them, and mind my steak is rare.'

'No blood in mine, please,' said Amiss to the waitress.

The Bursar looked at him askance. 'The blood is the best bit. I like blood.'

Amiss ignored her. 'With just a green salad.'

'Real men don't eat green salads. They eat chips, and plenty of 'em. What's got into you?' She noticed the waitress waiting patiently. 'Oh, thank you, Maureen. Please fetch us our claret as a matter of urgency.'

She turned her attention to Amiss. 'You will be able to force down a little wine? Or would you prefer some sarsa-parilla?'

'I shall be eating a large dinner tonight, Jack, and my stomach is less capacious than yours.'

The Bursar patted herself happily. 'I've decided to stop bothering about being fat; I've got to build up my strength to defeat the legions of Satan. Talking of which, what the devil happened this morning? I thought you told me Mary Lou was on our side. She's obviously either afraid to come out of the closet or she was having you on.'

'I'm sure she wasn't having me on.'

'She's probably hoodwinked you. It's those great eyes of hers. Has she been bestowing her favours on you?'

'I must remind you, Jack, that I am an engaged man.'

She laughed sardonically. 'I don't think even you can be as much of a prig as you make out. Enough of that. What's with Francis Pusey?'

'I intend to find out this afternoon, even if it involves me in more cake and a lecture on the development of over-mantles in the Tudor refectory.'

'And I'd better work over that little rat Crowley. I don't like the smell of any of this. I fear some deals have been done which can only lead to disaster.

'Ah, good. Thank you, Maureen. Just pour it. My friend and I are in urgent need.' She took a great gulp. 'Yum, yum.'

'Don't tell me. You like claret.'

'I like most things, but not any of those frightful bitches. Poor little Emily. She was dreadfully hurt.'

'Maybe you shouldn't have proposed her.'

'Who the hell else was there to propose? Anyway, the Senior Tutor always becomes Deputy Mistress. God help us, it's a tradition. Nor was I exactly spoilt for choice of candidate.

'The trouble is that on my side they're nearly all wimps. Old Maud was such a benevolent dictator that there was never any real need for the Virgins to think for themselves and by the time even they began to grasp that the Dykes were dangerous it was too late; they'd lost whatever political skills they ever had. Speaking of which, do you know the great line from Kipling? "Time and again were we warned of the dykes, time and again we delayed."' She chortled long and loudly.

'Perhaps you could get Francis Pusey to embroider it on a sampler.'

She ignored him: the Bursar always liked her own jokes best. 'Maud imported me because she realized she needed a robust ally and I imported you for the same reason, but the way things have worked out, I'd have been better bringing in an SAS squad. I must talk to Myles about it.'

'Myles is not quite my idea of an SAS man, Jack. With respect.'

'Never judge by appearances, old boy.' She closed one eye conspiratorially.

Amiss sipped his wine moodily. 'I think our side has had it. Dame Maud's death and its consequences have totally altered the balance of power. Fear has driven the Old Women to snuggle up to the Dykes and even the Virgins have not held firm.'

'Something's going on with old Windlesham, that's for sure. That speech about harmony and unity was hilarious when you think of it. It was only Maud's iron hand that kept her from stirring up trouble right through the years. She's a vicious old cow, so there was nothing in the notion that she might be following the precept of making the most trouble-some girl in the class Head Prefect. Bridget Holdness is a fascist who believes in acquiring power by any means available and if you know your history, you will know that when you hold out a hand of friendship to a fascist you find it's bitten off. To do her justice, I thought that Windlesham might have spotted that.

'Ah, excellent! This smells extremely good.' She probed her steak anxiously with her knife. 'Excellent, my dear, very bloody indeed. Robert, is yours as anaemic as you wanted?'

'Thank you, Jack, it is perfection.'

'Good. Eat up, drink up. We mustn't lose heart; we must find out the price the Old Women have exacted and try to top it.'

Amiss spent the latter half of the afternoon fruitlessly stalking Francis Pusey and Mary Lou. In the end, he went out for a long walk from which he returned bearing some bottles, for Pooley had virtually finished his whisky the night before. At 6.15 he arrived at Pusey's door and knocked once more.

His quarry was there. His initial slight look of alarm quickly turned to delight when Amiss, with a flourish, presented him with the best bottle of sherry the excellent wine merchant could provide. 'Francis, I can't go on sponging on you. I brought this to give us both an excuse.'

'Oh, goodness me, what a very sweet gesture. Isn't it, Bobsy? Do come in, Robert. What a treat. Sit down, dear boy. You look tired.'

'I had a long walk this afternoon. I needed to get away from the college. I was finding it a bit gloomy.'

'Gloomy! It certainly is. Sometimes I don't know how we stand it here. Bobsy and I went out too and bought ourselves something to cheer us up.'

Amiss tried to think of something which Pusey and Bobsy were likely both to enjoy and fixed on cake. The reality proved to be another paperweight to add to their already substantial collection, on which Pusey discoursed at length and in grinding detail. As they finished their second glass of sherry, Pusey put the paperweight back on its little table and smiled brightly.

Before he could start talking again, Amiss broke in quickly. 'It was rather dramatic this morning, wasn't it?'

'Well, it was all a bit horrid. I didn't like seeing Emily upset; she's a nice old thing.'

'I don't want to be intrusive, Francis, and you know college politics are beyond me, but I was frankly a bit baffled as to why you voted for Bridget Holdness after the things you said about her. It was largely because of your attitude that I voted for Dr Twigg, so picture my astonishment when you went the other way.'

'Oh, dear, I should have told you about it really, shouldn't I? We men should stick together and all that. But there really wasn't time. You see, the Mistress nobbled me after breakfast while Bobsy and I were having our little walk and,' Pusey giggled, 'she made me an offer I couldn't refuse. If I voted for what she called the dream ticket – well, I don't want to go into details . . .' He wriggled a bit in his seat. 'Oh well, I'll tell you. Have some more sherry. She said she'd give me a three-year contract.'

'You mean you're not permanent here?'

'Alas, no. I've been on an annual contract for quite a while and it leaves us very vulnerable, especially now that there's been all that pressure to change the statutes. If Bridget and her mob succeeded in all that I might have been out of a job and jobs in my world are very few and far between.'

'Wouldn't you have been able to get something in . . .' Amiss cast around desperately, 'the Royal College of Needlework or somewhere?'

'No, no. They would think what I do old-fashioned. Young people nowadays don't want old fogeys like me making pretty things; they want their own nasty designs.'

'And Windlesham has the power to do this?'

'That's what she said. And she said that Bridget wouldn't oppose it if I voted for her. So what choice did I have?'

Not a lot, you poor old sod, thought Amiss. 'Oh, I do understand, but aren't you afraid of what Bridget might do to the college now she's in a position of power?'

'Frankly, dear boy, I don't care if they teach theology, women's studies or windsurfing as long as Bobsy and I are cosy and safe. Now, mind you, I'd have much preferred that bequest to be used to make our lives more comfortable but there's no point in whistling for the moon.'

He looked at his watch. 'Goodness, it's dinner time. Come along.'

'I'm going out.'

'Lucky old you.'

Amiss stood up, paid his respects to Bobsy and withdrew. As previously agreed, he caught the Bursar as she went into dinner and they hastily exchanged their news. 'That's pretty staggering,' said Amiss when she had finished. 'Does he know you know?'

'Can't see how he would.'

'Mind you lock your door tonight, just in case.'

'Don't fuss.'

'If you don't promise to be careful and to lock your fucking door, I'll tell everyone your name is Ida.'

The Bursar grinned. 'I like blackmail. It's a very efficient way of getting things done. I just wish that at present I was better equipped to practise it on this mob. All right, I'll be careful. Now go off and carouse with your sergeant. I'll try and seduce Mary Lou.'

Amiss repressed a pang of anguish at the image that conjured up. As he walked down the drive, he focused his mind on Rachel. ' "How do I love thee? Let me count the ways" ', he muttered. By the time he reached the gate he had enumerated at least two dozen things he loved about her. However, the trouble was, he admitted to himself, that Rachel had one major defect: she was four thousand miles away.

21

'This job, if I may so loosely describe it, is ruinous to the liver. For a fellow of a temperance college I seem to have to do an awful lot of drinking.'

'Well, that's because it's not actually a temperance college,' said Pooley. 'Temperance, after all, is moderation and there's nothing wrong with moderate drinking. It's when they interpret temperance as a total ban that the problems arise and people overreact.'

'Quite,' said Amiss. 'Now, what are we going to drink?'

The restaurant was cosy, they had a quiet table and nobody looked familiar. After they had ordered and Pooley was well into his gin and tonic, he leaned back in his chair and closed his eyes.

'I'm knackered.'

'Why, particularly?'

'Because it's exhausting doing anything with Romford; he's so slow he wears you out. Everything that would take three minutes with Jim takes thirty minutes with Romford and it's a kind of contagious stupidity. By the end of a day with him your IQ has halved, your energy level is at rock bottom and the whole world seems confusing.'

'Is that why he runs his home the way he does?'

'Ah, you mean an oasis of order? I suppose that figures. Fundamentalists like making order out of chaos. I want another gin and tonic. What about you?'

'Why not? This is most encouraging, Ellis. Spend much more time with Romford and you'll end up a disorganized alcoholic rather than the anal retentive I occasionally fear you might become.'

'Does that mean that by spending too much time with you anal retentiveness becomes inevitable?'

'I expect so. So for perfect balance you should spend your life shuttling between the two of us. Now, what gives?'

'What gives is that the students and domestic staff appear to be out of it. You can't get into the library after nine o'clock at night without a key and Primrose Partridge, who was in there about 9.30, is convinced that the end-of-groove stoppers were still in place.'

'How could she know?'

'Wasn't used to them. The steps, I mean. Those back at her school are much heavier. So she climbed off them about three-quarters of the way down the room and gave them a sharp push, intending them to travel a couple of yards. Instead they flew ahead, clanged noisily on the stoppers at the end, shot backwards another couple of feet and hit her on the arm. Indeed, she was able to show us the bruise.'

'Was she lying?'

'Give me one good reason why she should.'

'Pass. And only the Fellows have keys?'

'Yes. There were some valuable volumes pinched from the library in the last year and it was decided to make it off bounds from the time it ceases to be supervised. So from 9.00 at night until 9.00 the following morning it's locked.'

'So any of us could have fixed the steps.'

'Except Sandra, Bridget and the Bursar, who all have alibis.'

'Surely Bobsy vouched for Francis? And vice versa?'

Pooley sighed. 'Shall we order, or do you intend to go on being silly?'

'Oh, let's order by all means. Now, let me choose something serious. A boiled egg, perhaps? And maybe a tiny tiny glass of tap water? Or would that be too self-indulgent?'

'Robert!'

'Oh, all right. I'll have the terrine and the *pot-au-feu* and a lot of red wine. I'm told it's very good for the arteries.'

'Now,' said Amiss, when Pooley had ordered, 'to recap. Do I gather that Sandra and Bridget spent the night together?'

'So they claim.'

'Romford must have been dead chuffed about that.'

'Nearly as chuffed as when he discovered that you had spent the night in the Bursar's bedroom.'

'Didn't you explain the circumstances?'

'Well, of course I did, but Romford's got a filthy mind.'

'I suppose a man who dwells so much on Sodom and Gomorrah has sex on the brain.'

'I think I did eventually convince him that your motives were altruistic, but he's not keen on your alibi. Are you absolutely sure that you didn't sleep heavily enough for Miss Troutbeck to have been able to sneak out unbeknownst to you?'

'I didn't sleep at all,' said Amiss testily. 'And as to her sneaking out, does she look like somebody who can sneak out? She's as heavy-footed as a bison.'

'OK. That's her in the clear as far as I'm concerned. But *you've* no alibi since she slept so well and neither Romford nor I are entirely convinced by the others.'

'What about alibis for the time when the Bursar was attacked? Or does Romford think she knocked herself out?'

'I don't think that's occurred to him yet. Sandra and Bridget were apparently together again; you were with Francis Pusey; Primrose Partridge says she was with the Mistress and that's it on the alibi front. But then any number of the students, and even Greasy Joan, could have done that.'

'Forensic has nothing to offer?'

'No. Any adult could have inflicted damage with that implement and the Bursar's head is so peculiar that it's impossible to assess the force of the blow.'

An elaborate performance by the wine waiter intervened before Amiss asked, 'Likely suspects?'

'Romford would like it to be the Bursar but he's not ingenious enough to find a way round the facts.'

'And how are you doing on the motive front?'

'Bridget and Sandra are strong.'

'Yes?'

'Deborah Windlesham, seeing as it's made her Mistress.'

'Yes?'

'We can't think of anyone else, although Romford would

like to think that the Bursar was fiddling the college funds and was in danger of being found out.'

'But her lack of opportunity has scuppered that scenario, has it?'

'He has suggested that you and she might have been in cahoots.'

'Christ, he never gives up, does he? I thought I'd won him over yesterday.'

'The whole effect was spoiled today when he saw you arm in arm with Miss Troutbeck. He's heard of toy boys and he's deeply suspicious.'

'She grabbed my arm,' said Amiss peevishly. 'She was feeling affectionate.'

'Exactly.'

'He can't see any career reasons why anyone else should have had anything to gain from the Mistress being murdered? Money doesn't seem to apply.'

'She didn't have a huge personal fortune that she was going to leave to the Rev Crowley?'

'She had a small nest egg that she left to the college.'

'Big help. Sex?'

'Well, Romford worries over that ground diligently enough but she seems to have been a good old-fashioned celibate. Has the Bursar anything to offer on that score?'

'The Bursar says that it's a pretty sexless Fellowship even by Cambridge standards. Apart from the capital "D" Dykes and possibly Anglo-Saxon Annie and Miss Thackaberry, she didn't think anyone did anything to anybody.'

'Crowley and Pusey aren't in a gay relationship, I suppose?'

'It would have to be a troika. And I don't think that's Bobsy's scene.'

'No vendettas?'

'Apparently not.'

Pooley disconsolately speared his fish and chewed it without any sign that he realized what he was eating.

'I can offer you another motive, Ellis.'

'What? Whose?'

'The Rev Crowley's. The Bursar found the incriminating evidence in her in-tray.'

'Tell me, tell me.'

'She has kindly provided me with a photocopy.'

He pulled it out of his pocket.

'Show me.'

'I'll read it to you. It took me five attempts to master the handwriting. It's from a pal of Dame Maud's in Canada.

'My dear Maud,

This is a quick letter just to deal with something urgent that emerges from your long letter of today. I was much struck by the few sentences you included anent your chaplain. It wasn't so much his name; there may be many clergymen called Cyril Crowley. Nor was it even his interest in East Anglian place names. What rang the alarm bells was your description of him as unctuous and linguistically orotund.

Even allowing for the tendency of clergymen to adopt both those habits of manner and speech, it is too much of a coincidence. This has to be the Rev Cyril Crowley we threw out of here a year ago. Does he look like a Trollopian Bishop? Smooth-chinned, pot-bellied, pink of countenance, elegant white hair? Yes? Then read on, for you have been lumbered with a bounder with the twin distinctions of being both a clerical and an academic fraud. He never got beyond deacon because he was thrown out of the Church before ordination, owing to a scandal over diocesan funds, which in the good old Anglican way was hushed up.

He then appears to have popped up at a few institutions throughout the Commonwealth on visiting fellowships. He won the first on the basis of a thesis written by somebody else which he'd appropriated by the simple device of changing the title page and slightly altering the title. Later, he had a lucky break in Australia when a friend of his died leaving a body of work behind him which Crowley raided and out of which he published some articles over his own name in learned journals. He is an attractive proposition for impecunious academic establishments in these secular days, because he can teach as well as being chaplain. However, a few years ago he was unmasked by an old colleague and was thrown out of his Australian university.

At St Ethelfreda's we found out about him only by accident.
He was caught by a visitor from Australia to whom he was
known and who found him, you might say, in flagrante,
performing a service. Even unctuousness didn't get him out
of that one; he was gone by the following morning.

Get rid of him with all speed, Maud. He is a nasty and
corrupt bit of work who deserves no charity.

I'll write at greater length shortly.

With my love, as ever,

Amy.

Pooley had cheered up greatly by the end of the letter.

'How did the Bursar get hold of it? What was it doing in
her in-tray?'

'Dame Maud popped it in an envelope with a note on it
saying, "I'll give him a week's notice. You will want to sort
out the financial aspect of this. I propose to offer him the
option of resigning for personal reasons rather than drag the
college through the gutter. So don't tell anyone else."'

'But what would have been the point of his knocking off
Dame Maud? He would have known she would have told
someone else.' Pooley was suddenly despondent.

'Not necessarily. If he thought she hadn't told anyone else
he still had a chance of keeping his job. He'd have had plenty
of time to search her desk after the body had been found.
He could have assumed the letter would have been easy to
find. Bad luck for him that she had already sent it on to the
Bursar.'

'It's going to be difficult to get Romford's mind on to this.
He's completely and utterly fixated on the notion that the
murderer has to be, in his words, "a woman given to abomin-
able practices", so he's settled on Bridget, Sandra and Mary
Lou as prime suspects and has only reluctantly given way
on the Bursar in view of her condition on the night of the
murder.' He paused. 'You know, I don't want to be a bigot
myself but I'm really not sure that fundamentalists are well
equipped to be detectives.'

'Stop being a wishy-washy liberal, Ellis. Romford was

always useless precisely because he was blinded by a closed mind.'

'And his stupidity,' said Pooley, sounding almost defensive.

'It's not that that singles him out in your organization, Ellis.'

Pooley winced in acknowledgement. 'Of course, he may be right. Maybe the Dykes *are* all in a conspiracy to murder their way to the bequest? After all, he's got divine inspiration on his side. His conviction on the matter, he assured me, has been enhanced by prayer. God was apparently pretty explicit this morning to him on the subject of perversion.'

'But from what you tell me, every woman in this institution is an abomination to Romford.'

'Oh, absolutely. But there are, you understand, degrees of wickedness. It is obviously wrong for a woman to pretend to be a scholar and to presume to teach; but it's decidedly worse if she's a sexual sinner as well.'

'I sometimes think enviously of how simple life must be if you are a fundamentalist. Imagine knowing exactly what you think on absolutely everything, never having to torment yourself with the other fellow's point of view and feeling righteous to boot. I think I might take it up.'

Pooley poured him some more wine. 'I can't off-hand think of a fundamentalist religion which wouldn't require you to give up drink, sex before marriage, reading unapproved literature and having a loose tongue. Add to that having to go to services and give up ten per cent of your income.'

'That last requirement would be little hardship,' said Amiss gloomily. 'Ten per cent of fuck all is fuck all.'

He sipped his wine appreciatively. 'I am glad you're rich, Ellis. Don't ever feel embarrassed about buying me superb meals. It will stand to you in heaven.'

'You're supposed to be earning this one,' said Pooley sternly. 'I'm looking for a bit of inspiration.'

'Well, I bear with me a recommendation from the Bursar which is that someone gets in touch with Amy to find out what else was on the Mistress's mind. Jack says that while she and Maud Buckbarrow were chums, they discussed col-

150

leagues only as much as was absolutely necessary for the "Doing Down the Dykes" campaign, for Maud was a woman of great discretion. Jack thinks that if she had any confidante it was Amy; she thinks they were lovers from way back.'

'So Dame Maud wasn't always celibate, then?'

'Apparently in her young and passionate youth there was this one intense affair and afterwards nothing.'

'Well, I'll suggest it to Romford in the morning when he's seen the letter. It's going to be hard to distract him from the path on which he has embarked.'

They broke up early. Pooley was exhausted from the sheer nervous tension of dealing with Romford; Amiss, rather listless from too much hanging about waiting for something to happen.

Something happened at 11.30, when he'd just switched out the light. The door opened and shut quietly and a familiar voice said, 'Don't panic. This is a friendly call.'

Amiss's conscience, faced with the temptation of a naked Mary Lou climbing into his bed, retired from active service.

22

'How do we know she's telling the truth?'

'Who, sir?'

'This Amy person.' Romford jabbed his finger at Pooley in a preaching gesture. 'She might just be trying to destroy the reputation of a fine man. For I have to tell you, Pooley, that the Reverend Dr Crowley is the only person in this establishment for whom I have any respect. A respectable widower, a man of the cloth, clean-living, decent in his language. That woman's probably just a malicious old gossip.'

'She'd hardly lie to her friend, sir, would she?'

'You don't know what these women do. Living an abnormal life makes them abnormal. Poison pen letters – spinsters are always at them. They get peculiar fancies when they don't have a man to look after.'

He sat there irresolute. 'What's more,' he said, 'the way they carry on infects decent women. My wife . . .'

Pooley did not dare speak. Was Mrs Romford writing poison pen letters? Or becoming a lesbian? Finally, he broke the silence. 'I hope Mrs Romford is all right, sir.'

'Hah! She thinks so. I think she's on the slippery slope. Mark my words, Pooley, when a wife goes against her husband's express wishes it bodes no good. A wife having a full-time job is something I'll never hold with – "Neither give a wicked woman liberty to gad about".'

'But she's not a wicked woman, sir.'

'We're all sinners, Pooley, but "all wickedness is but little to the wickedness of a woman". They are easily corrupted, you see. When you're a married man you'll understand more about that.'

152

Pooley's embarrassment grew. Finally, Romford gave himself a shake. 'I suppose we'd better see the unfortunate man. Find him, but mind you're polite. I'm not taking any of these accusations seriously until they're proved.'

Pooley thought he detected a certain wariness about the Reverend which vanished under the sunshine of Romford's welcome. For instead of confronting him with the letter, Romford encouraged Crowley to dilate at some length about how he approached his ministry at St Martha's and in Athelstan. Many judicious Romford nods accompanied Crowley's explanation of why young people today had to be helped to cope with the damaging secular influences of the godless media, the importance of emphasizing traditional values and the deplorable decline of standards.

After about ten minutes and with visible reluctance, Romford dragged himself away from pious chit-chat and on to the path of more immediate duty. 'I'm sorry to say, Dr Crowley, that there have been allegations made about you.'

'Allegations? Ah, yes, of course. You must be referring to that poor deluded creature Amy Braithwaite.'

'Could you tell us a little more, please, sir?'

'Alas, Inspector, how can I explain this without seeming unchivalrous. But you are a man of the world. You will understand . . .' He shot a concerned look at Pooley.

'It's all right,' said Romford gruffly. 'Sergeant Pooley has to learn about these things. Go on.'

'I fear I incurred the enmity of a lady of a certain age.'

'Ah,' said Romford. His nod was heavy with significance and masculine collusion.

'You see, since my dear wife died a couple of years ago, while I have given them no encouragement, it has to be said that the occasional maiden lady, perhaps simply from a Christian desire to look after the bereaved, has been known to entertain hopes that are entirely unjustified. For I, Inspector Romford, am a one-woman man.'

'I honour you for it, sir. I am the same myself.'

'And I fear I was at fault in the case of poor Amy. A colleague of mine in a university abroad – and at the time of life when women's fancies often take an unfortunate turn . . .'

Romford nodded vigorously. 'She wanted me to marry her, Inspector, and although I let her down as lightly as I could . . .' He shook his head sadly. 'You know what they say about a woman scorned.'

'Indeed I do, sir, and have often seen it proved in the course of my work.'

'I left there to get away from her. But at last she tracked me down in order to blacken my name.'

'What happened?'

'Poor Dame Maud.' Crowley sank his head briefly on his clasped hands. 'May she rest in peace.'

Romford bowed his head in sympathy.

'She called me in – goodness me, it must have been the night before she died – to tell me she'd had a letter making many allegations. She was understandably perturbed.'

'What kind of allegations?'

'Oh, terrible things. Casting doubt on my ministry, on my scholarship. Very, very distressing, Inspector. For a man who, since the death of his dear wife, has lived solely to serve God and scholarship, it is heartbreaking to be accused of being unfit in both spheres.'

'Did she show you the letter?'

'No, but she told me of the contents.'

'What happened?'

'The Mistress was a fair woman and she had, of course, known me for some time, so she had reason to know of my dedication and, if I may be so presumptuous as to say so, my proficiency. It did not, I am happy to say, take very long to convince her that I was innocent. I would have felt terrible if she had gone to her grave thinking me an impostor and a cheat.'

'So there was no question of your being dismissed from here?'

'My goodness me, no, Inspector. We parted the best of friends.'

Romford's tone was redolent of relief. 'Well, Dr Crowley, I'm most grateful to you. You've been frank about what are most painful matters. I am sorry to have had to put you through such distress.'

'That's quite all right, Inspector. You have your job to do. Now, if you'll forgive me, I have a sick parishioner to visit in Athelstan.'

With an angelic smile he got up, bowed at Romford, bowed at Pooley and oiled his way out of the room.

'There we are,' said Romford. 'I knew there'd be nothing in that.'

Pooley employed the trick that had seen him through many such moments. He breathed deeply for about twenty seconds and stayed quiet until he could fully trust himself. Then he asked mildly. 'Do you want me to run a check on Dr Crowley?'

'What sort of check?'

'On whether he is ordained. And whether the Canadian university backs up Miss Braithwaite's allegations.'

'When it comes to being ordained, I've no interest in that. In my church there is no need for such pernickety carry-on.'

'But there is in the Church of England, sir.'

'I know a man of God when I see one. And I've no doubt he's a true scholar as well.'

'Perhaps just a phone call to the head of Miss Braithwaite's college?'

'Now look here, Pooley. What you have to learn is that if the police were to follow every silly lead given them by hysterical women there would be no cases solved. We know who the guilty people are and that's where we'll be applying the pressure. Go and find that Holdness woman.'

Pooley was just about to leave the room when Superintendent Hardiman rushed in. 'I was just passing so I thought I'd get an update. Come on Romford, summarize.'

At the best of times, Hardiman was not patient; now he was under stress. Pooley felt almost a pang of sympathy for Romford, stuttering and stumbling through a confused monologue as Hardiman's fingers drummed on the table.

'Hm, you're certainly not making much progress,' he interrupted. 'Got to check out more of the facts. What are you doing about Crowley?'

'Well, sir, as I've explained, I found his explanation totally convincing.'

'You did, did you?' He turned to Pooley. 'Leave us for a minute, Sergeant.'

Pooley skipped out, closed the door firmly and applied his ear to the keyhole. 'How long have you been a policeman, Romford?'

'Thirty-six years, sir.'

'And still a sucker for charlatans, eh? If Dame Maud took those allegations seriously, why don't you?'

'I should have thought, sir, that a man of my experience would be a better judge of character than some spinster who knew nothing of real life.'

'Well, I've just been talking to the Bursar and she concurs with Dame Maud's view.'

Romford was outraged. 'You can't listen to her, sir. She's a freak and a pervert.'

Hardiman's voice rose. 'If you were to take the trouble to look in *Who's Who*, you would find that Miss Troutbeck was a most distinguished civil servant of immense experience. Her private life is no concern of yours except insofar as it has a bearing on murder. I suggest that you do not lightly ignore the opinions of your intellectual superiors.'

Remembering how deliberately unhelpful the Bursar had been to Romford, Pooley felt another stab of pity for him. Romford was mutinous.

'They're all atheists, sir. They can't understand the soul of a believer the way I can.'

'You're treading very close to the wind, Romford. Number one, your attitude to women is disgraceful for an officer of the 1990s; I do not wish my force to be accused of male chauvinism. Two, if you drag your religious beliefs into your work, I'll have your balls. Is that understood? Three, get the facts on Crowley and do it fast.'

The squeak as he pushed his chair back was just loud enough to give Pooley time to jump away from the door and appear to be gazing intently through a window. The superintendent was breathing heavily.

'Show me out, Sergeant.'

They sped down the corridor. 'Is he making a complete hash of it?'

'Er, mmm,' said Pooley.

'You're not here to be loyal to Romford. You're here to be loyal to me. Here's my card. Ring me when you need to on my mobile phone, keep me briefed and let me know when you need me to bollock him into doing something sensible.' He was out the door and into his car before Pooley could answer him.

When he rejoined Romford, he found him staring straight ahead of him, lips pursed. Pooley slid silently into his seat. Romford turned to him. 'On second thoughts you'd better do a bit of checking on Crowley. You can never be too careful.'

'Very good, sir. Is it all right if I make contact with Miss Amy Braithwaite? She might just give me a lead.'

'Do anything you like. I'm going back to the station to see if anything's come up.' He gathered up his papers and left.

Pooley rushed off in search of Amiss, whom he found eventually in the Bursar's office. They were sitting there companionably, she puffing her pipe, both of them drinking gin.

She hailed him. 'Ah, young Pooley. Where is your master?'

'Gone back to base for a while.'

'Have some gin.' She waved him to an armchair.

'I'm sorry, Miss Troutbeck . . .'

'Not while you're on duty?'

'Exactly.'

'Well, thank God I never joined the police force.'

She poured a healthy measure into her and Amiss's glasses and shoved the tonic over to him.

'So what's new? Robert has filled me in up to last night.'

As Pooley got to the end of his account of the morning's events, she exploded. 'He couldn't see through shifty old Crowley even with that evidence?'

'No. He didn't even show him the letter. I think he didn't want to hurt his feelings.'

'And he's a policeman!'

'But a believer,' said Amiss.

'Well that's not a sufficient reason,' said the Bursar, 'Some of my best friends believe in God and are perfectly sane into the bargain.'

157

'Gods of wrath who require unquestioning obedience?'

'Well, maybe not my best friends.'

'That's the difference. Can't be a copper if you're not a sceptic, can you, Ellis?'

'Well it would certainly be a little constraining,' said Pooley cautiously, still a little uneasy at discussing a superior in the presence of a virtual stranger.

'So what are you going to do?' asked Amiss.

'I thought I'd talk to Miss Braithwaite first.'

'I've got her number.' The Bursar opened a notepad, rapidly found the right page, copied an entry on to a piece of paper and thrust it at Pooley. 'I talked to her last night. Be nice to her. She's very upset.'

'I'm only supposed to ask her about Crowley. She didn't by any chance offer anything more on other suspects?'

'Last night was the weepy telephone call. I thought it would be indelicate to push for any more and I think she'll be a bit cautious of the police.' She took another puff and scratched her head. 'Tell you what. You get the gen from her on Crowley and I'll ring her later on and pump her more generally. Let's all meet up tonight. You're not going to be tied up with your inspector, are you, young Pooley?'

'Not if I have to murder him to get out of it.'

She beamed. 'Ah, good, you're learning sense. OK, Robert?'

'I'm having dinner with someone.'

'What, as well as lunch? What are you up to?'

'Nothing,' said Amiss guiltily.

'In that case you can cancel dinner.'

'You're a frightful bully, Jack. Oh, all right. I'll postpone dinner. Where and when?'

'Private room upstairs in the Gamekeeper Turned Poacher. And mind you arrive separately with paper bags over your heads. Can't have Pooley being drummed out of the constabulary for associating with perverts.'

'Speak for yourself,' said Amiss. ''Bye. See you later.'

'Who's he having lunch with?' Pooley asked as the door closed.

'He's being secretive,' said the Bursar. 'Not a thing I like in my protégés. It should be one of the privileges of age. I think he might be up to something. Let's try and get it out of him tonight.'

23

Amy Braithwaite was distressed but composed. The names and addresses of those who could corroborate the truth about Crowley were produced without difficulty.

'Do you think, ma'am, that he is a possible murderer?'

'He is wholly egocentric, amoral and without loyalty. Are those good credentials?'

'Excellent, I should have thought.'

'On the other hand, he seems to be used to being thrown out of institutions and moving on; he's a bit of an adventurer and a risk-taker. Of course, that latter quality could also make him predisposed to murder. Who can tell, Sergeant Pooley? That's your job. Now, if you'll forgive me, I have much to do. I am trying to reorganize my teaching so that I can get to Cambridge for Maud's funeral.'

'You're coming a very long way.'

'When your most beloved friend dies, you have to be there at the end.'

'You have my sympathy, ma'am. It is a terrible tragedy.'

'Oh well,' said Miss Braithwaite. 'There are worse ways of going. Maud always had style.'

Amiss had not expected Pooley and the Bursar to hit it off, but though Pooley's eyes occasionally widened with astonishment, his expression never became sanctimonious. It helped that the Bursar was on her best behaviour. Instead of mocking Pooley when she discovered his aristocratic parentage, she used it as an excuse to make common cause with him against Amiss. After the first rush of jokes about noblesse oblige, the duties of lineage, how breeding always

160

told and so on they proceeded to historical chit-chat. The Pooleys and the Troutbecks, it emerged, had been four-square with Henry VIII at the Reformation but they had followed different paths in the Civil War: the Pooleys had been Roundheads and the Troutbecks Cavaliers.

'*Plus ça change*,' said Amiss.

'Ah, the poor young deracinated Robert,' said the Bursar sympathetically. 'What must it be to have no link with your forebears? How wonderful it is, Ellis, not to be a member of the lower orders.'

'Jack,' said Amiss, 'knock it off. I didn't alter my social arrangements in order to listen to aristocratic triumphalism. I can get that from you any day of the week by just dropping into your office.'

'I have never claimed to be an aristocrat. We Troutbecks are yeomen – more sturdily independent than the aristocracy, who, after all, only got their titles by selling out to royalty or being screwed by them one way or another.'

She saw Amiss's glare. 'Have another drink, Robert. We have something to celebrate.'

'What?'

'Another suspect.'

'Excellent. Amy came across?'

'She certainly did. I played her like a stringed instrument. Turns out Amy is better informed about what's going on in St Martha's than anyone there. She was quite up to date with all the political machinations – nothing new though. But then in Maud's last letter came a great *crise* over Deborah Windlesham, our beloved new Mistress, and the murky business of the allegedly faked footnotes. I have to say, it was pretty saintly of Maud to keep quiet about this, even to me.'

'Pretty stupid as well, if it led to her murder.'

'But then she'd led such a serious life – no crime novels, no television – that she never knew that the first thing you do on finding out someone else's guilty secret is to make damn sure you blab it to others and let the guilty-secret holder know you have. The really dumb move is secretly to

161

put your thoughts on paper and dispatch them across the ocean.'

'So what's the story? And make it straightforward. I'm not in the mood for reading between the lines.'

The Bursar took out her pipe and its attendant paraphernalia, filled it and tamped her tobacco down firmly. Then, after a copious draught of claret, she began. 'The trouble arose because Maud was a true scholar and a woman of infinite integrity as well as being painstaking to a balls-aching degree.

'One day, a few weeks ago, having run out of filing-cabinet space, she decided to empty a particular set of drawers that nobody had looked at in years. Most of the contents were the sort of yellowed paper you'd expect in an administrator's cabinet: ancient applications for places at St Martha's, records on individual students, various odds and ends relating to disciplinary matters, parental complaints, arguments over interpretation of the statutes and so on. She threw out a lot of it, consigned some more to the archives and then settled down to read through a drawerful of Fellowship applications stretching back twenty or so years.

'Anyone less conscientious would have binned the lot unread, but Maud skimmed through the papers to see if there was anything potentially useful to historians of the university or of women's education or whatever and that was when she came upon the 1965 file on Nina Becker.'

'Sounds quite racy,' said Amiss.

'Sshh,' said Pooley, who was already quivering and was poised to take notes.

'She certainly would appear to have been a bit of a dish. In fact, that seems to have been at the root of her problem.'

The Bursar picked up her lighter. Amiss, who had experience of this device, moved his chair back slightly. She pressed the ignition switch firmly and a large flame shot out which simultaneously lit her tobacco and slightly singed the front of her hair. Even Pooley's concentration lapsed. 'That's extremely dangerous,' he said, 'it's like a mini-flamethrower.'

'I like a decent flame.'

'Oh, get on with it, Jack,' said Amiss, 'you're just trying to keep us in suspense.'

The Bursar puffed deeply and emitted a vast cloud of smoke which threw Pooley into uncontrollable coughing. She waved her hand vaguely through the offending cloud. 'That's the trouble with people who don't smoke. They've no resilience.'

'Jack!'

'Oh, very well, very well. Don't fuss.

'What Maud wrote to Amy was that the academic credentials of Nina Becker were impeccable, that she seemed perfect for a St Martha's Fellowship and that on the face of it she had been kept off the shortlist because Deborah Windlesham had told lies.

'In those days, because there were so few Fellowships for women, St Martha's always had a large number of applicants. Existing Fellows would sift the applications in their area of expertise, read the theses presented, write a brief report on each and whittle the list down to the outstanding. Then three of them would read the work of everyone on the shortlist.

'Maud skimmed the Becker thesis, thought it excellent and was therefore surprised that Windlesham described it as being of poor quality, sloppily researched, poorly argued, of little significance to scholarship and containing a host of inaccurate references.

'Now, some of these things are matters of judgement; honest mistakes can be made. I may think my discovery that Odwold the Magnificent had three footmen instead of the two favoured by his father to be of immense importance in discussing the development of the Anglo-Saxon court: you may not. You may think that only a peabrain could fail to see the huge importance of discovering that the holder of the Deanery of Hogswallop in the late fifteenth century was not, as was always believed, a scion of the family of Borspittle but instead someone from the distaff side – a Mugwump who had procured a papal document enabling him to supplant the Borspittles for a whole generation: I may not.

'But what Maud said to Amy was that while she thought Miss Becker's thesis extremely useful, it wasn't that which

163

was the point of contention. It was that she could see no evidence of either sloppy research or poor arguments. She wasn't suspicious – Maud didn't have that kind of mind – but she had the curiosity of the true scholar, so off she went to check the allegedly inaccurate footnoting.

'She started with every tenth footnote and on finding those accurate took a whole chapter and then another and found that everything she had the resources to check was perfect.' The Bursar drew heavily once more on her pipe. Exhibiting extreme thoughtfulness, she blew the smoke in the opposite direction from Pooley. It caught Amiss and sent him into a paroxysm of coughing.

'Oops, sorry,' she said, slapping him vigorously on the back and almost knocking him off his chair. When order had been restored she resumed.

'She wrote worriedly about this to Amy. The charitable explanation, she concluded, was that having – for some innocent reason – taken a dislike to the thesis itself, Windlesham had made an honest if ignorant error about the quality of the research and on randomly checking footnotes had by a fluke lit upon a couple that were faulty and made a hasty assumption that they were typical. If so, Miss Becker had been done out of a possible Research Fellowship because of her examiner's fallibility.

'But having spotted that Becker and Windlesham had been contemporaries at around the same time in the same Oxford college, St Mary's, Maud was slightly haunted by the fear that there might be something personal involved, especially since Becker's photograph showed her to be a stunner. "Should I challenge Deborah?" she asked Amy, "or should I let it go?" Amy advised her against causing unnecessary friction by challenging Windlesham and Maud agreed, but her conscience wouldn't let her leave it at that. Instead, she embarked on a little detective work to see if there was a case to answer.

'It didn't take long to come up with the information that Windlesham and Becker had read history in the same year, that Becker had got a slightly better first than Windlesham in her Tripos after which Windlesham had gone on to do her

Ph.D and Becker had vanished for a few years, coming back to do postgraduate research a year after Windlesham had moved to Cambridge to take up her St Martha's Fellowship.'

'So they must have known each other quite well?'

'Yes, but that didn't prove anything. Still, though it wasn't an absolute rule, it would have been proper for Windlesham to have noted that she knew Becker, so Maud went ahead and rang the Mistress of St Mary's, who was a pal of hers, with a general enquiry about the Becker woman. After some ferreting about among the St Mary's dons, Maud was put in touch with an academic who had known Becker well and was occasionally in touch.

'Under the seal of the academic confessional the story was pieced together and a man turned out to be the problem – a law professor who was young, brilliant and unmarried. He went out for a short while with Windlesham but on meeting Becker fell madly for her. They dallied, she got tired of him and rather than hang around Oxford feeding the fires of his devotion, she did the decent thing and decamped for a couple of years to Paris to teach English. Then, when she reckoned he'd be over it, she came back because she was seriously academically inclined and wanted to do research. Apparently Windlesham could never be disabused of the notion that he would have come round to her in the end had it not been for Becker – even though by the time Becker arrived back in Oxford he had married someone else.'

'So it was vindictiveness, pure and simple?'

'Yes, and an understandable desire not to want the person she most hated in her own institution. But it was very rough on Becker, who according to her old pal was a woman who did nothing to attract hatred other than attract men. Becker needed and deserved a Research Fellowship, worked immensely hard on the thesis and was absolutely devastated when she discovered she'd not even been shortlisted. She just threw in the towel.'

'Well, that didn't show much backbone,' said Pooley.

The Bursar puffed meditatively. 'I think there is something I'd better explain to you that people of your age don't easily understand. I am not, I think, regarded as a wimp?'

She looked enquiringly at her audience. 'It's not the first term of abuse I would hurl at you, Jack,' said Amiss.

'Yet I have no difficulty in understanding how the sheer number of obstacles that until recently stood in the way of becoming a female university teacher would break your heart. I was all right because I joined the civil service, which treated you more or less equally, but the opportunities for women were a joke in the old universities. For God's sake, it wasn't until 1948 that a woman could actually be conferred with a degree in Cambridge. You couldn't join the Union until the sixties. And to this day women cannot even be full members of the Oxford and Cambridge Club.

'There were so few places for women in Oxbridge that only a tiny percentage of the best of them ever made it there in the first place and their colleges were so miserably poor that jobs were few and conditions spartan. Can you imagine how high-minded you had to be to crave the kind of life they've been living in St Martha's for decades, while around them were countless male colleges full of overfed dons swilling vintage port and wooing privileged male undergraduates who would go out into the world, where they would become successful and rich and in turn leave legacies to their old colleges.

'Women were tenth-class citizens in Oxbridge. They were patronized by many of their male lecturers and made to feel highly unwelcome by others: it wasn't that easy to acquire the effortless self-confidence that made one take rejection light-heartedly. Becker had shot her academic bolt because a member of her own sex was jealous of her but she didn't know that was the reason – she assumed she simply wasn't good enough.'

'So what did Dame Maud do then?'

'Told Windlesham that the injustice must be remedied and the Becker woman hunted down and, if possible, tempted back to St Martha's.'

'My God,' said Amiss, 'she was a hardliner, old Maud. What was the point after so long? Didn't she owe more to a longstanding colleague, even if she is a cow.'

'Maud believed in the simple principle of truth, justice and intellectual integrity. In her way, she was a fanatic.'

'I suppose I understand intellectually, but not emotionally.'

'I do,' said Pooley. 'It's the same debate as in Dorothy Sayers's *Gaudy Night* – intellectual integrity as against the feelings of flesh and blood people.'

'Precisely,' said the Bursar. 'You and I might go for the flesh and blood people in many instances, but we're not scholars. The point of scholars is to give scholarship priority. You want honest cops, honest scholars, honest Bursars.' She looked at Amiss. 'How do we describe you?'

' "Honest scrounger". Pour me some more wine, Ellis.' As he emptied the bottle in his companions' glasses, Pooley asked, 'Do we know what she was proposing to do if Windlesham didn't play?'

'Bring the matter up before the College Council and tell Becker the whole story when she tracked her down.'

'Preserve me,' said Amiss, 'from the mercilessness of the good.'

'What next?' asked Pooley.

'I'm handing it over to you. I suggest you go back now when we've finished here, ring Amy and get the facts officially, so to speak. Then you and the blithering fool can decide tomorrow morning what to do about it.'

'I have to say, in defence of my boss, that for once this is something he might just about grasp. Idiot though he may be, he is honest and I think he'd be more in sympathy than Robert with a sea green and incorruptible like Dame Maud.'

'Oh, I'm not entirely out of sympathy,' observed Amiss. 'We need people like that. I'd be worried about public standards if everyone was a wishy-washy liberal like me who likes being liked. You need the whistle-blowers and the people who don't mind being unpopular and the people with tunnel vision.'

'But not too many of them,' said the Bursar. 'They're almost all Roundheads.'

24

Pooley was right about Romford: he seized on the story of Windlesham and Becker with cries of joy. 'Ah, this is more like it, Pooley. I'd say it's pretty open and shut. The woman's got a double motive. If the Mistress stayed alive, Windlesham would be ruined, whereas if she died her reputation is saved and she becomes Mistress as well. Go and get her. The thing to do is to lean on her. Someone like that, she'll soon crack up. They're not used to pressure in their ivory tower.'

'Quite a lot of them seem pretty tough to me, sir.'

'Well, those impertinent young perverts, yes.'

'And the Bursar?'

'She's not a proper woman. At least Dr Windlesham is a normal woman; they crack easier.'

The familiar sensation of grinding rage gripped Pooley's vitals. He breathed deeply. 'I'll go and look for her, sir.'

Ten minutes in, Pooley wished it was possible to shoot senior officers for incompetence. Even in his most anti-Romford moments he could not have envisaged that the man would throw away a set of excellent cards by simply placing them face up on the table in front of his opponent. There was no attempt to trap the new Mistress into a lie.

Impotently, Pooley ground his teeth as he thought of how he would have conducted the interview, coaxing out of her assertions of a warm, happy relationship with no trouble and no friction and then finally beating her over the head with proof of her own falsehoods. Romford's approach – 'I have reason to believe, ma'am, that you and the late Dame Maud had words over a Miss Becker,' had enabled her to produce a competent and unincriminating version of the dispute. Over and over again Romford tried to get her to alter her version and over and over again she refused to budge.

An hour into the interview even Romford realized they had reached a stalemate. Far from cracking, Dr Windlesham was becoming even more unpleasant as the morning went on. Pooley wished she wouldn't be so patronizing; Romford was going to be in a vile mood at having a subordinate listen to him being treated in this way.

'I must insist, Dr Windlesham, that you are in a very serious position; personal offensiveness will not assist you in your predicament.'

'Inspector Romford, we have been over the same ground, by my reckoning, five times. There is nothing more to say.'

Romford was goaded by the condescension of her tone. 'Can you give me any reason, ma'am, why I shouldn't conclude that you murdered Dame Maud to keep her mouth shut?'

'For the last time, Inspector – and this is the last time, for I have better ways of occupying my time even if you do not – we had an intellectual disagreement on a matter of college policy, we agreed to differ, Dame Maud intended to raise the matter for discussion among our colleagues, I concurred and the matter would have been settled amicably at the Council. I have every reason to believe that my colleagues would have taken my side, being unlikely to wish to see the college's good name dragged in the mud over a minor error I made twenty years ago.'

'It was not a minor error. You ruined her career.'

'For the sixth time, Inspector, I did not ruin her career. For the sixth time, let me remind you that she is a successful barrister, earning probably ten times what you earn, and if it is true that I came between her and a Fellowship at St Martha's she should be on her knees every day thanking me. Now, I have no intention of wasting any more time on this absurdity.' She rose up and picked up her book.

'You can't go yet.'

'I can and I will. I am the Mistress here now and I have urgent work to do. It may escape you, Inspector, but I have

169

a college to run and my predecessor to bury. If there is any further unwarranted persecution of me I will feel obliged to have a word with your chief constable. I wish you good morning.'

'Well, she's certainly unpleasant enough,' said Pooley. 'We knew that. She's a complete cow.'

'She's not all cow,' said the Bursar. 'Close to it, I grant you, but she has a couple of good qualities – guts and certainly spleen. I always like a woman who can push the rozzers around. Romford at least must be developing a healthy respect for the inhabitants of St Martha's.'

'I think he is. He referred to you collectively as "that monstrous regiment".'

'Dear old John Knox. What a splendid turn of phrase. I'd rather be loathed and despised than patronized. This'll shake up Romford – do him good.'

'That's all very well, but he may have let a murderer off the hook.'

'Maybe, maybe. My money's still on the Dykes. And of course, Crowley isn't out of it yet. I think old Deborah's revelation that the Becker sex-pot made it big in the law alters the picture pretty substantially. Certainly she's right that most of us would have voted against reopening the whole business. In fact, I would have probably been able to stop Maud doing anything about it, come to think of it; she usually listened to me.'

Pooley sank his chin on his right fist. 'I feel very dispirited. We're left with hardly a decent suspect now unless Romford can crack an alibi.'

'Romford!' said Amiss. 'He couldn't crack an egg if you gave him a hammer.'

'Trust in the Lord, Ellis,' said the Bursar. 'Something'll turn up.'

The new Number One suspect didn't show at breakfast. It was 9.30 when Greasy Joan, sent to Dr Windlesham's bedroom to summon her, threw hysterics at the sight of her body, which had been stabbed several times with a sharp paper knife bearing the legend 'Boston Red Sox'. The only clues yielded by the police search were a few wiry black hairs in her bed. By lunch-time, with the preliminary forensic report in, Romford was cock-a-hoop. 'Now that we know she was full of sleeping pills, we know even someone as small as that black girl could have done the stabbing, so my instinct was right. Stands to reason, nice quiet backwater like this, it's got to be a foreigner. She's American. They don't understand anything except violence, especially the blacks. I'm only surprised she didn't use a gun. Go and get her. We'll give her a going over and then we'll take her in.'

'Sir, just before I do. Why? I mean, what motive?'

'That lesbian takeover. She sees off Mistress Number One, so as to get that Holdness woman made Deputy, then she sees off Mistress Number Two. You'll see, Holdness will step into her shoes any day now and they'll get hold of all this money and use it to disseminate whatever filth they want. Plain as a pikestaff.'

'I wouldn't be certain, sir, that this lady necessarily sees eye to eye on everything with Dr Holdness.'

'Stuff and nonsense, Pooley. Which side do you expect black American lesbians to be on? Motherhood and apple pie?'

It was rare for Romford to make a joke. When he did he fully appreciated it. Pooley waited for the merriment to subside. 'Sir, I'm just suggesting that we might go a little gently with her. The evidence is, er, a trifle circumstantial.'

'Do what you're told. Go and get her and warn the boys to be ready for the arrest.'

Pooley hovered. 'The students are very edgy at the moment, sir. We need to be careful.'

'Are you telling me my job, Sergeant?'

'No, sir.'

'Good.'

Pooley quit the room unhappily. His first port of call was the phone box in the hall from which he rang Superintendent Hardiman; his mobile was switched off. His second was Amiss's bedroom, which was empty. So too was the Bursar's. Having told the DCs what to expect, he reluctantly commenced the search for Mary Lou, whom he found in the library.

Professionalism and inside knowledge fought within him as they walked to the interview room, exchanging desultory small talk. 'Dr Denslow,' he said finally, 'could I just warn you that Inspector Romford's bark is worse than his bite?'

She eyed him curiously. 'You mean he shouts a lot?'

'I shall deny it if you quote me, but what I mean is that he sometimes jumps too readily to conclusions.'

She stopped and looked him full in the face. 'Come on, call a spade a spade.' She grinned broadly. 'I'm not going to rat on you; I know you're a friend of Robert's. Are you trying to tell me Romford's attempting to pin this on me?'

'I can't say any more. Just that if you are outraged by what Inspector Romford says or suggests or even does, don't panic.'

Mary Lou smiled, 'I don't. But I'm very grateful for the tip-off.'

'I must warn you that whatever you say may be taken down and used in evidence.'

Mary Lou looked at Romford in a relaxed fashion.

'I'm from out of town, Inspector. What's all that supposed to mean?'

'It's an official warning.'

'Of what?'

'That anything you say might be used against you.'

'That's a pretty vague explanation.'

Romford looked helpless.

'Excuse me, sir,' said Pooley. 'It means simply, ma'am, that anything you say to us might be used in court, should you appear there.'

'In the dock?'

'Yes, ma'am.'

'Well, that would be some interesting experience. Just what are you fingering me for?'

'Murder,' said Romford.

'Why should *I* murder the Mistress?'

'Ha!' Romford looked triumphant. 'How do you know

she's been murdered? The one that found her's been taken off to the hospital and we didn't tell anyone yet that it wasn't natural causes.'

Mary Lou looked at him blankly. 'Everyone knows she's been murdered.'

'They do not. This is a matter known only to the police.'

'But it's been in the newspapers.'

Romford looked discomforted. 'Oh, I see. You were referring to Dame Maud.'

'Well, she was the Mistress, wasn't she? What's going on round here, Inspector?'

Romford cleared his throat and put on his impressive voice. 'There is a measure of misunderstanding at this point in time, owing to the fact that Dr Windlesham, the present Mistress, has been murdered too.'

'What! This is getting Shakespearian – no one else could explain matricide on such a grand scale.'

'What do you mean, matricide?'

'The murder of your mother.' Seeing Romford's perplexity, she added, 'I mean that the Mistress is the mother of the college.' Romford still looked blank. 'Oh, never mind,' said Mary Lou, 'it was just a thought.'

Romford went on the attack. 'I must ask you, Dr Denslow, about the nature of your relationship with Dr Windlesham.'

'Relationship, Inspector? I've only been in the UK for about five minutes. I never even spoke to her except to say hi.'

'Well then, how do you explain that she was murdered with your paper knife.'

'Was she? I was looking for that only this morning. Someone must have nicked it.'

'So you say, ma'am.' With a flourish, Romford opened the envelope in front of him and took out some black hairs.

'Do you recognize these?'

'How am I supposed to recognize hair?'

'But would it not be true to say, ma'am, that they resemble your own?'

'I suppose so. They have an Afro look to them.'

'You understand that we can do tests that will determine whether or not they are yours.'

'By all means, Inspector. They may well be mine. Blacks aren't exactly two a penny in this joint. Where did you find them?'

'In Dr Windlesham's bed.'

'Dr Windlesham's bed. Now there's a surprise. And where was Dr Windlesham?'

'Stabbed to death in the same bed.'

'So you're rounding up all the niggers in the neighbourhood?'

Romford looked shocked.

'It's OK,' said Mary Lou, 'I'm allowed to be politically incorrect. It's one of the perks of being from an oppressed minority. We can say what we like.'

Romford was in no mood for sociological observations. 'Within this college, ma'am, I understand that there are only two students and one Fellow who are . . .' He stopped, palpably embarrassed.

Amiss guessed he was struggling with an imperfect memory of what he had been taught in his last multicultural sensitivity course. Mary Lou looked at him with bright-eyed interest.

'Of African descent,' he suddenly came out with triumphantly. 'And you're the only one with the motive.'

'Which is?'

'There is very good evidence that there was a conspiracy to put a particular element in power in this college.'

'And you think I'm part of it?'

'I do, ma'am.'

'After less than a week in the country, I'm so carried away I jump into bed with people and then murder them?'

'I can only say that the circumstances look very suspicious.'

'Anyone could have taken hairs from my trashcan when they were pinching the knife. This is crazy. You don't murder people you don't know.'

'In America you people do it all the time, as far as I can see.'

'Usually with guns, though. Maybe I should have used mine rather than messing about with paper knives.'

Pooley tried willing her to stop making jokes. They were not helping.

Romford was at his most censorious. 'I hope you realize, ma'am, that we take the matter of unlicensed firearms very seriously in this country. Are you telling me you have imported such a weapon unlawfully?'

Mary Lou sighed. 'Gimme a break, Inspector. I'm not an imbecile and I've never owned a gun. I don't even recollect ever killing anyone.'

'Where were you last night between the hours of midnight and 6.00 a.m.?'

'In bed.'

'Whose bed?'

'My own.'

'Alone?'

'You haven't seen my bed, Inspector. It's only just about got room enough for me.'

'So you've got no alibi?'

'No.'

'And what are probably your hairs were in Dr Windlesham's bed? Not to speak of your knife.'

'So you say.'

'I shall have to ask you to accompany me to the station.'

'And if I say no?'

'You'll be put under arrest.'

Mary Lou nodded. 'I think I might just refuse. What happens then?'

'I fear we will have to use force.'

'That might be fun.' She crossed her legs demurely. 'I'm not going to move. I'll opt for passive resistance – the Gandhi approach.'

'Sir, could I have a word?'

'Do you have to?'

'Yes.'

Pooley and Romford left the room. 'Sir, if we take her by force out of St Martha's there'll be a riot.'

'What do you suggest I do?'

175

'Let her go for the time being. Anyone could have put those hairs in the bed and taken her knife to implicate her. And it really is highly unlikely she's going to be murdering people a few days after arriving in the country.'

'I can see you don't understand Americans, Pooley – or blacks for that matter. Those Yardies in Brixton shoot you as soon as look at you. I know about them.'

'Sir, this is a scholar of impeccable respectability.'

Romford was obdurate. 'I know my duty. Now come along, find the lads and we'll take her in.'

Pooley ran frantically to the Bursar's office. She was sitting with her feet on the desk reading a newspaper. He panted out his story.

She whirled her feet to the floor and jumped up. 'He's off his nut. Has he no idea what it will do to St Martha's, not to speak of the reputation of the Cambridgeshire constabulary, if an innocent woman – and black to boot – is dragged off in chains?'

'Well, I'm glad you think she's innocent,' said Pooley. 'So do I.'

'Was she asked about an alibi?'

'Yep. Said she didn't have one.'

'Well, well. Now I call that behaving like a gentleman in a big way.'

'What are you talking about?'

'She's protecting the fair name of young Robert, of course.'

'You don't mean . . . ?'

'Ellis, don't be an idiot. Where do you think he was off to last night. Where do you think he'd been the night before?'

Pooley suddenly remembered the two poured whiskies from two nights previously.

'They mightn't have spent the night together.'

'I was at breakfast with them this morning. Two cats who'd each swallowed a canary.'

'Well, why wouldn't she tell Romford that?'

'Because of Rachel, of course. If she's the sort of girl I think she is, she doesn't want to mess up Robert's life.'

'But she could tell us about it in confidence.'

'Would you trust Romford if you were her?'

'No, I suppose not.'

'Come on then. We'd better sort this out.'

'Are you going to get Robert?'

'Certainly not. I don't want to mess up his life either. I'll use a different stratagem. Now hurry up before Romford claps on the leg irons.'

When the Bursar crashed into the interview room, Mary Lou was gazing out of the window and Romford was rereading his notes.

'I ran into young Pooley. He tells me you are proposing to arrest my colleague.'

'I have no option, I fear, Miss Troutbeck. She refuses to accompany us to the station.'

'You bloody well do have an option. You can leave her alone. She's got a rock-solid alibi.'

'Not one that we're aware of, ma'am.'

'She spent the entire night with me, from about 11.15, was it, Mary Lou? Until after 7.00 this morning.'

'Why should I believe you? You could have been in a conspiracy together.'

'As anyone will tell you, we're on opposite sides in the college dispute.'

Romford looked at Mary Lou. 'Is this true?'

'Yep.'

'Why didn't you say so?'

'I didn't think it would be good for either the Bursar's reputation or mine.'

The Bursar smiled at her indulgently. 'It wouldn't be good for your reputation to be arrested for murder, you silly girl.' She leaned over and ruffled Mary Lou's hair. 'Now come on. Unless the inspector's got anything more to ask you I think we'd better be off. There are a few matters of college business I need to talk to you about.' As they left, the Bursar turned towards Romford and gave him an enormous wink.

25

'Don't you think, sir, that the likelihood is that somebody planted those hairs deliberately to implicate Mary Lou?'

'Who would do that?'

'The murderer.' Pooley was amazed at his own patience.

Romford looked uncertainly at the college list. For some reason that escaped Pooley, he seemed to be trying to find the murderer by the application of simple guesswork. 'Who should we call next, do you think?'

'Sir, wouldn't it be better to wait until the field has been narrowed a little? We should have the result of alibi checks shortly. Perhaps if you were to go back to the station and coordinate forensic I could hang on here and pull the paperwork together. Then we would have something to go on maybe later in the afternoon.'

Romford was too discouraged even to put up a fight.

After he had left, Pooley dialled the Bursar.

'We've got to get at Robert before he blows your alibi.'

'I've dealt with that. He'll play ball.'

'Where is he?'

'Half asleep in the library. Haven't you noticed he's getting tireder by the day?'

'She looked fit enough.'

'We women are made of sterner stuff, Ellis.'

'The shortlist is very short,' said Pooley. 'Crowley, Pusey and the Senior Tutor are now the only ones without alibis.'

'And me.'

'Except, Robert, that you really have one.'

178

'Yes, but Romford doesn't know that.'

'True. I can see you becoming top of the suspects any minute now.'

'Can we do a quick elimination exercise, based on the truth as we know it, as opposed to how it might seem?'

'OK.'

'Right, first list is of those who are definitely innocent, if one supposes the same person did both murders – and, of course, attacked Jack.'

'OK.'

'Me, the Bursar, Sandra and Bridget, if we believe them, and Mary Lou.'

'OK, so our suspects are Pusey, Crowley, Primrose Partridge, Anglo-Saxon Annie and Miss Thackaberry.'

'Well, I don't know about you, Ellis, but I do not find that an encouraging list.'

'Well, what about if somebody different did each of the murders?'

'That just means you can add Mary Lou and the nasty old Windlesham as possibilities for Dame Maud's murder and leave list two unchanged.'

'Except for the Bursar.'

'You're not seriously suggesting . . . ?'

'I'm not, but one has to be objective. At least, I have to be objective. Maybe she's plotting to become Mistress herself. Maybe she leaped at the chance of getting a false alibi.'

'Ellis, I'm not going to follow you down one of your mad routes. I can imagine Jack seeing off one of her opponents with an unduly enthusiastic uppercut, but I do not see her sneaking into their bedrooms in the dead of night and sticking paper knives into them. Anyway, if she did stab anyone she'd probably use a pitchfork.'

'Of course I don't really suspect her. But when you've got as few suspects as we've got you do get a bit desperate. And no one looks likely. Take Crowley. He thrives on minimum publicity. This murder's going to bring a lot of publicity to St Martha's and that's hardly welcome to someone who usually, when he's found out, folds his tent and steals away into the night. I just can't see him changing his tactics.'

179

'Unless things became intolerable. Maybe Dr Windlesham was blackmailing him. Or Holdness. Otherwise why would he have backed them?'

'It's possible.'

'It's time you worked Bridget over, Ellis. If it weren't for that alibi she would be Number One suspect. And I don't trust their alibis. You know Sandra would back up Bridget in any circumstances.'

'It's all very well to say work her over, but watching Romford interviewing Bridget Holdness is like watching a rabbit interrogating a stoat.'

'Where's that superintendent of yours? Surely now with two murders at St Martha's he's got to give it higher priority?'

'Cambridge just don't have the resources, Robert. They're stretched at the best of times and now, at one and the same time, they've got this grisly Fens serial murderer, a massive security operation going on for a conference which is expected to attract the attention of the IRA and now this. Poor old Hardiman is driven crazy. Still, I did catch him half an hour ago and he said he'd try to free himself up at some stage tomorrow if we still haven't got anywhere.'

'However, you're right. I'll lean on Romford to bring in Bridget Holdness. What are you going to do? Pursue Mary Lou?'

'You sound reproachful.'

'I am a bit.'

'Have you ever been knocked over by a wholly unexpected and inappropriate sexual passion?'

'You mean a consummated one? No, I can't say I have – at least, not the way you seem to have been. Are you going to ditch Rachel?'

'My dear Ellis, I am devoted to Rachel. I'm frantic for her to come back to London, I want to spend the rest of my life with her and if the option were open to me now I would probably run away from St Martha's to avoid further temptation but it's not and I'm not superhuman.'

'What does Mary Lou want?'

'A fling. Wouldn't you if you were marooned in a dump like this knowing nobody except the weird sisters? She's much less affected by it than me. She's more promiscuous anyway, and bugger it, she's lesbian as well as straight. I am but a toy with which to while away the hours.'

'Robert.' Pooley cleared his throat. 'Look, I don't quite know how to say this but if Mary Lou's promiscuous . . .' His voice tailed off.

Amiss took pity on him. 'AIDS?'

'Yes?'

'Well, to tell you the truth, it's the last thing I think of when I'm in the company of Mary Lou.'

'But . . .'

Amiss raised his hand. 'It's OK, Ellis. We've covered that. She's a forthright girl. The first thing she did was to ask me where I'd been and then to reassure me that she'd been confining herself to women for several years.'

'Well, why did she go to bed with you then?'

'Because I'm so devastatingly attractive.'

Pooley looked sceptical.

'Because she likes going to bed with men quite as much as women – it's just that on her campus it was easier to be exclusively lesbian or you were accused by some of the loonies of being a traitor. She was lonely, I was there, we got on well and we drank a lot and the sexual chemistry was right. Yes, I know, I shouldn't have and I particularly know I shouldn't have the second time, but I'm not a saint.'

Pooley sighed. 'Oh well, at least if she's normally a lesbian she's unlikely to get AIDS.'

'That's a disgracefully anti-feminist observation.'

'What?'

'Didn't you know that a lot of right-on lesbians have a sense of grievance at their low AIDS profile; they feel they're being left out of the limelight.'

'That's ridiculous.'

'Ah, you say that. But that's because you have no regard for wimmin. All this propaganda about wearing condoms shows that society values only heterosexuals and gay men.'

'It does?'

'Sure. Where do you see the great campaigns for using dental dams? You look foxed, Ellis. Don't tell me you don't

181

know what a dental dam is? Don't they teach you anything at Staff College.'

Pooley shook his head.

'Ah, well. Right. I'm an expert on this, owing to the fact that it has been an issue on the College Council. Jack tells me that one entire meeting last month ended in uproar over this. It's one of the great tragedies of my life that I wasn't present.

'Now, not only did the Mistress come under great pressure to install condom machines, which she refused on the grounds that it was a women's college and she had no intention of encouraging men to enter the building and fornicate, but the Dykes mounted a campaign for a dental dam dispenser. When the Senior Tutor asked innocently why the college had to take responsibility for the students' teeth, Bridget explained brutally what a dental dam was – viz, a piece of extremely thin latex, the kind of thing they make condoms out of, which can be placed over the female genitalia as a protection during oral sex.'

'How do you get AIDS from oral sex?'

'It can be done if you really put your mind to it. Let's say the contingency is pretty remote unless you're both actually suppurating.'

Pooley leant his head on his hands. 'Someday, I'm going to find a nice girl who has, in the past, had only one or two boyfriends, if that, and we will get married and settle down and have 2.4 children and be faithful to each other.'

'One isn't always completely able to live up to one's principles in this regard, Ellis. Believe me, I have similar aspirations and my present carry-on is out of character.'

'I know it is,' said Pooley with a rush of generosity. 'Besides, I'm jealous. She's very attractive.'

'Marilyn Monroe compared to the rest of my colleagues. And I have made a few weak efforts to stop. Unfortunately, Mary Lou believes in enjoying yourself when you get the chance, so she's not really cut out for heroic self-sacrifice.'

'Well, she was prepared to be arrested rather than blow the gaff on you this morning.'

'Sorry, I mean self-sacrifice on the sexual front.'

The door crashed open and the Bursar entered. 'What are you two gossiping about?'

'Duty versus desire,' said Amiss.

'Can't say I often find a conflict. However, you may, Ellis. The bonehead is back and is looking for you.'

She threw herself into his vacated chair. 'Now, listen here, young Robert, there's serious trouble brewing. Bridget's called a College Council for tomorrow morning.'

'So she can become Mistress?'

'Presumably.'

'How do the numbers look?'

'They don't hold steady for ten minutes together, as you well know. It's a bit hard to predict anything with any certainty when you don't know which of your colleagues is going to be a jailbird by the time the meeting commences and how many of them will be bribed into doing an about-turn.'

'Anything I can do?'

'Let me know what Pusey's price is. I'll see to Crowley.'

'Who are you running?'

'Emily, of course.'

'Do you think anybody really wants a job in which two of her predecessors have been murdered?'

'Emily doesn't think like that. All she knows about is service.'

'You'll feel pretty sick if you get her elected and then she's knocked off too.'

'I shall see that no harm comes to her.'

'That's a fine fat rhetorical statement. Why don't you run yourself?'

'Who'd vote for me?' she asked reasonably. 'I frighten the wits out of the Old Women and the Dykes all hate me. Anyway, I don't want it. I shall enjoy being the *éminence grise* behind Emily – her ventriloquist, her puppet master. Or do I mean puppet mistress? I was a civil servant; that's what I'm used to. Now, let's get to work.'

'When can we compare notes?'

'I don't know. It's a busy day ahead.'

'Tonight?'

'No, I've got a working dinner. Come to my office in the

morning, fifteen minutes before the Council meeting. You know what has to be done. Just get on with it.'

'But you want to know what Pusey says. And I might seriously need you.'

'Leave a message on my answering machine. I might even be lurking behind it.'

'I really hate answering machine owners who sit there auditioning callers before deciding if they're worth speaking to.'

'Don't be so sensitive. An answering machine is a convenient social prophylactic.'

'What does that make those attempting to, as it were, penetrate it?'

'Some metaphors, Robert, are better not taken to their logical conclusion.' With a cheery beam she waltzed out of the room.

26

'A cake. Oh gosh, a Sachertorte.' Pusey simpered. 'I think you're trying to bribe us, but we don't mind, do we, Bobsy?'

Amiss simpered back. 'I am a bit, Francis. I need advice. It's bad enough being new to an academic environment without having all this happen.'

'It really is frightful. I don't dare to think what's going to happen next. We're keeping our heads well down, Bobsy and I.'

He bustled around filling the kettle and getting out crockery and cutlery. Amiss and Bobsy gazed at each other, Bobsy uninterestedly, Amiss distastefully. Fortunately, one of Bobsy's few virtues was his lack of interest in nuzzling up to anyone other than his partner.

'There we are, then, all ready. Milk in first? I hope I've got it right? Yes? Oh, good. And now let me give you a great big slice.'

'Not a big slice, please, Francis.'

'Oh, don't be so coy. I'm going to have a great big slice.'

Resignedly, Amiss embarked on the miserable task of once more forcing loathsome stodge down his reluctant throat. Not until Pusey was replete could they get down to business.

'My fear, Francis, is that Bridget Holdness will become Mistress tomorrow and all the men will be out in no time. I bet you anything that mob will go in for gender cleansing in a big way.'

'You don't really think that, do you? She says she'll renew my contract for three years.'

'Just like Windlesham promised. Have you got it in writing?'

'She said that would be legally impossible since it would seem like a bribe.'

'You're a brave man, Francis. I can't say I'd be prepared to take the word of Bridget Holdness.'

'But she's going to win, anyway.'

'Why?'

'Because no one thinks Emily's up to the job. I mean, you and I would rather have her, but the waverers aren't going to vote for somebody who doesn't know what century she's in, and that means we have to back the person we think will win.'

'Aren't there any other candidates? You wouldn't run yourself?'

Pusey giggled. 'I don't think I'd get many votes.' Amiss did not trouble to challenge such an incontrovertible statement.

'Thackaberry?'

'Doesn't know what planet she's on.'

'Anglo-Saxon Annie?'

Pusey laughed.

'Jack Troutbeck?'

'Out of the question. They wouldn't have her. Too rough. No, I'm afraid we're stuck with Emily versus Holdness and self-preservation drives me into the Holdness camp. If you've got any sense, you'll try and strike a deal with her yourself.'

Amiss brooded. 'If you thought there was a good chance that Holdness could be beaten and your job would be safe, would you take the risk?'

'Oh dear, Robert. You are a naughty boy. You're making this very difficult. I'd quite made up my mind.'

'I just think we shouldn't throw in the towel.'

'Have another slice of cake and we'll talk it over.'

'I don't need this,' said Sandra.

'What?' asked Romford.

'This hassle. You're hurting my feelings.'

'I have no desire to hurt your feelings, ma'am, but I just have to ask you a few more questions.'

'You're harassing me.'

'I'm trying to find out the truth.'

'You're inferring I'm a liar. That's defamation.'

'Dr Murphy, all I ask is that once more you give me an account of your movements on the nights of the two murders.'

'It's here. That's the statement I wrote out for you before.'

'You have nothing to add?'

'No. And don't you try forcing a confession out of me. I know about British injustice. You won't trap me.'

'Excuse me, sir, could I have a word?'

Crossly, Romford marched out of the room. 'What is it?'

'Don't you think it might be a good idea, sir, if you asked her about the two nights she spent with Holdness?'

'What's the point? They've already coordinated their stories.'

'Well, they just mightn't have, or not fully. I mean, if we went into real detail . . .' Pooley cleared his throat. 'For instance, if we asked about . . .' he plunged on boldly '. . . if they'd, er, made love and if so, how and when, we might catch them out.'

'Sergeant Pooley, I'm surprised at you. We can't sink to that. Anyway, she'd complain. She's already threatened us with a lawyer.'

'She wouldn't have a good case, sir.'

'They can make a good case out of anything, those people. I'm not going to lay myself open to that kind of scandal. I'd be accused of asking improper questions for my own gratification. They wouldn't like that in church.'

'But we might catch them out, sir. I mean, we could ask about what they wore in bed and who got up first in the morning and . . .'

A whirlwind arrived in the shape of Superintendent Hardiman. 'What's going on, still floundering?'

'We're making progress, sir. I shall shortly be making an arrest.'

Pooley gaped at him.

'Well, thank God for that, Romford. You've caught the murderer?'

'No, sir. We have not as yet had a breakthrough in that

department. This will be an arrest on a drugs charge.'

'Who, what, where, when, how much?'

'In response to a tip-off which I received at lunch-time, I instructed that a thorough search be made of the bedroom of Mary Lou Denslow where DCs McMenamin and WPC Allen found a substantial quantity of what they recognized as marijuana, concealed in the woman's toilet bag. I have therefore instructed that she be apprehended, taken to the station and charged with possession of drugs.'

'Who tipped you off?'

'I don't know, sir.'

'Has it not occurred to you that this might be a plant?'

'Why should it be?'

'To stir up trouble. All we need now is a case of wrongful arrest.'

'Well, maybe she tipped us off herself, sir. Maybe that's what she wants. Trouble. Some of these people like being martyrs.'

'So we help them?'

'If she's guilty, she's guilty, sir.'

'Inspector Romford, cancel that instruction. What I want done this afternoon is an intensive attempt to break the two sets of alibis.'

'Well, I've just been trying that, sir, with the Murphy woman. We got nowhere.'

'Have you taken each of the four in minute detail through every stage of that night.'

'No, sir.'

'Why not?'

'I didn't think it appropriate, sir.'

'Romford, by the time you report back to me, I want you to know which of them took their knickers off first or if they took them off each other, if they did it standing on their heads or on the top of the wardrobe, if any of them got up to pee in the middle of the night, if the curtains were open or closed and what they talked about afterwards; then we will know if the alibis stand up. Do I make myself clear?'

'Yes, sir, but I don't like it.'

'You're not paid to like it, Romford. I should not have to

remind you after thirty-six years that police work is often sordid.' He turned to go. 'And don't let one half of the alibi out of your sight until the other half is in your clutches. Now, get to it.' He rushed off without another word.

Romford looked grimly at Pooley. 'Sometimes I think about early retirement.' He shook his head. 'Send for them. And since you wanted us to undertake all this unpleasantness, you can do the questioning.'

'I don't think I've ever been as embarrassed in my life.'

'I'm not surprised. Asking Bridget Holdness if she used a dildo is not something I would be enthusiastic about. Does she, by the way?'

Pooley went slightly pink. 'I didn't have to ask that. Both of them claimed they made love in a pretty perfunctory manner both nights. Just . . .'

'Just what?'

'Just oral sex.'

'With or without dental dams?'

Pooley laughed. 'That was the only bit I enjoyed. They didn't, by the way, but I thought it gave me a certain cachet being so well up on such matters. Mind you, it wasn't so good having to explain it to Romford afterwards.'

'So how did the various participants behave?'

'Very differently. Sandra ran true to form – victim language and legal threats and only came up with the answers when I told her she'd be charged with withholding information from the police in the execution of their duties and that there was no martyr status associated with that. Then she was as obstructive as possible and pretended to have forgotten nearly everything but even she couldn't avoid coming across with a few specifics.'

'Bridget?'

'Not as bad as I'd expected. I think she realized she just had to go through with it. Seemed pretty resigned. The Bursar and Mary Lou, on the other hand, each seemed to enjoy the interviews. One of them is as unembarrassable as the other.'

'But surely they were in a very weak position to tell the same story.'

'Well, that's the funny thing. Sandra and Bridget produced enough discrepancies for any clever prosecuting lawyer to cast severe doubt on their alibis on either night. The Bursar and Mary Lou, on the other hand, could not be faulted.'

'Had you rigged it with them beforehand?'

'What do you take me for, Robert? Anyway, I didn't have the chance. Either you've been fantasizing and Mary Lou was with the Bursar all last night, or they've had a pretty thorough rehearsal.'

'Good old Jack. You can see why she's ace at her job.'

'I can see why I'm glad she's on the same side as I am.'

'So has Romford taken Sandra and Bridget off in chains to the station?'

'No, because Sandra made such a song and dance about being under stress and under pressure that he's convinced that nothing that she's admitted would stand up in court even though she's signed her statement. He gives in very quickly to psychological terrorism, does old Romford. Now if Mary Lou had been in a similar position it would have been different. He's taken a rooted objection to her.'

'Because she's black?'

'No, in fairness to him, more than anything because she laughs at him. As far as he's concerned, Mary Lou and the Bursar are bats out of hell whereas Sandra and Bridget are barrack-room lawyers. He hates that sort less.'

'So what next?'

'Don't ask me. Romford's gone off muttering so I'm left to my own devices until tomorrow morning. Dinner?'

'Sure. Do you mind if I bring Mary Lou along.'

'Sorry, Robert. You know I can't take the risk of dining with a serious suspect.'

''Course you can. As long as you both pay for yourselves. Remember, you don't work for Romford, you work for Jim. He wouldn't disapprove.'

'All right. Against my better judgement. Will you still consort with me if I'm fired from the police?'

'I'll get you a job at St Martha's. It looks as if Greasy Joan is leaving.'

Amiss burst through the Bursar's social prophylactic early evening.

'How are you getting on?'

'Consolidating. Anglo-Saxon Annie and Thackaberry are pretty clear that they are to vote down Holdness. I've terrified them about the attitude of the Dykes towards medievalists. And you?'

'If you can convince Pusey that if your side gets in he'll get a three-year contract – which is what Bridget is offering – he'll rat on her if he thinks she'll lose.'

'OK, I'll get Emily on to it.'

'No point, he doesn't think Emily can deliver. You've got to guarantee it. He's prepared to take your word.'

'Done.'

'What about Crowley?'

'No dice. He did the same deal as Francis with Deborah and has been offered it again by Bridget. He says both were prepared to overlook what he calls the discreditable allegations about his past. That, incidentally, would seem to put paid to any motive he might have had to knock off Deborah. But while Emily and I are prepared to give him a few weeks' grace, we won't let a cheat stay on the premises. Things are bad enough here without having a bogus scholar/clergyman.'

'No room for manoeuvre?'

'None. I may be pragmatic but I'm not amoral.'

'But why can't you get the College Council to kick him out now?'

'Because obviously the Dykes won't go along with that. Anyway, if he's on their side and they win because of that, it might be possible to upset the election later on appeal.'

'Is it a Troutbeck trait to like belts and braces?'

'It's a Troutbeck trait to like winning. Speaking of which, has young Ellis reported our triumph this afternoon.'

'Indeed he has. Congratulations. What a pair of consummate liars.'

'Thank you. Why that fool Romford didn't question us the

first moment I gave her an alibi I'll never know. We'd have failed ignominiously. Twenty minutes homework did the job. She's a bright girl.'

'Where is she anyway?'

'Consorting with the Dykes. Spying out the land. She's my undercover agent.'

'Any idea when she'll be free?'

'Not this evening.'

'Shit. I'd hoped she'd join me and Pooley.'

'Well, you'll just have to have a Boys Night Out on your own. Now get off the phone, I'm busy.'

Disconsolately, Amiss roamed around the little garden, brooding. His mind felt like a washing machine, the same material going round and round and round and seeming to become more threadbare by the minute. The bright idea did not come to him until the moment when physical exhaustion threatened. You idiot, he said to himself. Why didn't you think of that earlier? He strode off into the building and headed towards the Senior Tutor's room.

'Will it work?' asked Pooley.

'Depends on the timing being got right.'

'I can think of better collaborators.'

'Do I have a choice?'

Pooley reflected. 'Can't say anyone comes to mind.'

'Pass the wine.'

'Go easy, Robert. You're going to need all your wits about you tomorrow if it goes wrong.'

'No, I won't. This either works or it doesn't. Either way, Jack's going to have to be the master strategist. Now, what has today yielded, other than the alibi mess?'

'Well, as per instructions, Romford's had the tip-off note examined closely by forensic, but there are no fingerprints, nothing special about the paper and the words were formed out of Letraset that you can get in any stationery store.'

'What did it actually say?'

'Oh, you mean are there any stylistic oddities about it? No, it was literate and straightforward. Something along the lines of: "DRUGS ARE AT THE CENTRE OF ALL THIS. LOOK IN THE BLACK BIRD'S ROOM."'

'Not a very PC way of putting it.'

'No. Even Romford grasped that, so he concluded it must have been written by a servant. But when he tried that on Hardiman, he told him he was a fool.'

'I have to say that I would be surprised if any of the put-upon domestic staff would care if they found them taking coke at the College Council. They've far more than that to worry about, like not starving to death on their rotten wages. However, the perpetrator has been admirably brief. The note doesn't give you much to go on.'

'Nothing does,' said Pooley sadly. 'I suppose all we can do is chew over motives again – who wanted to kill each of the Mistresses most.'

'I hope you're making plans to guard the next one. It seems a pretty high-risk occupation being Mistress of St Martha's.'

'Well, of course, you could always leave it to the good old process of elimination. If the Virgin candidate wins and is murdered we can be pretty sure the baddy was a Dyke. If the Dyke candidate wins and isn't murdered we can be equally be pretty sure it was a Dyke.'

'And if the Virgin candidate wins and isn't murdered, or the Dyke wins and is?'

'That enough hypotheses for one evening. Fill my glass.'

Amiss looked at his watch. 'It's half past ten, Ellis. I should be going.'

'You have another assignation?' Pooley tried not to look disapproving.

'More an expectation.'

'You're getting in deeper and deeper.'

'Well, Mary Lou isn't and that's my safety net. When this is over, I'll get out of St Martha's ASAP, I promise, but I just don't seem able to pass up this opportunity while it's so readily available. How could anyone turn down a temptation of this quality – it would be akin to refusing the Chateau Mouton Rothschild 1961 because you know you really should cut down on your drinking.'

Pooley sighed and called for the bill. 'And here am I unattached and nobody's crawling into my bed.'

'You frighten them, Ellis. You're so virtuous, so proper, so organized, well-behaved and sober. They're afraid they won't measure up. I reckon most of the success I've had with women has been because of my failings. No one has ever accused me of being perfect.'

Pooley had a burst of candour. 'I don't think I'd have the courage to go to bed with a feminist anyway. I wouldn't know how to do it in a politically correct fashion.'

'Mary Lou is most reassuring on that. From the outset she explained that she wasn't a feminist in bed.' He looked guilty. 'Now, that's quite enough kissing and telling. Let's be off.'

'I'm sorry', said the note Amiss found shoved under his door. 'Can't get away. Talk to you tomorrow.'

Amiss knew he should feel relieved. Instead he felt so disappointed he was afraid he might cry.

27

Breakfast was dominated by the newspapers. 'DYKES IN DOUBLE MURDER PROBE', said the *Sun*, 'SERIAL KILLER STALKS THE CAMPUS', said the *Mirror*, 'CALL INSPECTOR MORSE', said the *Mail*, 'ANXIETY AT CAMBRIDGE COLLEGE AFTER SECOND KILLING', said the *Independent* on page 3. For the first time in their lives, the Fellows of St Martha's focused their attention on the tabloids.

'Oh, what an awful thing to say,' said the Senior Tutor. 'How can they?'

The Bursar looked up. 'What?'

'It says here that St Martha's is known as a hot-bed of lesbian passion and militant feminism.'

'Well, isn't it?' asked the Bursar absent-mindedly.

'Not yet,' said Anglo-Saxon Annie. Amiss was amazed. He'd never yet heard her say anything other than 'hello' and 'goodbye'. The Bursar must have really been stirring her up about threats to scholarship.

Bridget glared. Sandra piped up dutifully. 'We can expect nothing from the paternalistic capitalist press but vilification, misrepresentation and homophobia.'

Amiss thought she sounded quite pleased.

'Listen to this,' said Miss Thackaberry. 'They claim to have got hold of a list of the papers read at the Gender and Ethnic Workshop.'

'Read some out,' said the Bursar. 'Give us all a good laugh.'

'"Out of the Drawing Room; Exclusion Strategies against Women Artists with particular emphasis on the life and works of Mbele Rafferty".'

'Who's she?' asked the Bursar.

'There you are,' said Sandra. 'None of you have heard of her, because she's been excluded.'

'Is she any good?'

'It is not for us to be judgemental about art. Elitism is . . .'

The Bursar groaned. 'I bet she doesn't even exist. What you might call the ultimate exclusion. Get on with it, Thackaberry.'

'"Embrace the Victim: the Politics of Gender in Modern Teaching"; "Alcohol Disadvantage Among the Irish in Britain".'

'What does that mean?' asked Pusey.

'That they don't get enough to drink, of course,' said the Bursar helpfully. Sandra's glare passed her by.

'"Sisters or Suckers: paternalist opportunism in the women's movement"; "Rap against Repression: Ice-T and the Police State".'

'What the hell is that?' asked the Bursar.

'There you are,' said Sandra. 'You're completely out of touch with modern literature.'

That was more than Amiss could bear. 'Literature's going a bit far. He's only got a vocabulary of a hundred words, and most of them have only four letters.'

'WASP values,' said Sandra.

Miss Thackaberry ploughed on. '"Damning the Dykes: lesbian invisibility in the contemporary novel"; "Strip-searched, Tortured and Marginalized: the Women of Northern Ireland".'

'What? All of them?' enquired the Bursar.

'No member of the oppressed minority,' said Sandra confidently, 'can walk down the streets of Belfast without being strip-searched at the whim of the British occupying forces.'

'What a load of bollocks,' said the Bursar.

Amiss was more tactful. 'Where did you hear that?'

'It was in the last issue of *Women Militant*.'

'Ah, indeed. A most reliable source,' snarled the Bursar. 'Are they raped as well?'

'That wasn't mentioned.'

'Good. I'm glad it's not yet compulsory.'

'Listen, everybody,' called Crowley, 'there's a nice obituary in *The Times*. Shall I read it out?'

'Why not?' said Bridget Holdness. Amiss wondered if she were being momentarily statesmanlike. 'It would be more edifying than those scurrilous rags.'

'Very well.' Crowley bowed his head for a moment to collect himself and began sonorously.

' "A daughter of the manse, Maud Theodosia Buckbarrow early showed that seriousness of purpose and high moral awareness that was to distinguish her as a scholar throughout her life. By the time she won her scholarship to King Harold's School for Girls in Birmingham, she was an accomplished student of classics and was already showing a precocious interest in medieval Latin.

' "At King Harold's, where she was Head Girl and Captain of Lacrosse, her capture of the 1951 Matutina Hobbiss Open Scholarship to St Martha's College, Cambridge, came as no surprise. There she was universally popular, for Maud Buckbarrow was never a prisoner of learning. She enjoyed nothing more after lectures and study than a hearty row or a vigorous team game. Nor did she confine herself intellectually to her formal studies: it was she who founded the Cambridge University Palaeography Society and organized many happy field trips to local archives. There were no surprises when she passed out with a double first in History and English, but such was her generosity that she was never to regret coming second to her friend Ida Troutbeck . . ." '

Crowley put the newspaper down: everyone looked at the Bursar.

'I never knew that,' said Miss Thackaberry.

'Well, if you were called "Ida", wouldn't you keep it quiet?'

'I meant about your academic record.'

'It was only exams,' said the Bursar impatiently. 'Maud was a proper scholar. I never was.'

Crowley resumed reading.

' ". . . who was to spend her life in public service before returning to St Martha's as Bursar and administrative support to her old friend.

' "Maud Buckbarrow was the finest kind of scholar. Truth was her guiding light: accuracy her driving force. Her integrity was a by-word. If sometimes she was criticized by young scholars as being overly dedicated to the values of the past, she could always defend those values as timeless.

' "She was, it is true, no innovator. Her critics could say with some justice that St Martha's remained static as the Cambridge world about it changed. There were those who felt her disdain for the modern obsession with creature comforts was carried a little far. And she was, too, a remorseless opponent of mixed colleges, believing that women did better when encouraged by women and that in a predominantly male environment the woman would suffer from prejudice." '

'They're making her sound rather like you,' said Miss Thackaberry waspishly to Bridget Holdness.

' "Although, as she would say laughingly, many of her best friends were men, she, like the feminists of her generation, believed that women had much to teach them and that putting scholarship before ambition was something that came more easily to the female of the species.

' "Yet she was no fuddy-duddy when it came to changing attitudes among women. 'The young women must have their chance', she told colleagues. Their ways might be different, their interests new, but as long as they held on to the core of the scholar – integrity and truth – she would back them.

' "It was to that end that Dame Maud encouraged the fellows of St Martha's to elect young women who might cause a fresh intellectual breeze to blow through the corridors. That there were stresses and strains along the way her friends and colleagues cannot deny, but Dame Maud herself always believed that harmony would prevail in the end. 'Feminism is not a new phenomenon', she said in an address to her old school in 1993. 'I look back to the great feminists of the past – those who helped the progress of women through reasoned debate. I think particularly of Mary Wollstonecraft, John Stuart Mill and Millicent Fawcett. Then there were the great pioneers like Florence Nightingale and Elizabeth Garrett Anderson who were for women what would nowadays be called "role models": they showed what a determined woman could do. Then, of course, there were the founders of the women's colleges – great and courageous people like, in Cambridge, Emily Davies and Professor Henry Sidgwick. I have not included the founder of St Martha's among this pantheon, for, grateful though we are for his munificence, it is true to say that his motives were mixed.'"'

The Bursar burst out laughing. 'Good old Maud. Honest to the last.'

'"It was the patient work of innumerable pioneers like these that made it possible for my Cambridge generation to forge ahead and even, from 1948, to take degrees for the first time. We hope that what we have in turn achieved has helped to open up a wide world of rich opportunities to our younger sisters.

'"You will notice that I have mentioned two men among our great feminists. This is to illustrate my hope that the next stage of feminism will not be an exclusive one. What I long for is respect and partnership between the sexes.'"'

Sandra shook her head energetically. 'She never understood, of course. How can the oppressed be partners with the oppressors?'

Everyone ignored her. Crowley took another sip of tea.

'"Maud Buckbarrow's scholarship was distinguished by a fastidiousness about accuracy and detail. She was, she confessed herself, not an easily accessible writer, smiling at the description of herself as 'a scholar's scholar'. Her best-known work was on early medieval parish records, but her interests took her over a much broader period: her distinguished monographs covered territory from Anglo-Saxon place names to early Tudor finance.

'"It is, though, as a woman of the utmost integrity that Maud Buckbarrow will be remembered. There was about her nothing meretricious, nothing self-seeking, nothing self-regarding. While the tragic circumstances of her death have caused her friends great grief, they take comfort from the fact that she died at the height of her powers, with the light of scholarly battle in her eyes. She will never experience that fate of which Rudyard Kipling, her favourite poet, wrote with dread.

> '"This is our lot if we live so long and labour unto the
>   end –
> That we outlive the impatient years and the much too
>   patient friend:
> And because we know we have breath in our mouth and
>   think we have thoughts in our head,
> We shall assume that we are alive, whereas we are really
>   dead.'"'

A subdued silence followed. As tears welled up in the Senior Tutor's eyes, the Bursar said gruffly, 'Got to be off,' and disappeared at full speed from the dining room.

Despairing of seeing Mary Lou on her own, for Sandra was talking to her agitatedly, Amiss sidled out. He found the Bursar sitting on the edge of her desk swinging her legs and puffing vigorously.

'Is that a new tobacco? It seems even fouler than the last.'

'You have no taste. This is particularly fine example of Capstan navy Cut Ready Rubbed at its best. Robust, I grant you. But then so am I.'

'How's the election looking?'

'Dicey. By a piece of vile luck Primrose Partridge has been summoned to the bedside of her aged mother.'

'Shit.'

'But if Pusey and Mary Lou both play the white man, we should still make it. But you never know with the Dykes. They might have done some other secret deal or be at this very moment murdering Emily.'

'That's a bit unsubtle even for them.'

'We can't all be subtle. Did young Pooley come up with anything?'

'He was awestruck at how you and Mary Lou had managed to perfect your alibis at such speed.'

'Ah, well, I'm not just a pretty face, you know. I learnt a lot of tricks from MI6.'

'Come off it, Jack. You were never a spy.'

'Let us say that in the course of my civil service duties I was not averse to helping intelligence colleagues on the side. You pick up a few useful tips that way.'

'I must try it sometime,' Amiss said absently. 'Where was Mary Lou last night?'

'Am I her keeper just because we concoct a mean alibi?'

Amiss moodily kicked the desk.

'Snap out of it, my lad. We may need all our wits about us this morning. I have learned that the Dykes have called a meeting of students for immediately after the Council meeting, presumably to announce the glad news that their leader-ene has been elected. It may be a bit hairy if dear old Emily makes it.'

'Have you written a victory speech for her?'

'I think on this occasion I'll have to be her mouthpiece. Emily is not cut out to be Mark Antony.'

The telephone rang. 'Troutbeck. Yes, yes.' She looked up at Amiss. 'I'll be a while. You'd better get along. Get some fresh air. Go and walk Bobsy.'

Obediently Amiss trailed off to the garden and joined Pusey and Bobsy on their morning constitutional.

'Is it really less than a week since we had that horrid experience?'

'Indeed it is. So much has happened since. One forgets.'

'Bobsy and I have forgiven but we haven't quite forgotten,' said Pusey, 'the Bursar was really . . .'

'I know, I know,' said Amiss hastily. 'But although her faults are blindingly obvious, we must remember her virtues. At least you know where you are with her.'

Pusey sniffed. 'Usually somewhere you don't want to be. However, I accept that she won't go back on her word.'

'She gave you a clear-cut guarantee?'

'Yes, as much as she could. What she said was that she would do everything in her power to ensure that I was given a three-year contract if the right man won.'

'Have the others been after you since we last talked?'

'They haven't had the chance. I haven't answered my phone since the Bursar rang, and Bobsy and I have lain low. There were several knocks on our door but we didn't answer.' He looked at his watch. 'It's time for Bobsy to go up. Oh dear, I'm not looking forward to this. It could be very, very horrid indeed.'

'*Courage mon vieux*. Let us show the ladies what can be done when we are on our mettle.'

Pusey tittered nervously and headed for the stairs.

28

There was little eye contact visible at the Council: the certainty that among them was a murderer seemed to be a dampener on the Fellows' spirits. The Senior Tutor's hair was wilder than usual, perhaps in sympathy with the agitation visible on her face. Amiss sat beside her and discreetly pressed his knee against hers; she responded gratefully. That little bit of clandestine human contact made them both feel slightly better.

Bridget Holdness opened the meeting. She looked, Amiss was pleased to observe, a little shaken. 'It was only yesterday that our new Mistress was talking about the need for us to all pull together in the face of tragedy. This is even more true today. All I can say is that I was looking forward to working in partnership with Dr Windlesham, whose death, I know, we all greatly regret.'

Amiss was amused at this departure from Bridget's usual frankness; she was being positively anodyne. And the use of 'Dr' was a huge concession.

'Now, I think we'd better get on with the main business of the morning immediately. There is much to be done in calming the fears of the students. It is our job now to choose the right person to take us through a time that requires remarkable energy and leadership skills.'

Rather well done, thought Amiss. These were certainly not the two first attributes one could apply to dear old Emily Twigg. The Bursar, he noticed, was looking uneasy.

'Nominations, please, colleagues.'

Amiss kicked the Senior Tutor under the table. She broke into speech. 'I wish to propose the Bursar.'

'Seconded,' said Pusey. His voice was so low as to be almost a whisper.

Jack Troutbeck looked as thunderstruck as the majority of her colleagues.

'Sorry, Bursar,' squeaked the Senior Tutor, 'but you're up to it and I'm not.'

'Other nominations?' asked Bridget levelly.

'I propose the Acting Mistress,' said Sandra.

'Seconded,' said the Reverend Crowley.

Amiss was impressed; absolute gender balance on both nominations.

'Bursar,' asked Bridget, 'do you accept the nomination?'

The Bursar shrugged. 'Yes.'

'All those in favour of the Bursar, please raise your hands.'

The hands went up slowly. First, the Senior Tutor, Pusey and Amiss, then, after a quick exchange of whispers, Anglo-Saxon Annie, Miss Thackaberry, the Bursar herself, and finally, Mary Lou. 'Traitor,' hissed Sandra in Mary Lou's direction.

'That's it then,' said Bridget. 'Congratulations, Mistress.' She got up and gestured to Jack Troutbeck who pushed her chair back with a resounding scrunch, walked to the head of the table and plonked herself into the Mistress's seat. She gazed around her colleagues. 'I appreciate Dr Holdness's courtesy in conceding defeat so graciously.

'I am surprised, I won't say pleased. No one could feel pleased at inheriting a job in circumstances like these, but I will do it as well as I can – in my own style. And, I can assure you, I have no intention of being murdered.

'Item two on the agenda – the election of a Deputy Mistress – I suggest should not take place today; one press-ganging is enough. With your agreement, I shall refer it to the next meeting along with elections for other vacancies.'

There was a squeak of protest from Sandra. 'But Bridget is Deputy Mistress.'

'Not so. If you read your standing orders you will find that on the election of a new Mistress, the Deputy Mistressship also becomes vacant. My predecessor had not done her homework.

'Item three, "Any other business." Under this heading, Dr Holdness, I think it would be appropriate for you to tell us about the student meeting you have organized.'

'It was a meeting properly called under the auspices of the Gender and Ethnic Workshop.' She sounded defensive.

'So that's why most of your colleagues were not told about it? Despite the subject being the future of St Martha's?'

'In a feminist context,' said Bridget. As an answer it was clear it seemed weak even to her.

'Hah! It was intended as a victory rally,' said Pusey, emboldened by his success as Mistress-maker.

'Let us avoid recriminations, Dr Pusey. We have to clear up the mess we're in as fast as possible. Where and when is this meeting, Dr Holdness?'

'Twelve o'clock in the library.'

'Do all the students know about it?'

Bridget looked at Sandra. 'Yes,' she muttered.

'Sure?'

'I put a leaflet under all the students' doors this morning.'

'Very good. I'm sure you'll be pleased, Dr Holdness, in your capacity as' – the new Mistress paused for a brief consideration of the appropriate nomenclature – 'chairman of this group to call the meeting to order, announce my election and hand over to me.' She paused. 'Quickly.'

'Yes,' said Bridget Holdness.

'Very good. Now, I shall require you all to be there standing around me showing solidarity. This college will not survive any further dissent.

'I declare the meeting closed. I shall see you all later.' She rose, bowed low and left the room. Within half a minute the only people remaining were Amiss, Pusey and the Senior Tutor.

'Well done, both of you,' he said. 'Worked like clockwork.'

'Well, you should have the credit,' said Pusey.

'Oh, it's such a relief.' The Senior Tutor looked happier than he had seen her in days. 'You took such a weight off my shoulders when you suggested this. She's to the manner born.'

'Fancy Mary Lou coming over to our side,' said Pusey. 'Was that anything to do with you?'

Amiss shook his head. 'I haven't seen her since I had the idea. But she's got a mind of her own. I think you and she will have a great deal in common, Senior Tutor.'

'I suppose I'm not the Senior Tutor any more. How nice.' She gathered up her belongings. 'It's all very muddling. I do hope this meeting goes well. I'm so happy I don't have to do anything at it.'

'I wonder what the Mistress has in mind?' said Pusey.

'Let's just enjoy the surprise,' said Amiss. He smiled at his co-conspirators and set off once again in pursuit of Mary Lou.

'Could I have a look at the drug tip-off note, sir?'

'You've got that on the brain, Pooley. I read it to you over the phone. It's plain and straightforward and could have been written by anyone.'

'Please, sir.'

'Oh, all right, all right. I think I've a photocopy here.'

He hunted through his file and drew it out. As Pooley looked at it he felt murderous. 'Excuse me, sir.' His voice was almost level. 'Just one point occurs to me.'

'Yes, yes. What is it?'

'The way the word centre is spelt.'

'Oh, it's spelt wrong, I saw that, but everyone's illiterate these days.'

'It's the American spelling, sir – "center".'

'Well, so if it is, that's a coincidence. It's just a spelling mistake.'

'It's not a common spelling mistake, sir. It's much more likely to be a cultural slip by an American.'

'You mean that black girl sent it herself?'

'I can't think it very likely that she set out to frame herself.'

'Maybe she wanted to be a martyr, be able to sue us after-wards. You know what Americans are like.'

'Maybe somebody else wanted to make a martyr of her. Someone like Sandra Murphy; she's American too.'

'I know that, I know that.' Romford was grumpy. 'Oh well,

I suppose we'd better have her in again and ask her how she spells "centre".'

'I don't think that would get us very far, sir. If I might suggest . . .'

There was a knock on the door.

'Come in,' called Romford.

Amiss's head appeared. 'May I interrupt you for a moment, Inspector?'

'Certainly.' Romford sounded almost cordial.

'I thought you'd like to know that the Bursar has become Mistress and that she'll be making a speech to the whole college in the library in ten minutes. I think you might find it interesting.'

'I doubt it,' said Romford. 'We're trying to solve a murder here, not get involved with what all these women are up to.'

'I think it might have some bearing, Inspector. You see, Bridget Holdness and Sandra have lost a campaign they expected to win and I think it's just possible there might be a little bit of a breach between them. Disappointment can cause allies to fall out.'

Romford chewed that over. 'You mean they might shop each other?' His brows knitted. 'I suppose we'd better bring them in, then.'

'Forgive my meddling,' said Amiss hastily, 'but they are likely to be in even lower spirits after the meeting and it really is in any case very important for college morale that they should be at it.'

'Oh, all right, we'll go to the meeting. Come on, Pooley.'

'I'll be with you in a second, sir. I just have to make a quick call to my hotel to pick up messages.'

Failing to think of any good reason to object to this, Romford nodded curtly and followed Amiss out. Furtively closing the door, Pooley dialled Superintendent Hardiman.

There was a full turn out. Even Greasy Joan was there, apron removed for the occasion to reveal an impressive, if sagging, cleavage protruding from a fake leopardskin close-fitting tracksuit. Bridget Holdness played her part exactly as directed. Pausing only to offer congratulations, she stood back. Jack Troutbeck strode forward carrying a chair on which she climbed. 'Can you all hear me?' she bellowed.

'I'd be surprised if they can't hear her in Alabama,' whispered Mary Lou to Amiss under cover of the shouts of 'Yes'.

'I want to read you the obituary of a fine woman, of whom we should all be proud.'

She read brilliantly, rather to Amiss's surprise – the timing perfect, the voice rich, vibrant and full of controlled emotion. What had been poignant read out by Crowley was elegiac read by Jack Troutbeck. When she had finished there was an absolute silence.

The new Mistress folded the newspaper and stuck it in her pocket. She looked slowly around her audience. 'Colleagues, friends, sisters and brothers, we have a simple choice.

'As you all should know, St Martha's was set up by a man who believed that women were inferior creatures who might be driven insane by too much intellectual effort: if he were alive now he would be saying "I told you so". Yet despite his vision of womanhood restricted, protected, cosseted, forced down the so-called womanly paths, the women in this college proved him wrong. They were self-reliant, honourable, hard-working, proud of each other's achievements, supportive of each other's endeavours and devoted to their students.

'If, under them, St Martha's lacked glamour, it never lacked integrity. Generations of its students, among whom I am proud to number myself, were sent into the world to play a useful part and behave honourably. We were taught that to die with one's self-respect intact was more important than to be laden with the honours and baubles of the self-seeker and materialist.

'Yet recently as a college we began to lose our collective sense and to experience a fragmentation of our historical common purpose. Factions developed. I will not deny that many of those anxious to take St Martha's in a new direction were motivated by idealism, though I cannot pretend that I thought all were. I freely admit that on occasion I may have been less than generous in my assumptions, tactful in my speech or subtle in my battle against radical change.

'At the root of the dispute over the future of St Martha's were two opposing views of the nature of women and the importance of sexual proclivities. On the latter, I believed, and I still do, that sex is a private matter and that the nature of one's sexuality or sexual appetites should not dominate one's thinking. My generation of Fellows was, I believe, right in tolerating but not highlighting each other's sexual inclinations; we all had the courtesy to keep the issue out of the public domain.'

'*You* didn't,' called out a voice from the back. The Mistress was unabashed. 'Until the other day, I did. You must view my recent outspoken comments as uncharacteristic and a consequence of an unhappy struggle between colleagues which is, I believe, now over.

'That issues of sexuality became such a divisive force within the college was serious enough. What was much worse was the attempt to encourage students in a new, dangerous and joyless direction. For my generation, female liberation was about casting off the shackles imposed on women by society and rejoicing in the freedom to be human beings. It is therefore with alarm that we have seen the trend on the campuses of America, and even here, towards the pursuit of victimhood: I believe our job is to escape it, not pursue it.

'I want St Martha's to be a college in which liberated women follow their stars, not one in which feeble throwbacks to the Victorian era whimper about hurt feelings, bitch about political correctness and act like frightened virgins if a man touches them without a pre-witnessed contract. We must take control of our lives. In the world I envisage, anyone attempting a date rape will be dealt with by a strong right hook.'

Recognizing that the Mistress showed signs of going over the top and losing her audience, Amiss nudged Mary Lou and whispered. 'Three cheers for the new Mistress,' she shouted. 'Hip, hip . . .' 'Hooray', yelled Amiss and several colleagues. 'Hip, hip . . .' Slightly uncertainly and then with a gathering enthusiasm, the audience responded. Amiss was delighted to see Pippa shouting loudly. The cheering continued for several minutes. The Mistress, flushed and delighted with herself, bowed in acknowledgement, waved furiously, descended from her chair and finally jumped up and down in enthusiasm, both fists clenched in the air in the victory salute. Then abruptly she wheeled round and disappeared through the nearest door. Amiss and Mary Lou followed.

'Well, well, well,' he said. 'How very interesting. And where were you last night?'

As she began to tell him, Pooley and Superintendent Hardiman closed in on Bridget Holdness.

29

Hardiman had Sandra consigned to a nearby room under the friendly gaze of DC McMenamin. Flanked by Romford and Pooley, he faced Bridget Holdness across the table. 'There are only two suspects with convincing motives who do not have rock-solid alibis.' It was a lie, but he told it convincingly. 'And those two are you and your colleague, Dr Murphy.'

'But we do have alibis.'

There was an unfamiliar note of uncertainty in her voice.

'Very leaky alibis. Let me remind you, Dr Holdness, there were a dozen discrepancies from the time at which you went to bed, the sexual practices in which you indulged, the order of events . . .'

'Yes, yes, yes, I know. It's easy to muddle up such matters.'

'In any case, the alibis make no difference, for it is clear that you and Dr Murphy are involved in a conspiracy centring round your desire to gain control of this institution and the Alice Toon bequest. You wanted to be Mistress and most of your colleagues testify to your ruthlessness in the pursuit of your objectives. You and your co-conspirator appear to be most unpleasant pieces of work; I would go further – you are double murderers.'

'We're not.'

He ignored her. 'And contemptibly, you attempted to pin the blame on a young woman whom you pretended to befriend.'

'What are you talking about?'

'Dr Denslow. You chose a murder weapon which was her property, planted drugs in her room and tipped off the police with an anonymous letter.'

'I never even heard about any anonymous letter.'

Hardiman handed it to her. She read it twice and pushed it back. 'Is it really true that all the other suspects are out of the running?'

'Yes, ma'am.'

She rested her forehead on her hands. No one spoke. After a couple of minutes she looked up. 'All right then. Here goes.'

Half an hour later, Pooley replaced McMenamin and sent him back to guard Bridget Holdness. Sandra was scowling. 'What's going on?'

'Superintendent Hardiman and Inspector Romford will be along in a moment to ask you some questions.'

'This is persecution. You're picking on me because I'm foreign.'

Pooley said nothing.

'I'll sue for wrongful arrest.'

'As you wish, ma'am.'

She got up as the others entered. 'You've no right to keep me here like this.'

'Shut up,' said Hardiman. 'I'm charging you with the wilful murders of Dame Maud Theodosia Buckbarrow and Dr Deborah Windlesham and the attempted murder of Miss Ida Troutbeck and I must warn you that . . .'

'You can't,' she screamed, 'I've got alibis.'

'Not any more you don't,' said Hardiman. 'Your mate Bridget has blown the gaff.'

It took the three of them and two reinforcements Hardiman had brought with him to subdue her, for she managed to produce a show of strength that would have impressed a Troutbeck. Finally handcuffed, she was removed to a police car. Hardiman tenderly mopped the scratch she had planted on his right cheek. 'Jesus Christ.'

Romford looked at him sternly. 'You are speaking about a friend of mine.'

Hardiman narrowed his eyes. 'I warned you before, Romford. This time I'm going to fucking castrate you.'

*   *   *

212

'Yippee!' said the Mistress. She brandished the empty bottle in the air and shouted. 'More champagne!'

A scurrying waiter disappeared to fulfil her command.

'Mind you, young Pooley, it was about bloody time. Talk about making heavy weather of it . . .'

'If Hardiman hadn't come along, I don't think we'd have resolved it unless Sandra had murdered every member of the College Council.'

'I hope Hardiman gives Romford a pretty hard time,' said Amiss.

'I think he's getting a choice between being hanged, drawn and quartered and being sent on secondment to the Falkland Islands.'

'Let's drink to the Falklands,' said the Mistress. 'He can convert the sheep. They're about his intellectual level.'

They clinked their glasses gravely. More champagne arrived and was uncorked and the trio settled down to serious ordering.

'Right,' said the Mistress when they had a respite. 'So what made the Head Bitch come across?'

'Seeing the anonymous letter. She guessed it was Sandra.'

'How?'

'The Americanized spelling of "centre". That's what Romford had missed, needless to say, and I spotted.'

'You mean Bridget jibbed at Sandra framing Mary Lou but not at her murdering a brace of dons?'

'No, no. Don't be silly, Robert. She didn't believe that Sandra was a murderer because she didn't want to believe that Sandra was a murderer, so she didn't allow it as a possibility. Then the anonymous letter forced her to face facts. As she said when she came clean, it all suddenly fell into place.'

'You're making her sound rather like a human being.'

'I wouldn't go quite that far,' said Pooley cautiously. 'You, Jack, however, always alleged that she was pragmatic rather than principled.'

'True, true, I did. And it's the idealists that are really dangerous.'

Amiss fiddled with a bread roll. 'You mean that Sandra believed all that crap but Bridget just used it for effect.'

'She didn't just believe it, she believed in it like a religion. She was as bad as Romford.' Pooley checked himself. 'What am I saying? At least Romford doesn't murder people to bring them to Jesus. Sandra murdered to bring Jesus, i.e. Bridget, to power for the creation of a PC heaven in a dank corner of Cambridge.'

'Heaven preserve me from idealists,' said the Mistress, swilling her champagne. 'Whoever they are and no matter how high-sounding their motives seem to be, they are usually in the business of gaining power for themselves or their own faction. It doesn't matter if they call themselves National Socialists or Basque Separatists or Red Brigaders or IRA or whether they call it freedom, justice, democracy or power to the people or even flower power – what they really want is to control other people and bend them to their will.'

'It seems a bit much to spill so much blood just to stop St Martha's being insufficiently multicultural.'

'You know bloody well that wasn't what it was about. First you control language; then you control thought; then you send your evangelists forth to spread your dreary message.'

'She must be mad.'

'So Holdness charitably thinks.'

'Now let me be clear about my colleagues,' said the Mistress. 'The alibis were completely false?' She began on her venison.

'Yes. Holdness thought it was perfectly sensible when Sandra suggested it, that they should cover up for each other in case the unjust cops pointed the finger at them because they were lesbian.'

'Who did she think had done it?'

'The attack on Jack she thought could be anyone, since she's so annoying.'

The Mistress grinned proudly.

'Number one murder she'd fingered Windlesham. Number two, she thought was Jack. Then she had some second thoughts during Jack's speech because of the effect it had on Sandra.'

'Which was?'

'Rage. Holdness admitted to us that she thought Sandra

214

unhinged by Jack's election and feared she might do something violent and it was then she began to wonder if she already had.'

'And Sandra's admitted it?'

'Yep. She was so out of control that she let it all out. Killing Jack proved too difficult, so she decided to murder – or at least seriously injure – Dame Maud. That, she thought, would knock the stuffing out of the Virgins. But then, although Windlesham was prepared to cooperate to some extent with Bridget, Sandra decided it would be simpler to see her off and put Bridget fully in charge. One successful murder made a second seem logical.'

'The doctored ladder is one thing,' said Amiss. 'Even the blunderbuss. But stabbing someone seems unlikely for such a wimp.'

'She took anatomy at college; she knew what she was about and she had sharpened up Mary Lou's paper knife most efficiently.'

'Any remorse?'

'No. She blames the victims.'

'I look forward to her defence,' said the Mistress. 'It should be entertaining.'

When they had chewed over the previous several days as well as their dinners and the Mistress was at the brandy-and-pipe stage, she leaned back and surveyed them both benignly.

'Happy endings in prospect, then. Presumably you, Ellis, go back to London festooned with laurels from a grateful Cambridgeshire police force?'

'Well certainly a few nice words from Hardiman.'

'And Romford?'

'It's not too bad for him really. He was fed up anyway and the early retirement deal is very good and now that Mrs Romford's got a full-time job they'll be financially pretty comfortable.'

'Doesn't he feel humiliated?'

'No, he's got a touch of the Sandras really – always blames everyone except himself. He complained a bit about how disgraceful it was that there was no room for God in the modern police force, reminisced nostalgically about that peculiar God-cop who used to be Chief Constable of Manchester and cracked down on a large range of people he considered undesirable, but then told me that God moved in mysterious ways and that no doubt all this persecution was designed to give him the opportunity to evangelize more.'

'I suppose that's good news,' said the Mistress. 'Mmm, this is extremely nice brandy. Now, Robert, what about you? Are you going to stay on and fulfil the task for which you were nominally hired?'

'I think not, Jack. I have fulfilled the task for which I was really hired and a lot more to boot. I adopted the advice of the college poet:

' "If you can make one heap of all your winnings
    And risk it on one turn of pitch-and-toss . . ." –
    and did so.'

'Well, you've certainly shown initiative. Can't complain about it really. I'm enjoying being Mistress. I intend to make things hum. How did you pull it off, anyway?'

'Easy. You underestimate yourself, Jack.'

'No one ever accused me of that before.'

'In the popularity stakes, that is. Pusey couldn't stick you but he grudgingly admired you and the Senior Tutor was rather frightened of you but thought you would be an absolutely ideal Mistress and so I'm sure you will be. A touch unorthodox perhaps, a little coarse and not quite what the founder had expected but one can't have everything.'

'Does this mean,' asked Pooley, 'that you are going to have to acquire some scholarly interests?'

'I have scholarly interests, dammit,' said the Bursar. 'I have, in my time, written the occasional monograph on military history. And I am no mean student of Kipling. But you don't have to be scholarly any more to run an Oxbridge college. In fact, scholars are passé: it's administrators and glorified fundraisers these days. I shall be swanning around, milking the trusts and squeezing the rich until the pips squeak. It's my firm intention to ensure that St Martha's becomes comfortable as well as intellectually respectable. Now, to get back to where we were. Robert, why don't you stay?'

'Because I mustn't and you'll easily find someone to do the Whitehall and academe job. I'm getting out of the path of temptation.'

'Oh, I don't think temptation is going to rear its head again. I have taken the necessary steps to ensure that henceforward you remain pure. Haven't you noticed?'

Amiss was alarmed. 'What have you done? You're surely not kicking Mary Lou out?'

'On the contrary, my dear boy. Mary Lou and I look forward to continuing our already intimate working relationship.'

'Christ Almighty.' Amiss looked at her in horror. 'You're kidding. You haven't? You're not? You couldn't?'

'I could and have and will. It's in both our interests.'

'You treacherous old cow.'

'Did you or did you not say that you would stop cavorting with Mary Lou if you could?'

'I did.'

'Are you or are you not concerned to preserve your relationship with Rachel?'

'I am.'

'So what are you bleating about then? I thought I should focus her attention elsewhere before you really screw things up.'

'You're all heart, Jack. Always thinking of others. I hope it's not too much of an imposition on your good nature.'

'Don't worry too much about that, my dear Robert. As you well know, the lady is scrumptious.'

Pooley's brows were knitted. 'This is none of my business but I thought . . . I thought all that badge-wearing and so on was put on. I mean, what about Myles Cavendish?'

'Oh, Myles,' she said carelessly. 'Myles, I suppose, you could say is my steady. But I am a woman of appetites: there is plenty of room in my life for both Myles and Mary Lou.

What's the matter with you, Robert? You are looking decidedly pissed off.'

'How do you expect me to feel when I discover a desirable lover has just been stolen from under my nose by a fat, elderly woman?'

'That's ageist and sexist. You're just piqued that Mary Lou has fallen for a woman of experience. You should be thanking me. She is; her conscience was beginning to stir.'

'Well, nonetheless I'm still not going to stay and that's not because of pique. I'm taking off for Delhi and Rachel; then I'll take stock.'

'What about Plutarch? You can't leave her locked up in that cathouse forever: it would be heartless.'

'I bloody well can leave her in that expensive cattery for another few weeks. If you're so worried, why don't you look after her yourself?'

'I'll think about it, though I rather fear that Francis would stamp his exquisite little feet at the very notion. Well then, if you must go, go. And when you get back you and Ellis must come down to Cambridge and the three of us will have a reunion. Or maybe we'll make up a quartet with Mary Lou.'

'If I can bear it by then, you're on.'

'Oh, and Robert, I urge you to take the advice of a woman of the world and don't tell Rachel. There are limits to what even the most understanding person can bear.'

'I was fretting about that.'

'Fret not, my boy. This is a time to be pragmatic rather than principled. Sacrificing Rachel's peace of mind to salve your guilty conscience would be bad for everyone. After all, if she's been at it with the local embassy Lothario, do you want to be told?'

'No.'

'QED. Now why don't you both join me in a celebratory cigar and let us cease bandying ladies' names. For as Kipling so wisely observed: "A woman is only a woman, but a good Cigar is a Smoke."'

EPILOGUE

'Congratulations.'

'Thank you,' said Mary Lou.

'When were you appointed?'

'A couple of weeks ago. Unanimous vote at the College Council.'

'I wouldn't have thought that being Bursar was exactly your scene.'

'This girl has hidden talents,' said the Mistress. 'I've discovered she's an administrator *manqué*. And now we have the power and the money to sort the college out there's a hell of a lot to do.'

'Bring us up to date.'

'Well, a large chunk of the Alice Toon money is going as Maud broadly wanted – in the direction of scholarship, but only some in the direction of the balls-aching scholarship that was so near to her heart. We're going simultaneously for excellence and élan.'

'E.g.?'

'Tell you later. Additionally, I've found a way of diverting two million towards licking the fabric of the college into shape and making it a pleasant place to be.'

'Good God! Not wine cellars and *haute cuisine*?'

'We can manage a reasonable wine cellar and a decent chef as well as central heating and roofs that don't leak. I've put little Francis Pusey in charge of working out schemes for our corporate acquisition of some creature comforts. He's having a wonderful time poring over catalogues and making lists and snapping up bargains in the food and wine department and subject to strict vetoes from me and Mary Lou, he's doing all sorts of dreary work on choosing fabrics and carpets and paints; he's never been happier. It was that bribe that made him agree to have Plutarch stay while you were away. How is she, by the way?'

'Horribly well. Are you sure you don't want her back?'

'I'd be delighted. Unfortunately, she is not a universal favourite with my colleagues. Devouring the salmon destined for high table was not the best way of winning friends and influencing people. Give her my love.'

'I'm sure she will reciprocate. Any other changes?'

'The Statutes are getting a reinterpretation that will have old Ridley spinning in his mausoleum. No more drill, for starters. And accomplishments are going to cover a multitude of gastronomic treats.'

'What a disappointment! And what about people?'

'Well, now that Emily is Deputy Mistress, she's at peace. She no longer has any official duties since I don't give her anything to do. Thackaberry is a not bad Senior Tutor and Emily's other job as Director of Studies had been taken by an outsider who's a humdinger on the intellectual front.'

'What happened to Bridget?'

'She's doing exactly as she's told.'

'You mean you let her stay?'

'Yep. I have a magnanimous streak. I gave her a simple choice: accept she'd lost, turn constructive and she had a future. Otherwise she'd be drummed out and because of the scandal of the court case she'd find it hard ever to get a job anywhere else. She still doesn't know what Sandra's likely to say about her when the case comes up.'

'Doesn't sound like much of a choice.'

'It wasn't.'

'So she's given up all the gender and ethnic crap?'

'Sure. You knew she was an apparatchik. Today's fashion at St Martha's is vigorous scholarship, so Bridget has returned to her old intellectual pursuits as a Tudor historian and is working diligently in the hope of landing a university lecturership. She willingly takes on all the dreary administrative jobs we give her and seems quite content with her lot.'

'The Rev Crowley?'

'Skulked out of the college with his suitcase the day after you left, leaving no forwarding address. No doubt he's already ensconced in a visiting professorship in Ohio.'

'How's morale in general?'

'Going up by leaps and bounds.' Jack Troutbeck waved in Mary Lou's direction. 'You tell 'em.'

'To discover what Sandra had done really threw the kids. Then they found Bridget had reneged, and it rapidly emerged that life under Jack was going to be fun.'

'I think you could say that the ethnic/gender forces have been comprehensively routed,' said the Mistress complacently. 'The Dykes have indeed been downed.'

'By two dykes,' remarked Amiss acidly.

'Don't be a sore loser. Anyway, we're not dykes; we're women of catholic tastes who eschew labelling and who are devoting ourselves to the welfare of our charges.

'Poor little wretches. Maud really was guilty of driving them into the arms of Holdness and co. I'd have gone mad myself if I'd been forced to be solemn and rigorous all the time and always pushed in the direction of land tenures and acres of footnotes. Our priority is arranging for them to have excellent teaching, lots of intellectual adventure and encouraging them to have a good time into the bargain. We aim to turn out a band of happy, tough sceptics.'

Mary Lou broke in. 'One of the best things has been the lecture series taking the piss out of intellectual fads. Our new Director of Studies brings in people to take a comic look at the screwier bits of the academic world. With the right person you can both explain and amusingly savage everything from Marxist criticism to structuralism.'

'Not forgetting the gurus,' said the Mistress. She smacked her lips over her wine.

'Sure. The assassinations of Jacques Derrida and Mary Daly were a riot.'

'Mary Lou's being modest. She had them rolling in the aisles with her *tour de force* called "Black Studies as a Floating Signifier".'

Amiss seized the claret. 'What's the female equivalent of an Uncle Tom?'

'I'll have to ask Sandra,' said the Bursar cheerfully. 'When are visiting hours?'

'You couldn't really get a blacker joke,' observed Amiss, 'if you'll forgive the expression. Sandra goes to all that trouble to rub out poor old Maud and the dreadful Deborah and the net result is to put you two in charge. I wonder how she feels about it all. What's the news on her, Ellis?'

'The word on the grapevine is that she's still in a state of culture shock. Her parents were over within twenty-four hours and the three of them seemed pretty confident of getting her off on the grounds of the persecution she suffered at the hands of Dame Maud and Deborah Windlesham which had eroded her self-confidence and driven her to violence.'

'Oh, God,' groaned the Bursar. 'It sounds just like home.'

'However, the lawyer they tried with that one told them it wouldn't wash, that Britain is a sensible place still, just, and the notion of murderer as victim hasn't quite taken off here. Unless they could have her declared insane, in which case they could go for diminished responsibility, she'd had it.'

'I'm surprised she didn't try the pre-menstrual tension defence,' observed Amiss. 'I seem to remember her bleating on about how it excused any violence.'

'She said that to me once,' said the Mistress. 'I asked her if that made it all right for men to be excused rape if they had an excess of testosterone. That shut her up for a while at least.'

'And then?' prompted Amiss.

'They pursued the insanity angle, but couldn't find a compliant shrink.' Pooley shrugged. 'What was left to Sandra but the child-abuse angle? Her father had abused her sexually, her mother had abused her psychologically, she had been unattractive, she hadn't got good grades at High School because her teachers didn't like her and so on and so on. This not only failed to impress the lawyers but caused her parents to take deep umbrage. They disappeared back to America leaving her to work out her defence with a solicitor and barrister provided by legal aid. She's feeling very aggrieved about that.'

'So what'll happen?'

'Life imprisonment,' said Pooley.

'Is it fair,' asked Amiss, 'when Bridget gets off scot free?'

'Not really scot free,' said the Mistress. 'She's working out a very long penance. Besides, I think she truly has learnt her lesson.'

'Nobody as duplicitous as that could ever be relied on.'

'Oh, we won't rely on her, will we, Mary Lou? We'll use her. She's not the sort of person you make a friend of but there's plenty like her in public life. You just make sure they're channelled in the right direction and their success is dependent on yours.' She burst out laughing. 'Mind you, you haven't heard the best of it.'

'What's that?'

'She's not a lesbian.'

'Who?'

'Bridget.'

'How do you know?'

'She told me,' said Mary Lou. 'That's one of the reasons they mucked up so badly over the alibi. Sandra was always pursuing her but she wouldn't succumb. She had a boyfriend in Ely, rather rough trade and is as straight as they come. It was just convenient to pretend otherwise.'

'So poor old Sandra wasn't even getting her oats.'

'Poor old Sandra, my foot,' said the Mistress. 'It's people like her get women a bad name. St Martha's is going to produce robust feminists, isn't that right, Mary Lou? And they're going to have some fun as well.'

'Female cavaliers,' said the Bursar with a grin.

Amiss smiled at her. 'Two months in, you've achieved high office, you've turned your back on all you were taught at your alma mater, you have conspired to bring down your sisters, indeed you sleep with the enemy. I hope you feel a sense of shame.'

'Balls!' said the Bursar.